Lust, Money, Envy

Lust, Money, Envy

by Antonio Harriston

iUniverse LLC
Bloomington

LUST, MONEY, ENVY

iUniverse books may be ordered through booksellers or by contacting:

iUniverse LLC
1663 Liberty Drive
Bloomington, IN 47403
www.iuniverse.com
1-800-Authors (1-800-288-4677)

ISBN: 978-1-4917-2848-2 (sc)
ISBN: 978-1-4917-2849-9 (e)

Library of Congress Control Number: 2014906193

Printed in the United States of America.

iUniverse rev. date: 04/22/2014

Special thanks

I would like to thank all of those who have supported me from day one watching as my work manifested itself. I know it's been a long time coming, but thanks for patiently waiting because the book is finally here. I would like to give special thanks to the woman that inspired me to write this book my lady, my friend, my everything Shaniqua. I would like to give another special thanks to my mother for giving me life. She has always believed in me no matter what I was doing she always supported me and encourage me to do better I love you for that mommy. I also would like to thank my sisters Jenny, Angie and Christina who has always been there for me when I needed someone to talk to for advice. It might not have been what I wanted to hear at the time but y'all gave it to me straight and I love y'all for that. I would like to take my brother Vinny who always been my best friend since we were babies. My brother Earl who always been my right hand man and my soldier you are a trooper Kid. My brother Junior for being Junior you are a real loyal brother. My brother Pee Wee he's the oldest you installed so much into me growing up, although we used to fight all the time like boys do before they become men. My brother toTerrelll I just want to say I love you but I miss you even more, I ain't mad at yah.To my brother Malcolm I'm proud of you keep doing what you doing and don't let nobody change you. To my youngest brother of the pack Ahkeem, I hope you take what you learned from us weather if it's good or bad and use it to your advantage. And to all my official Homies out there, you know who you are stand up and put your chest out and salute, because I see you. Finally, but most of all I would like to thank God for giving me this opportunity to be here and for blessing me with the talent to tell this story.

Dedication

I would like to dedicate his book to all the people that doubted me, you gave me the energy to push forward and to do better. This one is for you. To let you know that if you believe in yourself anything is possible. I'm just getting started.

Chapter 1

"The Birth".

It all started in the early seventies, just before I was born. Around the time when black people were still fighting for their Civil Rights. My mother was born in Jacksonville North Carolina. She was the oldest out of her siblings. My father was born in Kingston Jamaica, one of the wildest parts in Jamaica, where people died every day trying to survive.

My father was a humble person for the most part of his life but his whole demeanor was gangsta a true "G" in his days. I still remember it like it was yesterday when my father use to tell me stories about how it was for him growing up in Jamaica. How him and his brother use to own a dry cleaning business that was very popular in Jamaica. Everyone throughout Jamaica brought their clothes there to get cleaned because they loved the services that they provided. There was this guy that was from Jungle another part of Jamaica that everyone feared throughout Jamaica except for my father. One day he came to the shop to pick up his clothes that he had dropped off days ago but they wasn't ready yet when he came to pick up his items. The man got very upset and started going ballistic yelling from the top of his lungs at my uncle that was at the shop at the time, holding it down for my father as he made his runs.

What kind ah "blood clot" ting you ah tell mi bout say mi ras clot clothes dem nah ready yet, "mi fi just shot yah pussy clot" dead in ah yah face boy. He yelled at my uncle.

Before my Uncle realized it, the man and the other guy's that he was with, had their guns drawn out ready to bust him. The man walked up to my uncle and pressed his gun against my uncle's cheek bone, rubbing it in his face. My uncle started pleading for his life.

"Just cool nah mon." It soon ready trust me, just come back in a hour no worry yourself big mon, It soon ready mon trust me." My uncle said. Seeing his life flash before his eyes. He looked at my uncle with the devil in his eye. And said to him.

Look ear boy, mi ah give uno one "blood clod" hour fi have mi tings them ready. Anyway dem nah ready yet uno ah go dead in ah this blood clod place ear. Yah ear wah mi ah say "batty boy".

Then he slapped the shit out of my uncle with the back of his gun. He damn near knocked his ass out. By the time my father returned to the store they were gone. When he walked inside the shop he noticed his brother sitting in the back of the store holding his face with a towel soaked with blood and it was still leaking down the side of his face. My Uncle explained to my father about what had happened to him while he was gone. My father became furious about what had transpired and went and got his A-K 47 that he kept in the in the store for situations like this and waited patiently for them to return. When they did they drove up to the front of the Cleaners. My father spotted them immediately but he waited until they were all out of the car and he had all of them in sight before he made his move. He began slowly emerging from behind the car that he was hiding behind before he got their undivided attention.

"A boy, ah me you a look fah?"

Before any of them could breathe again or even realize that was death was at their door step shots riddled their bodies leaving them with more holes than Swiss cheese. Back in those days there wasn't any police to protect the local business owners from street nigga's like these dudes. My father had to do what he had to do to protect his self, and his family. After that happened my father sold his business and came to America. My father also had older children that lived in Jamaica, that he had by another woman he was married to. He tried to keep that a secret as long as he could but you know how the saying goes what's in the dark shall come into the light. My mom's already had a son before they had me from a prior relationship. I always use to get excited when I heard my father tell me stories like that. Not knowing that I would have my father's instincts but a lot worse. My older brother, Jay from my mother was the total opposite of me. We grew up in Harlem in the mid 80's, when the Crack Era was strong and niggas was making crazy paper then. We were just little niggas still playing seven eleven or catch and kiss with the girls that lived on my block. I was the second to the youngest out of the Crew. It was Me, My brother Jay, Rob sometime we call him bo legged R but he hated when we called him that. My man Boo was the oldest, he was a spoiled child cause he was the only one his parents had and then their was my nigga Butta. He was the youngest, he lived in my building on the fifth floor. We use to watch all the older nigga's in my hood coming thru stuntin with all the Bitches, Car's, jewelry and Money. We even had Italian niggas that lived in my hood that was connected to the Mafia. They had the whole Pleasant Avenue on Smash. When any type of major holiday came around, they always had fun filled events for the whole hood. They was always showing love to everybody. Back then we use to argue about sports and who was going to be the next Michael Jordan, Patrick Ewing or Charles Barkley. We were all was nice in basketball. But me, Boo and E.B. were just better at it even though Rob had a mean jump shot. The niggas that was getting money in my hood (Drug Dealers) use to pay us to play for them in tournaments around the hood. Rob use to get upset (Jealous) about it because they never picked him. His mother was even jealous of my mom's because she wanted to fuck my father. She love the way he talked with his Jamaican accent. But he never paid her no mind because my mom's would of killed both of them if she ever found out. His mother even went as far as trying to take my mother out of the picture completely by throwing a can of vegetables out of the 6 floor apartment window that her friend lived in. I beat Rob ass so bad that day because of her. He understood tho and he took it like a champ and came back outside to fuck with us that very next day. Rob was my nigga. My father's oldest son name was Wicked. Wicked moved from Jamaica, and was living with us. From the first day Wicked stepped on to the block, I already knew it was going to be a problem with him and somebody else on the block, because of his attitude he was on that "Me a bad boy Shit." Sure nuff was I right. Wicked, and one of the Italian's son that lived up the block from us had got into a fight. I don't even know why but it showed me that there was bad blood between them. After a few months of staying with us, Wicked moved out and moved to Brooklyn with our cousin Tony. Because he couldn't get his way living with my pops.

So he decided to leave and live with Tony. My pop's was very strict I got my share of ass whippings growing up from him. My cousin Tony was never up to no good, he was Jamaican also. Tony was always looking to rob or kill someone. "A true Shotta" just like the movie. My brother Wicked always told Tony that there was a lot of food for them to eat in Harlem whenever he was ready to eat food (Catch a Juke's).

*   *   *

It was about one o'clock during a hot summer day, when E.B. and Butta called the crib looking for me. My brother Jay answered the phone.

"Yo Dice" . . . "Yo Dice". My brother Jay yelled.

Yo what up. I said.

"Pick up the phone, it's E.B." He said.

"Aight! Hold on give me a second, I was taking a shit. I said. Then I got up from the toilet cleaned my ass and washed my hands then grabbed the phone.

"Hello"? I said.

"Yo Dice, What's up?" What you doing? E.B. Said.

Ain't shit my nigga, just chilling in the crib for now cause it's hot as hell right now and I don't be fucking with that heat like that.

I know, but check it, Rock and them having a game today at the Laguardia Houses and they want you to come thru and do what you do E.B. Said.

Aight, so I'll meet y'all at the gym when I get there, I said.

"Aight Dice" I see you then. E.B. said.

Later! (Click) I hung up the phone.

"Where you going Dice?" Jay asked.

"I'm going to the Laguardia Houses to play ball the streets are calling me. Why what's up you wanna come with me?" I said. Acting like I was taking a jump shot.

"Yeah of course I do, you know I gotta see my little brother put it on them dudes out there, so you know I'm a be there for you Dice." Jay said. Taking a seat on the bed.

"That's what's up Jay cause you know they can't stop me especially when I get down low in the paint I'm a beast down there. I said.

"You ain't lying about that, but let me ask you a question. "Little brother" are you still taking that "dirty money" from them Drug Dealers?" He said. With a curious look on his face.

"Hold up, Hold up wait a minute "Whoa", mic check, what you mean "dirty money I work for "mine". I said, putting on my B-ball sneakers.

"But you don't even know where it's coming from." Jay said.

"Listen Jay, I don't give a flying fuck where it's coming from, as long as I'm out here playing ball for these niggas and they looking for me to play for them. They gonna be paying me fuck that, cause I need the money. I said. Patting my chest.

"Aight, Dice have it your way you'll learn one day, all that comes fast goes fast, and believe me I understand you might need the money, I'm just saying that it's other ways of getting money other than taking it from them "drug dealers" like you do." Jay said. Expressing his concern.

"Are you putting any clothes on my back?" NO! So why are you worrying about how I'm getting mine, when I'm not out here selling drugs. I'm not doing anything like that, I know you just trying to look out for me and all but I know how to take care of myself, so let me do me Aight.

Aight Dice have it your way. Jay said. Brushing it off avoiding an argument.

Once that was over we finished getting dressed, and started heading to the Laguardia House gym. When we got there we were amazed to see the amount of people that showed up to the game. All the hustlers, pimps, and bitches from the neighborhood were there to see the game. See in my mind I knew at an early age I had to get money any way I could. I had my mind made up already, if I couldn't get it the professional way or the legit way. I was going to get it my way. "By any means necessary."

* * *

My moms and father was in the house trying to relax on this hot day taking it easy after a long week of working for pennies. My pop's worked for a yellow cab company he drove taxi's cabs for a living. He also had a gambling problem and that didn't mix. My mom's worked for a cleaning company. They rarely got the chance to see each other so they were happy to be home alone spending quality time.

My brother Wicked and my cousin Tony were on their way to Harlem to pick up some coke from Crazy Louie. They called him Crazy Louie, because this nigga was straight crazy. We heard so many stories about this nigga Crazy Louie about what he did in the past to people or had done to people. Even after getting shot 11 times in front of my mother's bedroom window this nigga was still on his shit. One of them I don't give a fuck type of niggas. Many people would say that he was living with a death wish. He was Italian, but he hung around the Blacks and Spanish people like he was one of them. He lived on the block longer than anyone of us did. He knew my family for along time ever since we moved on the block. One time when my father was on his way home from work he spotted a familiar face being chased down by two niggas that was shooting at him. When my father was close enough to recognize who it was, he came to the rescue pulling his yellow cab into the middle of gun fire. Crazy Lou immediately jumped in and was relieved to see my fathers face as they sped down First Avenue. A few month's ago before Wicked moved to Brooklyn with Tony he got into a fight with Crazy Louie's cousin Peter. It wasn't nothing serious tho that would prevent them from doing business in the future. Crazy Louie was on Pleasant Avenue, and 118st waiting for Wicked, and Tony to show up. When they got there they was driving in a black Maximum with tinted window's. Soon as they pulled up to the Corner of 118th street, they spotted Crazy Louie sitting in a green Cherokee Jeep. He got out of the jeep and got into the maximum with Wicked, and Tony. They drove two blocks near Benjamin Franklin High School, and parked there to conduct the business at hand. Crazy Louie showed them the drugs that they wanted to purchase. He was carrying it in a Louie Vuitton bag.

"What's up my boss" Wicked said. As Crazy Louie entered the car.

Same ole shit man! Just a different day. Crazy Louie Said.

"Ah, it that Louie?" Tony Asked. Referring to the drugs.

"Yeah," that's that shit right there, pure as it gets, you know how I do, I only fuck with quality shit. Crazy Louie Said, as he was lighting a Cigarette.

"Yeah mon", that's why we ear now, you know mi no say yah have it. Wicked Said.

Aight let's do this shit now y'all can test it if you want but you know my shit is official let's make it happen so I can get the fuck out of here. Crazy Louie said.

Just cool nah mon mi ah grab it fa yah now. Wicked said. Trying to stall Crazy Louie before the transaction was done.

Wicked reached his hand in the bag that the money was supposed to be in and pulled out a .380 Simi automatic weapon turned around and dumped three slugs in his chest area then they pushed him out of the car as they sped off heading for the highway on 116 St. Everybody that was outside on the block saw what just happened to Crazy Louie in broad day light. This was a regular thing in my hood seeing someone getting robbed or shot. Crazy Louie was lucky he was wearing a bulletproof vest or it would have cost him his life. Crazy Louie laid there on the pavement feeling like he got hit by a semi truck. His peoples immediately rushed to his aid.

"What the fuck happened to you," Are you alright? One of them asked.

Do I look alright to you Mother fucka, them fucking bastards robbed me, and tried to kill me." Crazy Louie said.

"Who? Who you talking about?" They asked confused not knowing who he was talking about.

"That Jamaican motherfucker that use to live down the block, I'm a kill that bastard."

"Who?" His homie Mark yelled.

"Dice brother Wicked, you dumb mother fucka, stop asking me so many questions and go get the fucking guns. Crazy Louie Said.

Mark ran immediately and did as Crazy Louie said, when he returned he had a Mac-10 and a Tech 9. The other drug dealer that was with Mark had a 9mm. When Crazy Louie was able to gain his composure back they started heading down the block to my crib. Crazy Louie was trying to get his breathing under control because the slugs that landed in his chest knocked the wind out of his ass. Once they was in front of my building. My man Butta was coming out of his apartment on his way to the Laguardia House to see the game. Butta had no idea as to what was taking place at the moment. As he was exiting the building, Crazy Louie and his crew forced Butta back into the building and made him knock on apartment 1A. Which was my mother's apartment. Butta was so afraid of Crazy Louie and by the sight of gun's that he urinated on his self. Butta knocked on the door three times hoping that someone would save him. Mark cocked his Mac-10, and told Butta to knock harder . . . .

* * *

When we walked in the "Laguardia House" we heard the roars and cheer's before we even entered the gym. Today was a big game for us. The East Side vs. West Side, being that I was from the east side, you know I had to represent for my hood. The whole game was tight the lead kept changing back and forth. With about ten seconds left in overtime, my team had possession of the ball, the game was tied 86 to 86. Boo inbounded the ball to me. I was making my way up the court crossing over breaking niggas down. Once I made it thru the full court press I was pass half court, I threw E.B. the ally-oop pass, he then slammed it in the rim, and the game was over. This was the second time that we had beat them in the final's for $10,000. It was a good day for us. We won a little cash, and beat the West Side" for the second year in a row that was something to brag about for us. After the game we went and got some pizza for "Patsy's" It was the best pizza in Harlem it was located on the corner of my block. After we ordered our food we noticed all the Police and Ambulances surrounding my building. At first we didn't think nothing of it, we thought it was just another dead fiend overdosed on some shit. To my surprise we was wrong. I overheard these two ladies talking about what happened that live on the block when they walked inside the pizza shop.

Damn girl, um, um, um did you see what happened to that lovely family they all died in that house. Just like that pow and don't nobody know what happened. It's a damn shame it's time for me to move from around here. One of the ladies said.

Child, I ain't see shit either. Them jokers around here crazy, I was in the kitchen cleaning some chicken for dinner tonight when I heard the shots go off. That shit scared the shit out of me, you know I got bad nerves already. The other lady said.

I thought I was about to have a heart attack. Lord knows I was praying up in here you hear me. I'm just glad that it wasn't my baby out there getting hurt or in any trouble because I can't take any more stress. I have enough problems as it is already dealing with these crack heads.

* * *

My mother opened the door when she looked through the peep hole and saw it was Butta.

"Hey butta" She said greeting him. The boy's ain't . . . . Ah!" Before my mother could finish her sentence Crazy Louie and them were forcing their way into the apartment dragging Butta along with them inside the apartment. My father was in the bedroom sleeping but was awaken by the commotion coming from the living room. As he was pulling the covers off of him to get up and see what was going on. Mark walked in the bedroom with the Mac-10 pointed at him. At first my father thought he was still dreaming until he felt the cold steel pressed against his forehead. Then my father calmly made his way to his feet and let Mark, escort him into the living room where my Mother and Butta was being held hostage. My father made no sudden attempt to become a hero because he knew that could cost him and his Wife their lives. But if he was going to do something, he was going to have to do it fast.

What the fuck is your problem running up in my house like you some "kinda ras mon" My father said. Trying to control his emotions.

"First of all you not in the position to be asking any question's now and second of all what the fuck is your sons fucking problem robbing me for my shit and then he tried to kill me. See that's where he fucked up at, I would a charged it to the game if he would of just robbed me, but that mother fucker tried to kill me." Crazy Louie said.

My father and mother both looked at each other puzzled cause they didn't know what the fuck Crazy Louie was talking about.

"Me nah no what yah a talk bout mon." My father said.

"I'll tell you what the fuck I'm talking about your stupid ass Jamaican son. He's gonna die when I catch his silly ass. I'm a cut his fucking balls off, and stuff' em in his mouth." Crazy Louie said.

Everybody that was there knew that Crazy Louie was serious about what he was saying. My Father couldn't believe what he was hearing Crazy Louie say. That his son Wicked would come all the way from Brooklyn to Harlem where him and his family lived and do something like this. That would put them in Jeopardy.

Now before I kill your ass, get that bastard ass son of yours on the phone now! And I mean Now!!! Crazy Louie said.

My father hesitated for a minute because he wasn't sure about what he was going to do next. But the way things were looking he didn't have much choice.

"Hurry Up!" Mark yelled.

My father looked at my mother again and saw her crying and praying to herself. He felt in his heart that Crazy Louie and them wasn't playing at all and they were gonna kill them anyway. But he couldn't let my mother die like that so he picked up the phone and called Tony's house looking for Wicked.

Ring, ring, ring, ring . . . . No Answer! Then he tried again.

Ring, ring, ring, ring . . . . Still no Answer!

For a moment there was pure silence as the tension filled the air . . . Then the silence was disturbed by the sound of gun "shots" Boom, Boom, Boom,

Boom, Boom! The smell of blood, and death filled the room. They died instantly.

* * *

When we got to the building we saw everything close up. All the police, detectives and the E.M.S. Units were in the front of our apartment door. My heart stopped and my mouth dropped in disbelief. I couldn't believe that his happened to my family. Who would do something like this and for what. I was Clueless about everything. I forced my way through the yellow tape, the cops tried to stop me, but I had to see for myself, to see if it was true. Once I was inside I couldn't believe what I was seeing. Blood was everywhere all over the walls and furniture. My father was laying on top of my mother like he was trying to save her before they died. At that point my heart stopped again this time I passed out. It was too much for me to bare. When I came back to reality I was laid up in the Hospital surrounded by detectives asking me a million and one questions. They also had my brother Jay in the corner asking him the same thing over and over again. Did you see who did it? Do you know who did it? Did your parents have any enemies. We didn't know shit. I was sitting there in a daze it felt like I was dead. But I did die I lost my Mother, my father and a friend. Then I got up out the bed and walked away. That's when my nightmare started.

Chapter 2

"Turning Point"

After the funeral Mrs. Ruby took us in. She was E.B.'s mother. They lived across the street from us. His mother and my mother were close friends. My mother use to be at her house every other day talking and cooking for hours at a time when she was alive. Every time I use to go with her to Mrs. Ruby house I use to make up all types of excuses to leave because they annoyed me by talking and saying don't he looks just like his father. Or they would start talking about shit I really didn't want to hear like gossip. I wish I could hear her say it now tho. It took a lot out of me when they died, cause when they left they took my heart along with them. I had to find out who did this and why? I didn't care if it took my whole life to find out no matter what. I didn't have any emotions left nothing else mattered to me anymore but revenge and thats what I was out to get at all cost. Somebody owed me a lot and I was going to make them pay. Everything in my life changed right in front of my face in a blink of an eye. I knew life for me and Jay was going to be a lot different. We just had to be strong and take it day by day. I still hadn't shed any tears yet my body was numb to everything. The first couple of weeks were real hard on me. I stop doing what I was normally doing, like basketball and chilling on the block. It took a while for me to come outside cause I was tired of people coming up to me asking me was I Aight. Because I wasn't aight and if one more niggas asked me if I was aight then they wasn't gonna be aight. I wanted somebody to feel the pain that I was feeling, I didn't care who it was, I wanted them to feel pain.

* * *

Four years later. I was still learning how to deal with my parents death, and my man Butta. I was still living at E.B.'s mothers crib. Jay had moved down south a year after my parents were murdered. I wasn't ready to leave as of yet and go anywhere until I had answers. I felt all alone without my family around for me like they use to be when they were still here. All I had was my niggas to cheer me up by bringing bitches through to fuck with us. It helped while they was around for the moment, while we was doing our thing, but after that it was back to the same ol thing. E.B. knew I was fucked up in the game and I needed some new gear and the only way for me to get it was by getting money, and that was something that I didn't have at the time. I was 19 years old now and a nine to five wasn't for me. One day when me, E.B. and Boo were on 115th street and Lexington Ave at the chicken spot ordering some snack boxes for all of us to eat. E.B. and Boo kept bullshiting around snapping on each other the whole time we there. After we got our food we were heading back to the block. That's when a all white 600 Benz came creeping up next to us as the passenger side window slowly came down. I didn't recognize the passenger at first, because I haven't seen this familiar face in a long time since I wasn't around in the hood like that anymore or playing ball. When I did it was Rock wearing a black expensive suit sitting in the passenger seat.

Yo, what's up Dice? Where the fuck have you been I haven't seen you in a minute playboy. Rock Said.

"I've been chilling, that's all" I said.

Damn "youngsta" do you know how long I been trying to find you, I thought you moved or something, and went down south with your brother Jay and shit." Rock said. Plucking his cigarette out the window.

"Nah," I ain't going nowhere no time soon, I just been a little fucked up that's all.

"Well, I'll tell you what!" Since I always took a liking to you, cause you my little nigga, Here, take my number and call me and I'll take care of you when you do. Rock said. Passing me his number.

"Aight". I said.

"Yeah, you make sure you do that, and get at me cause I can't see you out here fucked up like that, you my little man, so do the right thing and make sure you call me, trust me you won't regret it when you do." Rock Said.

As they drove away in the white 600 Benz.

We watched the tail lights of the 600 Benz disappear into traffic as it made its way down Lexington Ave.

"I didn't know who the fuck that was rolling up like that" Boo said.

Stuffing his mouth with some chicken.

"Word! Me either" "So what you gonna do?" Dice you gonna call him or what, cause you know we need some money anyway, you never know it might be something that might work out for us, you know I don't give a fuck what it is cause I'm with it regardless. E.B. said.

"Word, I'm here for you dog." Boo said. Agreeing with E.B.

"I don't know I'll think about it." I said. As we continue to walk down Lexington Ave.

My intentions wasn't to call him back because I wasn't with playing basketball for him anymore and if that's what he thought he could've of kept it pushing.

On our way back to the block I decided to call Rock and find out what exactly he had planned for me. When we were back at the crib I gave E.B. the number for him to contact Rock, and set up a meeting for us.

* * *

When we arrived at Rock's place it was 8 o'clock later that day. We meet up with him at his pool hall that was located on 125th and Second Ave.

Rock was in the back in one of his private rooms that he had there. When we walked in Rock was sitting behind his desk counting stacks of money while his two body guards were sitting on the leather sofa that they had in the office. They were in there watching Boxing on Pay Per View. They immediately stood up when they noticed me and E.B. walked in.

"Easy Boys," I was expecting them. What's up Dice and E.B.

I'm glad to see that y'all could make it. Rock said. Standing up extending his hand to give us dap, have a seat." He said.

"Ain't shit, you already know what it is." I responded. After sitting down. Then through the corner of my eye, I noticed that "Rock" had one of his females hanging around while we was about to get down to business. She was off the hook she looked like Trina the rapper and had a body like Lisa Ray. Her name was Cookie it should of been diamond because she was rare like one. I stared at her like I wanted to taste her.

"Yeah, I had a lot on my mind and I didn't feel like being bothered so I laid low for a minute to get my head right. I said.

"I understand," and I'm sorry for what happened to your family, you have my sympathy if it's anything that I could do for you just let me know aight. Rock said.

"Yeah" that's what's up, but I didn't come here to talk about them, or to have your sympathy, you said you had some business for us to handle and that's what we here to talk about. I said. Getting directly to the point.

"Yeah" you right, let's get down to business. Are y'all niggas ready to make some real paper for y'all self's instead of running around with lint in your pockets. Rock said. Leaning back in this chair.

"That's why we here now! E.B. said. With emphasis.

"Watch your mouth little nigga" speak when spoken to, not before. One of Rock's body guards said. Getting defensive.

Nah its aight," let'em talk these "little niggas" hungry I like that type of attitude. I need these niggas on our team. Y'all "motherfuckers" ready to bust your gun's and do whatever it takes to get it, I need to know now before we go any further cause I ain't "fucking" with no scared shit later. I'm giving y'all niggas the opportunity to leave now. Rock said.

"Do we look like a bunch of fucking cowards to you?" I said.

So y'all niggas ready to get your hands dirty, "huh" well "aight." I'm a see what y'all niggas really bout, there's some shit coming in tonight that I was gonna go pick up cause they was expecting me, but I came up with a better idea. I want y'all to go and take that shit for me. It's going to be a lot of cash and five keys of coke coming through tonight, I want y'all to go up in there and get everything, I mean clean that shit out then come back here and I'll take care of y'all. Rock said. Observing us for any weak signs.

Why don't you tell some your goons to go up in there and handle that shit for you. I said.

"Cause I want y'all niggas to go and get it that's why." What y'all thought that y'all was just gonna walk in here with your hands out like this is a charity club or some shit. If y'all got a problem with it y'all can take your broke ass's and get the fuck out of here cause you starting sound like you scared to me. Rock said. In a agitated tone of voice.

I ain't never scared and we didn't this far to waste nobody time. I said.

"Well good," that's what the fuck I'm talking bout y'all gonna need some burners I got them here for y'all but y'all gotta supply your own set of wheels. Rock said. With a slight smirk on his face.

Then one of Rocks bodyguards reached in the duffle bag that he had next to him on the sofa and pulled out two forty glock's with extended clips and handed them to us.

"Cookie" smiled and licked her lips slow and seductive teasing me with her sexy ass. She had on a skin tight Fendi full body suit with the matching Fendi shoes to go with her outfit. I glanced at her one last time before we headed out the door. Then Rock gave me the address that we needed, and we were on our way.

*   *   *

We needed a car to get to the location that we were going to. Since none of us had a car at the time we had to steal one. Car jacking was out of the question for us, because by the time we jack somebody for their shit and let them go they gonna run and call the police and we were gonna be hot before we get to where we was going. The best thing for us to do was to steal a car. None of us knew how to steal a car, so we had to call this big mouth ass nigga name "Twin" to get the job done for us. He was the only one that we knew in the Hood that knew all about stealing cars and when it came to that Nascar driving (Good get away driver) he was one of the best. After we called him we all met up in Wagner Projects located in

Harlem. No sooner than we go there he started running his mouth, about what was going on in the hood. He was like one of them nosy ass bitches that lived in the hood, that did nothing but mind other peoples business all the time running around like a damn "News Reporter." He had dirt on everybody. We knew we were taking a chance by fucking with this nigga but we didn't have no other choice, but to use him for what he was good for.

"Oh what's good "E.B.", "Dice" my nigga what's up dog what's so important that y'all wanted me to rush over here and meet up with y'all. I know y'all two niggas ain't up to no good, I could see it written all over your face so what's good fill me in. Twin said.

"Slow down killa," we just need you to get a car for us and drive, its some paper involved for you after we take care of what we gotta do.

"Like what," let me know what's up" you know I gotta know the 411 about everything's that's going on, what y'all don't trust me or something." Look! Shut the fuck up, why you so fucking nosy about shit that don't got nothing to do with you, you getting paid driving and getting us a car. I said.

"My bad dog," I just wanted to know where we was going and shit that's all no harm done. Twin said.

You'll find out when we get there, now hurry up and do your thing so we can get the fuck outta here! I said. As we was leaving the projects.

We got on the train at 125st and Lexington Ave we took local 6 train to 86st. When we got off the train it took us no time to get a car we got our self 's a Toyota Corolla. It wasn't the best car for the job but it would have to do for now. We arrived on a 171st and University Ave in about thirty minutes which was our destination. We parked the car one block away from where we was going so no one could identify the car we was in when the jukes was done. We made Twin stay and watch the car there was no reason for him to come with us, bad enough he knew to much already.

The apartment that we was looking for was located on the fifth floor.

The front door of the building was locked, so we had to wait until someone was coming in or going out to let us in. After about five minutes of waiting a old lady that was pushing a shopping cart was coming out of the building. We helped the old lady out the building and made our way into the building and up the stairs. We could hear the loud Spanish music playing in the hallway coming from one of the apartments and that was a good sign for us because it would help muffle the shots. All we had to do now was find the apartment that we was looking for, knock on the door and ask for Freddy. Freddy was the code name that they used to let them know that you was there to do business with them just the way 'Rock" had explained it to us. When we knocked on the door a short stocky Dominican man opened the door for us when he heard the name Freddy. We rushed in the apartment like we was "ATF" but it was us (Them Stick up Kids) the wrong mother fucka's.

"Don't move, don't move." I whispered as I came towards the Dominican man with the nozzle pointed directly in his face. Then I grabbed him by his collar and forced him down to the floor.

E.B. quickly ran through the apartment looking to find anybody else that might have been inside the crib before we snatch up what we came for.

When E.B. returned from doing his search throughout the crib he found a mother fucka trying to hide in the closet. E.B. escorted him into the living room. E.B. smacked the Dominican man in the back of his head, and told him to get the fuck on the floor with his partner. The fat motherfucker started yelling at us in Spanish saying all type's of shit like Conyo this, putah, mathi con. Like he was trying to disrespect the juke's.

Shut the fuck up you fat mother fucka, and stop crying like a bitch before I smoke your ass. I said. He still didn't shut up, this mother fucker must think that we was playing with his ass because we two young niggas. I thought to myself. "That was a sad mistake."

Bang!

The first shot went off hitting him in the stomach, he slumped over clutching his stomach and started moaning feeling the pain, as the slug was burning his insides.

"You still think I'm playing with you mother fucka." I said. With my gun still pointed at him.

"That nigga started speaking English immediately." "No poppie, no poppie please, please no kill me. I give you everything just leave us! Please I don't want any problems papa please." He said. Begging for his life.

"Then tell us where all the shit at and the fucking money."

What money papa, we don't have no money only drugs here." He said.

"Oh, so you still wanna play games with me, huh?" Like you don't know what I'm talking about. I said.

Ok, ok just take it and go it's inside the refrigerator at the bottom.

E.B. quickly searched the refrigerator and found the drugs and money wrapped up in plastic. Then E.B. grabbed everything and put it all in a garbage bag tied it up and put it by the door.

I took one last look at them than I cocked my 9mm back and said thank you for your assistance but we won't be needing your services anymore. E.B. looked at me with a blank expression on his face like what the fuck he about to do. When he saw me raising my gun he figured it out quickly. Bang! Bang! Bang! Bang! Bang! Bang! E.B. followed suit.

We bodied both of them bitch ass niggas without any hesitation and I didn't feel a thing it was like nothing. That was the first time I ever squeezed the trigger of a gun and the first of my many bodies that was to come. Before we made it back to Rock's place we stopped at E.B. crib to see how much we caught off the jukes we did and to get rid of the guns. It was more than we expected it to be six keys of coke and two hundred, and thirty thousand dollars in cash. We never seen this much shit before in our lives it felt like we hit the lottery the way it came so fast and easy. We stashed a 100g's, and a brick of coke for ourselves. He wasn't getting everything, fuck that unless he was gonna take it in blood. I thought to myself. We then drove to Rock's place and gave him the rest that was left over. He gave me and E.B. 20,000 for us to split after what we just did all the dirty work and we left niggas stretched out in the crib with their heads open. I'm glad we stashed the rest because my next thought would have been to kill his ass next. From that day on we became thirsty for blood shed especially when it was money involved.

Chapter 3

"Step your Game Up"

Several weeks after we ran up in them poppie niggas spot, we started making our own money. The money and drugs that we stashed we divided between all of us. We use to dream about getting money like this, now it wasn't a dream anymore we were living it and we wanted more. We was on the come up. We all brought cars with the money we had stashed and the money we was making off the coke we was moving. Bitches were all on our dick's like crazy now seeing us in the flyiest shit and pushing them big boy whips. Even that chick Cookie was feeling the kid. She was a little older than me but I didn't give a fuck the older the berry the sweeter the juice. Cookie had slid me her number one night I had bumped into her at the Club. But I knew that this was Rock's Bitch so I had to watch my self, and make sure that she wasn't trying to set me up by playing me close. I never intended to call her back anyway. Rob and Boo was driving in a new .325 BMW that Boo had copped. Me and E.B. was in my SL500 Benz. We were heading downtown to the steakhouse on 42st. We picked up 3 keys more earlier that day and now we were going to celebrate due to ur new found success. We had spots set up from L.E.S (Lower east side) all the way back to Harlem. Breaking it down, and supplying spots. Rob and Boo took care of the spots. Rob wanted us to set up shop in Brooklyn with his cousin Blinky because Blinky was doing good numbers out there but he didn't have enough work that he needed to supply the demand, and that's where we came in. With the product we got we could make a killing out there. especially if we doing it right we could step on it 3 times. Rob was a chef when it came to whipping that coke up. His wrist game was sick when we were out playing ball all over when we was younger. Rob was running around with hustlers and pimps. Big

Ant was the one who threw him under the wing and showed him about the drug game before he got locked up. So flipping work for him wasn't a problem we trusted his judgment when it came down to this shit. We decided to fuck with his cousin Blinky but I gave him all responsibility over Blinky. It wasn't a real risk for us because we knew how to get it back if we took a lost down line in this game you have be prepared to take one.

* * *

The word on the streets was that Twin was running his mouth about the jukes we did that time when we paid them Dominicans a visit. We couldn't have this type of shit floating in the air cause if it got back to the wrong people it could become a problem. To prevent that from happening we had to bring it to the source. We called Twin and told him that we had another job for him. It was about 11:30 at night when we picked him up.

It was business as usual, Boo was driving, E.B. was riding shot gun and I was in the back of the car with Twin.

"Yo what's up Dice," big dog I see y'all niggas blew up off that shit, I see y'all buying new cars and shit from the gate can a nigga hold some'em. Twin said.

Don't worry boy you gonna get some real paper tonight, you gonna be riding like us in a minute watch. I said. While rolling up some weed.

"Where we going now dog, you got me all hype and shit right now." Twin said.

There you go again baby boy "speed balling," don't worry like I told you, you'll find out soon enough I'm a make sure you're the first to know when we get there. I said.

"Yeah chill nigga you know we gonna take care of you. Boo said. As he was driving looking through the rear view mirror.

After "E.B." took his couple of pulls off the blunt he passed it to Twin. That nigga was pulling on the blunt like he had a vacuum cleaner built in his lungs. Puff, puff pass nigga what the fuck you doing trying to smoke up all the shit acting like you the only one that wanna get high in here. I said. Everybody busted out laughing.

You know a nigga gotta get right before he do what he do you know what I'm saying dog. Twin Said. But you ain't the only one that put in on it man." E.B. said. Snatching the blunt away from Twin.

As we continue driving, I started loading up my .45. We were only minutes away from our destination. Twin was staring out the window viewing the scenery. He must have had a thousand thoughts running through his mind at that time. They say right before you die you have a quick flash back of your life as it comes to a end. I asked Twin what time it was, he looked down at his watch and said it's . . . .

Before he had a chance to answer the question a bullet was traveling through the left side of his head. His brains splatted on the glass. Then we pulled over and threw him off of the Tappin Zee Bridge to swim with the fishes. He was playing a deadly game with his life dealing with us. At the level's we was taking it to we couldn't afford any loose lips. That goes for everyone.

* * *

Three days after our little trip it was Friday night. Rock wanted us to meet up with him at the club called the Tunnel. When we arrived at the tunnel it was packed to its capacity, wall to wall with niggas and bitches drinking, smoking, and dancing everywhere.

After they searched us we headed straight to the bar. We check our surroundings before we made any moves. Once everything appeared normal I ordered me a bottle of Hennessy. Me and E.B. stayed by the bar Rob and Boo was mingling with the crowd fucking with the fly honeys that was there. There was a lot of fine ladies the type niggas call wifey that you take home to meet mommy and put a ring on it especially the one that was sitting next to me at the bar.

"The next one is on you." She said.

"What?" I Said. Shock by her assertiveness

"You heard me," is the next one on you because the way you looking at me is like you about to take my drink away from me. She said. With a grin on her face.

"Oh yeah", I see you got jokes I like a lady that can make me smile

Oh really, you probably say that to every booty and a smile. She Said.

Nah, just you. I said. Staring into her green eyes examining her from head to toe with her beautiful smooth brown skin. She was looking right in her Gucci outfit.

Aight, Shorty just one drink because I ain't no trick but I do like what I see.

First of all, my name ain't shorty, I'm a lady its Shaniqua and I never said you was a trick what you got a complex or something. She said. Playfully rolling her eyes at me followed by a smile.

Well Miss Shaniqua, my name is Dice the infamous one. I said extending my hand

"Please", anyway nice to meet you and nice name it sounds unique. She said.

It's like you, "Unique." I said.

"Stop it boy, you killing me." She said. Blushing feeling herself.

"Nah" I'm Serious, Where you from?

"Queens," She replied. As the word came slowly off her tongue.

"Who you with?"

"I'm with my friends they somewhere in here they wanted to come and have a girls night out to unwind from working so hard all week. We haven't been out in a while." She said.

"That's what's up."

"Who you with?

"It's just me and my mans and them."

"So y'all come here often?" She said.

Nah I came here to care of some business, but it was a pleasure meeting you in the process.

"Ok that's cool."

So what's up, what you getting into after the club or you got a curfew?

"No" I don't, and you gotta call me to find out yourself." She said.

Taunting me.

Then she wrote her number down and gave it to me and walked away giving me a full glimpse of her sexy body.

"Damn!" Dice who the fuck was that, I ain't never seen no bitch that look that good she straight outta a magazine for real. E.B. said.

"I know, I thought the same thing the first time I laid my eyes on her." I said.

She had me hypnotized for a minute watching her walk away. I had to find out who she really was, for a moment I almost forgot why we was there.

Rock was in the V.I.P. section of the club waiting for us. The speakers were thumping in there they was playing my shit the hood anthem by "Nas and Mobb Deep" (We don't give a fuck). We stepped through the crowd making our way towards the V.I.P. section. As we entered Rock greeted us like he always did.

"Dice my man what's up." Rock said.

"Chilling my nigga, that's it, what's up with you, you the man of the hour." I said. Giving each other dap before we sat down at the table.

"Same as always, out to get that motherfucking money and keep getting it nah I mean." Rock said. Then he gave the bodyguard dap.

That's what's good my nigga cause if it ain't about a dollar then it don't make cents." I said.

"That's right Dice, I see you learn quick, but I also never got the chance to tell you that I appreciate the way you handle that situation for me, It was messy but that's how I like it." Oh by the way I see your boy finally got what he had coming to him, I always told that nigga that he talks to much running around worrying about shit that don't have nothing to do with him, "Nah I mean," he got what he had coming to him but enough about him, fuck that nigga. That's not what we here to talk about tonight. I hear y'all niggas making big moves out there right now." Rock said. With a devilish look on his face like he knew something we didn't.

"Yeah, we doing a little some'em but nothing major though just trying to live."

"Cause that would be fucked up Dice if y'all niggas making moves out there and ain't showing me no love, when I was the one that put y'all on and got y'all started. So if we going to continue to do business with each other, y'all better hear what I'm saying I want in on everything that goes on, cause I hear and see everything that goes on in these streets." Rock Said.

I couldn't believe this greedy motherfucker bitching about paper. When he got damn near everything from that jukes we did for him. Oh hell no who the fuck he think he is, coming at me sideways. If I would've had my hammer on me I would empty the clip in his face right now, cause this mother fucka is gonna be a problem. I thought to myself. Staring at him face to face trying to control my emotions.

"Ok", now with that of the way we can proceed and get down to business. I got another job for y'all. There's this warehouse down by the pier that got crazy weight in there I'm talking big time. Bigger than that last shit we did. It's about 300 keys and a 1000 pounds of weed in there. The niggas that run that spot think it can't happen to them. They be up in there fucking with bitches and shit like it's a fucking game they don't deserve to have any of that shit. It's four niggas with some heavy shit. But all y'all gotta do is be patient and watch them for a minute to see how they moving and from there all you gotta do is run up in there with your gunz out blazing mother fuckers from the door, from there you know the routine take everything and one more thing before I let y'all go make sure you watch them bitches in there and when its over we gonna break it down 50/50 so its worth it for everybody, we'll all be happy." Rock said. Popping a bottle for Moet.

It didn't sound like a bad idea plus it would be a nice come up for us if we were able to pull it off and get away with it. My niggas were super hype they were ready to go and do it the same night. But to me it just didn't sit right I felt it in my gut. He was willing to break it down equally a little too easy. Being that it wasn't going down tonight I had time to let my thoughts marinate. We all made separate plans for the rest of the night my plan was to get up with shortly who I met earlier in the club Shaniqua. I made my way to the dance floor leaving E.B. with Rock and his bodyguards and in the VIP section smoking and drinking. Rob went to Brooklyn to holla his cousin Blinky to let him know that we were going to be supplying him soon. When I left the club I called shaniqua to see what's up we got together a little after 3 a.m. We went and got some breakfast from a local diner in the city by the West Side Highway. Shaniqua was from Laurington, Queens area of New York. She told me that she lived alone ever since her father was murdered during a car jacking by a couple of crack heads a few years ago and she never got the chance to meet her mother because she died giving birth to her. The only family that she had that was close to her was her grandmother.

Her grandmother comes to visit her from time to time. She also explained to me that all she does is work and hangout with her friends when they have free time and that's once in a blue moon cause they always busy. She hates being alone because she always been alone. When we finished eating our Steak and eggs Shaniqua decided that we should go back to her place. She drove in her Acura Legend Coup, I followed behind her in my SL 500 Benz. When we got off the Van Wyck Expressway we parked in her drive way. She had a very nice house I was impressed even more when we walked inside with the fine things like her imported Italian furniture set, 65 inch Television mounted to the wall and her large 100 gallon fish tank with tropical fish with flowers all over the place. It definitely had a woman's touch.

"You can make yourself comfortable and just relax while I go and freshen up, I'll only be a few minutes. I have to get out of these sweaty clothes." Shaniqua said.

"Aight, I'll be right here." I said. Then Shaniqua headed for the bedroom. I made myself feel right at home I turned on her stereo system and started listening to the late great Marvin Gaye as his soothing lyrics filled the air. (Let's Get It On) I closed my eyes and laid my head back and enjoy the sounds that was playing. Being there just felt right to me. My thoughts were interrupted when I opened my eyes and I saw Shaniqua standing in front of me in her birthday suit. Her skin was flawless, the dim lights made her body look like it was glowing, she was curvy in the right places her body was perfect. Her nipples were so hard and long they looked like missiles. Water was still dripping off her body from the shower she had took. She was ready to melt in my mouth like sweet chocolate on a hot summer day.

"You just gonna sit there and stare at me all day." Shaniqua said.

Shit, I damn near nutted on myself, just by looking at her gave me an instant hard on. I took off all my clothes in a hurry leaving me wearing nothing but my chain and a stiff hard dick. I got up from where I was sitting and picked her up and carried her into the bedroom, and began kissing, caressing her all over her body from head to toe. Everything started moving in slow motion. I placed her legs over my shoulders and started using my tongue all the way down to her love box playing with her clit, I was tasting all her juices. She started moaning and groaning moving her body like a snake. My tongue motion was making her orgasms come repeatedly. Shaniqua got up and changed her positions placing my 10inch dick between her soft juicy lips that was covered with lip gloss. Her head went up and down on my dick like a porn star. Then I put her in the Boston crab position, her body started shivering feeling me all up in her making her weak. Then we switched positions again, this time I was hitting her from the back doggie style. Shaniqua's pussy felt so good I thought I was in heaven for a minute the way her ass cheeks spread apart when I slid inside with all my manhood. I was fucking and eating that pussy right. She got on top of me like she was at a rodeo and was riding that dick. Shaniqua felt herself cumming again, and started screaming as I was taking her to ecstasy.

Oh, oh, oh that's it Dice, yes that's it baby "oh my god" yes, I'm cumming, I'm cumming yes!

"I'm cumming," I'm cumming," Yes!

The sex was the shit we went on for hours tossing and turning flipping and licking. Once we were done we just laid there sprawled out ass naked exhausted until we drifted off into deep sleep. I woke up that afternoon feeling like a new man. Shaniqua was still sleeping when I got up to get dress. Today was going to be a busy day for me and crew so I had no time to lay around and play hubby plus my thoughts wouldn't let me. Before I headed out the door I woke Shaniqua up to let her know that I was leaving.

"Do you have to Dice?" Shaniqua said.

"Yeah baby," I gotta go but I'll call you later when I'm done handling my business. I said. Grabbing my car keys, she got up, and kissed me with her soft warm lips and said

"Ok Dice, I'll be waiting for you Aight." I said. Then I walked out smiling from ear to ear.

* * *

On my way up to Harlem all I did was think about Shaniqua until my cell phone started ringing.

"Hello," I said.

"Yo, What up Dice?" Boo said.

"What's good my nigga Boo, Where you at?"

I'm at the crib, what happened to you last night I was calling your phone all morning it was going straight to voicemail.

I was caught up with this shorty, that's all where everybody else at?

E.B. and Rob right here with me waiting on you to show up." Boo said.

"Aight" I'm almost there anyway, I'm on the F.D.R. Drive right now I should be there in about 15 minutes the most, did you pick up them thangs for da night?"

"Yeah I did, I got some shit you gonna love you'll see when you get here."

"Aight, so I'll see you when I get there."

"Aight one!" Boo said. (Click) hanging up the phone.

As I resume to driving my cell phone began vibrating indicating that I have a new voicemail, when I called my voicemail to find out who it was from. To my surprise it was Cookie Rock's bitch. I immediately thought to myself how the fuck did this bitch get my number.

Hey, what's up Dice, this is Cookie I know you wondering how did I get your number well let's just say I have my ways but anyway I was thinking about you and I wanted to see you cause I have something very important to tell you. So call me back when you get this message please and don't worry about Rock answering the phone cause he ain't here he went to Florida this mourning ok baby, I'll be waiting. Then at the end of the message I heard a kiss. This bitch is Crazy. I said to myself out loud.

When I got to Boo's crib E.B. and Rob was there smoking on some sticky icky.

"What's up my niggas" I said. Giving the daps. "Y'all ready to take care of this shit tonight."

"Hell yeah" They all responded.

"You know, I don't give a fuck cause I'm down for whatever as long as my niggas eating I'm with it." E.B. said. Taking a drag of the weed he was smoking.

We all agreed with him on that note.

Then we examined the gunz, we had a 12 age Marshburge Sawed off pump, Two Mac-11's, .357 automatic, Russian mini AK and a Chrome 44 Desert Eagle. We went over the plans a few more times to make sure everybody understood what they had to do when it was time. It was now 5 o'clock the jukes wasn't going down until 10 o'clock tonight. So we had a couple of hours to burn. I decided to call Cookie back to see what she wanted.

"Hello Cookie." I said.

"Yes this is she!"

"Yeah what's up this is" . . . . she interrupted me.

"I know who it is, Dice. She said. Flirtatious with her sexy voice.

"Yo what's up, I got your message that you left me on my phone, what's good talk to me." I said.

"Where you at?"

"I'm around, why? I thought you had something important to tell me." I said.

I do Dice but not on the phone o.k. just meet me on 106st and Lenox Ave in thirty minutes and I'll tell you everything you need to know trust me it ain't no funny shit involved. Cookie said.

"Aight."

"Make sure you there Dice"

"I will." Then I hung up the phone. (Click)

When I arrived Cookie wasn't there yet. I parked and waited for her to show up. I was thinking was she really going to come until I seen her pull up five minutes later driving a Lexus GS300, she parked her car then got out and walked over to my car and got in. She was wearing a while hulta top with a D&G mini skirt that revealed her thick thighs. She was definitely eye candy.

"What's up baby?" Cookie said. Closing the door behind her.

"You, Now what's good?

"Calm down Dice! I'm not here to waste your time or play any games with you. I told you that I had to talk to you about something and I couldn't wait to tell you and I couldn't tell you on the phone what I have to tell you." Cookie said.

"Well we here now face to face, tell me what you got to say to me now!"

"Alright, alright okay Dice . . . You know I'm feeling you and I been feeling you for a long time now and I just didn't know how to express myself to you to let you know exactly how I truly feel about you for a long time. Dice ever since I first saw you from that first day I knew it was something about you that attracted me to you. That's why I gave you my number at the club but you never called me to find out how serious I am about being with you and only you, that's why I'm here taking a chance with you."

"We both taking a chance by being here." "I know."

We both stared at each other for a few seconds, then Cookie continued. "And I know you want me too Dice . . . . I see the way you be looking at me the eyes don't lie, you can't tell me that you don't feel the same way about me."

"Why are you telling me this?" "How do I know you not trying to set me up over some bullshit that I ain't with." I said.

"You really think this is bullshit well I guess I gotta show you". Cookie said. Then she reached over me to recline my seat back, unbutton my jeans pulled down my zipper and pulled out my dick and started giving me head. Cookie sucked it like it was her favorite chocolate blow pop. I couldn't resist the sensations I was feeling it was driving me crazy so I just let her do her. I was enjoying every moment of it rubbing on her thighs making my way up under her D&G mini skirt. That's when I realized that she didn't have on any panties. Cookie climbed on top of me then slid my hard penis in her wet pussy. It was tight like a virgin's pussy. She was screaming like she never fucked before biting her bottom lip, pulling on my clothes, her grip on me was so tight on me when I came, I came right inside of her. After I finish fucking her she told me that Rock never had sex with her and to be exact he was getting fucked by both of his body guards and for all she knew they could be somewhere fucking each other right now.

"Why you still with him then, why you just don't leave." I asked.

"He takes care of me, he gives me anything I want, but I don't love him. I never did that's why I'm here with you now cause I need you, I don't want to be with him anymore, I can't hide my feelings for you no more he sees the way I look at you and . . . . She paused.

"And what?" I said.

Dice, you can't trust him, he knows about the money and drugs that y'all stashed on him, he is not happy about that shit at all. I think that he's going to do something crazy that's really why I had to talk to you. . . . She paused and took a deep breath and said. I really don't want nothing to happen to you, you gotta believe me Dice, he's crazy who knows what he might do. Cookie said.

"What makes you think you could trust me?"

"I don't know but I do."

So that's how Rock knew about Twin, cause Twin must have told his bitch ass about that shit. I thought to myself.

"Dice you have to be careful baby, I'm not gonna let anything happen to you." I promise.

"When is he coming back?"

"Tomorrow, Why?"

"You'll find out soon enough, I hope you know what you doing by coming here today telling me this shit."

"I do trust me, I couldn't just sit back and not say nothing about it."

"So you really wanna be with me, or you just playing games with me cause (B.G.T) Bitches Get It Too. I said. With a serious expression on my face with my hand under my seat gripping my .9mm.

"Yes Dice I'm all yours, you don't have anything to worry about me." Cookie said.

"Aight' listen to me, I need you to do something for me first and after its done we could be together when its all over so pay attention real good, do as I tell you and don't fuck up. I said.

"Yes I understand anything for you Dice anything just tell me." Cookie said.

"Aight", this is what I need you to do . . . .

Chapter 4

"Never say Never"

The time was now 9 o'clock. We were on our way to the pier. I had informed E.B, Boo and Rob about the news that I had found out earlier from Cookie, and that we had a change of plans.

"Word! Get the "fuck outta here," you mean to tell me that, "that nigga" knew the whole time and he was fronting like he didn't know shit about it, I wonder if that nigga knows everything that happened with Twin and the jukes?" Boo said.

"We should just run in there and blast that nigga and say fuck everything." E.B. said.

"Chill, we already know who opened and ran their mouth about this shit it's not a mystery anyway. I guess this was his way of rocking us to sleep.

Plus I got plans for his ass we gonna handle this nigga before he think he could get the drop on us Cookie already let the cat out the bag so it's time for the dogs to come out and play." I said.

That's what he was talking about when we was all at the club then huh,

"well fuck that nigga." E.B. said. Aiming his gun at the wall.

*   *   *

When we arrived at the pier we noticed that there was activity out side in front of the warehouse. The females entering through the bay area. We were well equipped for the jukes we were using night vision heat seeking binoculars. After about 10 minutes of observing the scenery the females came back out and started heading towards the cars.

They opened the trunk of one of the vehicles that was parked out front of the warehouse. They pulled out six large bags from the vehicle that was parked next to a black Land Cruiser. They carried the bags back into the warehouse while one of the men that were there held them down with his MP-5. Making sure they made it back inside safe.

That's exactly how we going to enter through the bay area. I thought to myself.

We going to creep up and wait until one of them comes out and grab them and then make our move. I said.

We slowly emerged from the cargo van one by one, moving in a single file until we got close enough. Now that we were in position all we had to do was wait until we made our grand entrance and make our presence felt immediately. We were all dressed in all black the darkness played in our favor we blended in perfect. There was only one light and it hung over the warehouse door that the females went in. Several moments later the door was opening again from the inside. That's when we started moving in. I quickly grabbed the door as it opened. Boo was the first one to make it in with his finger squeezing on the trigger of the Mac-11. Hitting the first man that was opening the door dead in the throat sending him flying off his feet blood started flowing from the side of his neck. They we all strapped with MP-5 assault rifles. But we caught'em slipping. I smacked the shit out of one of the niggas that tried to sneak up behind Boo with the back of my Desert Eagle sending him crashing straight to the floor causing the back of his head to split open. One of the bitches tried to be fast, she must have thought she was superman the way she caught them bullets in her chest. R-R-R-R-R-R-R-R-Rah! E.B. grabbed one of the niggas that had his pants down to his ankles and forced him to lay down on the floor then he put two slugs in his head blowing off a piece of his skull. Then we had everything under control everybody else that wanted to live had their hands up in the air scared of the sight of death. We gathered all the keys of coke and pounds of weed that we came for. Before we left we made everyone that was still alive get down on the floor on their knees and told them that we don't leave no witnesses behind to tell stories. We open fire on them B-B-B-B-B-B-B-B-B-Braat!!

Murdering everything thing that was moving bodies were scattered all over the warehouse and the scent of blood. We made it back to the cargo van the same as we came. Rob started acting all emotional about the shit, like we was suppose to have sympathy for them.

Damn, Dice we ain't have to kill all of them like that they were surrendering, we could've just tied them up and left them there, they were harmless. Rob said.

"Man," what the fuck is wrong with you, are you crazy, fuck that shit this ain't the love boat, niggas die out here everyday over this drug shit, we ain't the first, and we damn sure ain't the last. E.B. said.

Stop bitchin up like that. what you scared nigga, them niggas would've done the same thing to you if they had the chance to catch you, why you think they had them machine guns for, huh," declaration nigga you bugging the fuck out." I said.

I'm just saying. Rob said.

"Ah man, fuck that shit." Boo said.

We drove to one of our stash houses to unload everything. Cookie called me to tell me that Rock was back from Florida. We planned to give him a surprise visit that he would never forget. He wasn't expecting us to arrive until the following morning. I told Cookie to make sure she had the basement door open for us before we got there, cause we were on our way.

Rock and his bodyguards were upstairs in the day room playing a game of pool, and drinking champagne while they were discussing some issues that they wanted to take care of. But all that change in a heartbeat when we walked in the day room. Rock dropped his glass of champagne causing it to shatter all over the floor because he was surprised to see us uninvited. The bodyguards tried to reach for their guns, but it was too late for them, to try and react. E.B, Boo and Rob had their guns pointed at them . . . 45s and Mac 11s. They never had a chance.

Oh there's no need for that, as you can see y'all "niggas" are to slow you gotta be ready for this type of shit man, didn't Rock teach y'all better than that I know he did. If you gonna plot make sure that you on point yo Rock what's good my nigga, why you don't look so happy to see us, I thought you had love for the kid what's good?" I asked. Laughing my ass off.

"How the fuck did y'all get in my house?" Rock said.

Your Bitch let us in, oh my bad that's my bitch now!" Who let us in nigga, she got some good pussy too, but you wouldn't know that cause you got these big head mother fucka's fucking you, "what's up with that?" I said. Looking at his bodyguards.

"Come on Dice", talk to me, what's this all about?" Huh, Money, you know I got that. What is it Cause if it's that, that's not a problem if you need money all you gotta do is ask me for it. There's no need for all this that you doing here, you like a brother to me. Rock said.

"Nah dog that's not the problem cause I got my bitch Cookie bagging all that shit up for me right now as we speak, you know why the fuck we here man, don't play dumb with me nigga, cause we all adults here so let's keep it official." I said. As I pulled my shirt up revealing my .44 Desert Eagle handle.

"All right man, you got me, you happy now?" Huh? What you gonna do, what you gonna kill me now "huh" all the "shit," I did for y'all niggas y'all gonna come up in my house and disrespect me like that, I showed y'all niggas how to get money when yall didn't have shit, I brought y'all niggas in, Now y'all wanna "bite" the hand that feed you, yall were the ones that "stashed" on me . . . . Come on Dice, let's forget that any of this ever happened here today, and let bygones be bygones and, just start over fresh from the beginning no more secrets. Rock said.

"Man . . . Stop Crying like a bitch I always thought you was a gangsta ass nigga, I had mad respect for you, but you aint nothing, but a gay ass homo motherfucker in a suit, you thought you was smart you was praying that you caught us slipping didn't you, but we fooled your ass, the whole shit, blew up in your face. Let me ask you a question, what kind of niggas did you think we were? You couldn't be satisfied with what you got. Nah, you want everything, now it's gonna cost you everything, you greedy mother fucka, nigga you must be crazy as hell, if you think that I was gonna let that happen. But now the time has come for a change, you had a nice run while it lasted, it's time to pass the throne, but before I kill your ass, why don't you say goodbye to your toy soldiers." I said.

Rock looked over at his bodyguards with the sad puppy face and watched them die. Boo, Rob and E.B. ripped them apart with bullets. B-B-B-B-B-B-B-B-B-B-Braat!

Rock started begging for his life.

"Please! Oh my god, Dice, please, please don't kill me, please I'll give you anything, just tell me what you want, huh, what is it? I'll tell you who killed your parents, please, just don't kill me."

What? . . . What the fuck did you say motherfucker, Whoa, wait a minute, wait a minute, did you say what I think you just said." I said. As I was approaching him. You mean, to tell me, that you knew all this time who killed my family, and you didn't tell me shit, you sorry mother fucka, you ain't worth shit, you fucking bastard."

Then I punched Rock dead in his face causing him to flip over the chair landing flat on his back.

"Now I got your ass, under the gun, you wanna cry like a bitch, and try to save your shitty life, that ain't worth shit!" But I got news for your homie that's not gonna happen, not today mother fucka you gonna die like the rest of them." I said. Standing over Rock, Rock was curled up like a scared dog.

"Please Dice, just hear me out, Please listen to me, it was your brother, Wicked, he robbed Crazy Louie for his shit, then he tried to kill' em, but he didn't he shot him three times in the chest, and he still lived. "So that's what made them kill your family, because they couldn't get to him, Dice you gotta believe me, it's the truth I wouldn't lie to you."

Two cold tears came rolling down my cheeks feeling the pain of what I was hearing Rock tell me about the day my family was murdered. I've been waiting to find out for so long now who was responsible for their deaths. I gritted my teeth together then I reached in my waist where I was concealing my .44 Desert Eagle and said you deserve to die then blew his fucking brain out." Boom! Boom!

"You fucking faggot." I said. Then I spit on his dead corpse.

Chapter 5

"It's a New Day"

A year after Rocks death, everything was moving smooth for us. We had found out that Crazy Louie was in prison serving a three year bid for an assult charge. He was scheduled to be released next year, and we were going to be waiting for him when he got out. I wanted him so bad, I could barely sleep until I knew I had go my revenge. It was personal between us,

I also had my people looking for my brother Wicked. Wicked and Tony haven't been seen since my family was murdered. I knew that one day I was gonna see them again. Me and Cookie were together now, ever since she gave me the drop. So far she proved her loyalty to me, for that I spared her life. I took her under the wing and kept her close. We had brought a house in Long Island next to where my family was buried at. Cookie was also pregnant by me. She was very excited about it, I was too. I also was still fucking with shorty that I had met at the Club Shaniqua. My feelings for Shanigua had grew strong for her over the past several months. Me and Shanigua could relate on a higher level, she was my soul mate, and I was hers. Even though me and Cookie lived together, I was with Shaniqua every chance I got. Me and Shaniqua shared a lot in common that connected us to each other. My love for Shaniqua wasn't just physical, it was mentality, and spiritually. Shaniqua was also expecting my child.

*　*　*

At this time period, the whole crew was balling. We were at the top of our game, we had everything cash, cars, jewelry, bitches whatever we had it or we were doing it. We still controlled Harlem and L.E.S. (Lower East Side) but we expanded our operators to Virginia and Baltimore. With money, power, and respect who was fucking with us. Throughout all the hoods our names rang bells like the president. We were them niggas now that everybody wanted to be. But with all the money and shit we had it still wasn't enough to wash away the pain that I was feeling and the memories that remain. I wanted to let my brother Jay know that I had found out who had murdered our family, and who was responsible. But I didn't want to cause him any more pain than what he was already feeling. I sent E.B. to go see Jay, and give him 50,000. He didn't want to take it, so I had to promise him that I would change my life and move down south if he took the money. It worked for the moment, but I knew he was going to be holding it over my head. Jay was still living down south with my grandmother. She was always mad at me for not moving down there with her and Jay to stay. She always told my mother that the city life was too fast for her and that she should move back down south to raise us, where she came from. My mother was a very strong and independent woman. She didn't like help from any of her family, she wanted to do things her way. Sometimes I wish she did, maybe it would've been different for all of us. In the mix of it all, I was living my life young, healthy, and wealthy. God had plans for us, that haven't revealed itself yet.

* * *

Today it was hot ass hell. Summertime and everybody knows what that means (stunt 101). Big boy toys, bitches, and block parties everywhere.

That's when people like to get together to enjoy the weather and everything else the summer has to offer. Especially niggas that's balling, you know it's like a car show, Stunting in the latest shit riding on chrome. Even the females wanna show who's that bitch, who got the fattest ass and the biggest tits. Boo called me cause he wanted us to go to the Rucker game Uptown. He begged me to go with him. At first I wasn't gonna go with him cause I had other plans that I wanted to get into, but I said fuck it and went with him, anyway. I drove my new candy paint cherry red Danali sitting on 28" inch rims. I had it laced with T.V.'s all around in the head rest, and in the dash, with a crazy mean system that you could hear blocks away.

I was blasting that Jay-Z, and Jermaine Dupri shit (Money aint a thang).

When I picked Boo up from his crib. It was about 1oclock in the afternoon we stopped to get a fresh car wash even though I didn't need one, but I like to keep my rims shining when I'm riding. From there we went straight to Rucker Park. When we got there, there were so many celebrities there

I thought it was a red carpet event. They were there representing for their teams that was playing in the tournament. We scanned the crowd to see if we notice anything funny or anybody we knew. There were a few cats that we recognized from back in the days but we ain't never fuck with them in the past, so we gave them daps and kept it moving. It was crazy bitches out there trying to stunt with their asses out. Some of them looked like they were wearing nothing hoping to catch a ballers eye and get lucky by becoming a baby momma. And just like every hood you go to, there were them grimy looking nigga around. I took notice to these two dudes that stood out like a sore thumb wearing hoodies hot as it was. I didn't really pay them to much attention cause we had that thing with us, and we was always ready for war. There were so many people out there flossing, they could've been there for anyone or maybe they were just there to watch the game. After we finished smoking a blunt I realized that I had left my cell phone in the truck. I tapped Boo on the shoulder to let him know that I was going to the truck to grab my phone.

"I'll be right back." I said.

Do you want me to come with you? Boo Said.

"Nah;" "I'm good," I'll be right back.

"Aight."

When I got back to the truck, I opened the door reached inside and grabbed my cell phone. I turned to holla at this chick that was walking by with a banging body she didn't even stop to holla at a playa. I checked my cell phone I had 5 missed calls and 2 new voice messages. That's When I peeped two shadows standing behind me I turned around quick to see who it was, when I did it was them same niggas that was wearing hoodies standing right behind me. I wasn't even scared when I saw their guns pointed at me. I stood there because they already had the drop on me. I had to respect that I already knew what it was. Until one of the gunmen took his hood off revealing who he was. It was Twin's Twin brother he just came home from up north. I wasn't even thinking about his brother coming back after me. But when you fuck with family, you always gotta expect that somebody is gonna try to retaliate one day.

"This is for my brother, mother fucka." He said Squeezing the trigger. Blam! Blam! Blam! Blam! Blam!

Everybody started running after hearing the shots go off. All hell broke loose out there. The last thing I remembered is when I saw Boo running towards me with his .9mm in his hand then I blacked out.

*   *   *

When I woke up, I was in the emergency room the Doctor said that I need about 3 weeks of recovery. I been down this road before with my family this time it was me laying stretched out on a hospital bed. God wasn't ready for me yet, I had a purpose to be on this earth. Like the saying says the good die young and I was far from that. My left arm was numb, and my stomach was burning. At first I didn't know what I was doing there until the Doctor walked in and saw me trying to get up.

"You have to relax, try not to move around too much and you'll be just fine. Someone must be watching over you, cause your lucky you survived you were shot four times, and you didn't damage any of your arteries. You have some visitors that been waiting to see you, do you want me to send them in." He said.

"Yeah." I uttered.

When my visitors walked in it was Cookie and Shaniqua. Here comes the drama! I thought to myself. If looks could kill I would have been dead four times the way Cookie and Shaniqua was looking at me.

You all right baby? Cookie said. Kissing me on my forehead.

Shaniqua stood there staring at me for a moment with tears in her eyes and a big belly. She didn't know if she should slap me or hug me shit I don't blame her. Then she reached over and hugged me.

"Ouch." I uttered

"Oh", I'm sorry Dice you ok? Shaniqua said.

It's aight baby girl its not your fault, I'm just in a little pain right now, the doctor said I'll be fine they didn't hit nothing major."

A little pain, boy are you out of your mind, you've been shot four times and you talking about you aight, you better thank god you still here cause I wasn't gonna let you leave me like that, hell no not while I'm carrying your baby." Cookie said. Staring at Shaniqua with her hands on her hips.

I knew that the drama was about to erupt and I wasn't ready for it.

"Who the fuck is this bitch Dice? Cookie asked. Snapping her fingers in Shaniqua's direction.

"Excuse me, that's miss bitch to you boo, the question is who the fuck are you, cause this is my man." Shaniqua said. Rolling her eyes.

"Dice you better tell me something cause I'm about to beat this bitch ass right now." Cookie said. Taking off her jewelry.

"Why don't both of y'all shut the fuck up. "Damn! Y'all don't see I'm shot the fuck up right now with holes in my ass, I don't have time for this shit, y'all both having my baby, what the fuck y'all want me to do huh? Shit . . . a nigga damn near died today.

"What?" "What you mean, we both having your baby Dice, you never told me no shit like that, what you was trying to hide it from me." Shaniqua said.

"Damn!" "What the fuck did I just say to you, matter of fact I don't wanna talk about this shit right now. I just been shot four times, let's deal with that right now, and deal with the other shit later."

I stayed in the hospital recuperating for a week and a half. I wasn't a hundred percent better but I had to get outta there I was gaining my strength back. The doctors said that is wasn't time for me to leave yet, I needed a few more days of rest. I said fuck that and signed out. E.B. heard the news from Rob that I was shot while he was still down south with Jay. He rushed back to New York to see how I was doing. Boo and Rob were on the hunt for Twins' twin brother and his man. When I got released from the hospital E.B. came to pick me up in his black Range Rover.

"Damn Dice", I can't even leave town for a minute without you getting in some shit, huh? I heard it was Twins' Twin brother who did it, y'all didn't peep him when y'all was out there?

Nah, it was so much people out there man I couldn't see everybody's face, that punk ass mother fucka, he needs to learn how to shoot."

"When did he come home from up north?"

"I don't know, but imam make'em wish that he didn't. You know we got a location on Twins brother we could go check this nigga tonight and push his wig back, plus I know where his bitch stay at and his grandmother, so don't even worry about it we got you.

That's what's up, but fuck that I wanna see his bitch ass before he dies. What y'all was doing out there without any burners anyway?

What you mean, we had that thang with us, they just caught me slippin that's all, but I put money on it, it wont happen again bet that. I know that's right, where you want me to take you to?

Drop me at the crib, and I'll call you later when I'm ready to ride.

E.B. drove me to my house in Long Island. When I walked in the house Cookie was outside on the patio, soon as she heard me she came running back inside happy to see me home.

"Hey Baby, I was waiting for you, I thought you wasn't coming straight home, why you didn't call me to let me know that you was on your way, I called the hospital they said you was discharged hours ago. Cookie said.

As she was approaching me with her arm extended out to hug me. She had on some sexy lingerie that enhanced every curve on her body.

"I know ma, I was a little busy. I didn't have a chance to call you, but I'm glad E.B. dropped me off." I said.

Sitting down on the suede sofa, then I grabbed the remote control to turn on my 88 inch flat screen HD television. I took off my T shirt, Cookie sat down next to me on the sofa then she leaned over and kiss me on my cheek her lips felt nice and soft.

"Oh my god" Dice, look at your bandages, you need to change them baby, when was the last time you changed them." She asked.

"When I was at the hospital. Oh no baby I'm a change them for you now." Cookie said.

Then she got up and went in to the bathroom to get some bandages and alcohol to clean it. As Cookie walked away her ass was bouncing like she was dropping it like it hot. After retrieving the first aid kit she squatted down next to me to change my bandages.

"Ouch" I Said. As she removed the tape from the bandages.

"You have to relax Dice, and let me do this for you. You know you had me worried about you when I first got the call that you was shot, then to see you laying there in the hospital and the doctors working on you. I didn't know what to think, I just kept praying that everything would be alright, because I can't live my life without you. I'm so glad you here with me now, now it's my turn to make it all better for you.

Cookie stood up in front of me slid off her robe that barely covered her hips. Then she slowly went down on her knees. She planted her lips on my chest, slowly moving them down pass my stomach pass my navel till her lips were wrapped around my dick, even my balls were being attended to. My body started shivering feeling a tingling sensation run through me. Then she got up and turned around and put all her ass on me. Her ass was bounced up and down on my dick until I felt her juices flowing on my legs. We both came at the same time. After we were done we took a shower together, she washed me up, then I washed her up as the water splashed on our bodies. I walked in to the bed room when we were done, to dry myself off and to get dress. I had Shaniqua on my mind the whole time. I wanted to see her. I put on my Sean John Jeans and my Julius Erving New York throw back jersey.

You leaving already Dice, you just got here a little while ago, you do have to get some rest, I don't know why you wanna rush and go back out so soon.

"I know, I'll get some rest when I get back, but right now I gotta go. I Said. Grabbing my .45 auto

Where you going with that? She Said. With a puzzled expression

Antonio Harriston

"What this? This is my American Express, I don't leave home without it."

I said. Referring to my .45 auto.

Dice, are you mad at me for finding out about Shaniqua? Cookie Asked.

"No! Why should I, you was gonna find out anyway that she's pregnant by me, y'all both having my baby, it ain't nothing to hide it is what it is. I know one thing though, I'm not gonna have that baby mama drama shit with y'all, that right there is a no, no for me. Y'all gonna learn how to deal with each other or I'm a deal with y'all."

Cookie stared at me as I was walking out of the house like she wanted to kick my ass. I jumped in my SL500 Benz stashed the burner in my stash box. And was on my way to Shaniqua's house I turned on the system in my Benz, popped in my mixed Cd and let that Jay-Z shit play out mid-level (Don't Cry my Nigga) till I got on the high way and turned it up. I rolled my windows down half way to feel the breeze. I started thinking about my family, what would I be doing if they were still here. Would I still be out here running these streets the way I do, or would I be doing something totally different like a 9-5 or maybe worse. All I had now was my niggas, Shaniqua, Cookie, and the streets

*   *   *

When I made it to Shaniqua's house, she was sleep when I walked in, until she heard me walk in the bedroom where she was.

"Ahhhh, hey baby I didn't hear you come in, damn I'm tired." She Said as I sat down on the bed, next to where she was laying at.

"What's up, you was up all night?"

"Yea, plus the baby got me tired, I was sleeping all day." Shaniqua said.

Sitting up in the bed to kiss me.

"How you doing baby, I missed you."

"I missed you too." I said. Rubbing her stomach.

"I'm glad to see that you feeling better now."

"Yeah, I'm aight."

"I was worried about you."

I know, I'm here now everything's gonna be alright, so don't worry yourself about me."

Then I pulled the covers off of her, and told her to stand up so I could examine her belly to see how my baby was growing.

"Dice, you know you really hurt me, I found out about Cookie and she's carrying your child, I thought I was the only one, I thought you loved me, why you never told me about her, you thought I wasn't going to find out, Dice, why did you do this to me, Why?"

"Listen to me Shaniqua" Cookie got history with me, she did things for me, you wont believe she did, and that's the only reason why I fuck with her, it just so happened that she got pregnant by me, I'm sorry that it happened this way but it did. So now we gotta deal with it, just like I told her, I'm telling you, Cause ain't none of y'all going anywhere. I'm not one of those lame ass niggas, I claim what's mine you mean the world to me.

Shaniqua, but I have my reasons for keeping Cookie close to me."

"But, if you say you love me the way you say you do then why did you do this to me?" "I would never do anything to hurt you in any way from the first day I had you in my life, I always been true to you Dice, I thought we was happy together, I didn't think that you would ever let anything come between us, I'm so hurt, and mad at you right now I don't know what to do."

"Damn baby, just hear me out, shit happens, I didn't mean for this to happened, but it did, this is life people make mistakes, I made a mistake the only thing we could do is learn from it so it don't happen again, I'm sorry that it happened this way, "Yes" I'm very happy with you, more than you could imagine, my heart, my love, and my soul belongs to you, and only you, If I gotta spend my whole life apologizing to you and doing my best to make it up to you, I will, I'm sorry." I said sincerely.

Staring into her eyes so see could see that I meant every word I was saying. Then I pulled her close to me so that we could feel our hearts beating together. I lifted her pajama top over her head and began kissing all over her stomach soft and passionate making her feel at ease. I rubbed and sucked on her breast as my tongue glided across her nipples. Then I said.

"Baby I love you."

I slowly laid her back on the bed caressing her silk like skin with my hands and tongue, making a trail with my tongue until it reached inside her wet juicy love spot. Shaniqua always loved when I ate her pussy, and I always enjoyed doing it. Ain't nothing like some sweet pregnant pussy from the one you love. I thought to myself while I was making love to my lady for the rest of the night until we were sound asleep.

Chapter 6

Bang! Bang!

The next day, E.B., and Boo were in Brooklyn at the barber shop getting haircuts. I called them to tell them that I was on my way there. But first I dropped Shaniqua at my house in Long Island with Cookie. I gave them both 5,000 a piece for them to go shopping at the mall. When I made it to the barber shop I parked my Danali behind E.B.'s Range Rover. I walked in the barber shop, E.B. was in the barbers chair getting fresh. So I walked to the back of the shop to sit where Boo was sitting at.

"Yo what's up Boo!" I said giving him dap.

"Ain't shit my nigga, what's good with you, you aight?

"Yeah I'm good, but it could have been a lot worse, you know what I'm saying, you know we gonna check them niggas tonight." I said.

"Hell yeah, they some dead mother fucka's when we catch'em." Boo said.

"Word! Cause that shit burned like a mother fucka." We both started laughing.

"You a crazy ass mother fucka." Boo said.

"I know, what's up with Rob though, he aight."

Yeah he good he's over on Nostrand and Fulton in Bed-Sty collecting some cash from Blinky."

"That's what's up.

Shouldn't you be home laying up Chilling with your feet up watching T.V. or some shit, cause you did just get out of the hospital yesterday, I know you a soldier and all, but damn."

"Man! Fuck that, they need more than four slugs to stop me, ya heard!" I said. With a smirk on my face."

Oh, so now you 2pac, huh?

"Whatever man."

What you getting into after we finish getting our haircuts, cause I wanna show you my new crib I got, it's crazy big, 4 bedrooms, two full bathrooms, large living room, dining room, a patio and of course a smoke room, and you won't believe where it's at of all places but you'll find out plus I got some fine bitches coming over, you probably don't even have enough energy anyway."

"Nigga you crazy, I'm strong like an ox, I don't know what you talking about.

"Nah, I'm just fucking with you, but if you don't have nothing to do when we leave here, you should fuck with us." Boo said.

"I was gonna go back to the crib and fuck with Cookie and Shaniqua to see how they getting along with each other, cause you know they ain't happy about it anyway."

"I know you got your hands full dealing with them two, you better watch it, they fuck around and kill each other by the time you get home."

We both chuckled. "But anyway, you fucking with us or what man?

Yeah, Fuck it, I'm coming."

"Aight, that's what I'm talking about, cause its gonna be a lot of fucking and sucking going on today boy." Boo said. Giving me dap.

"Shit, I got enough pussy yesterday."

We started laughing again.

When we left the barber shop, I drove behind them all the way to Boo's new Condo. The freaks were already on their way. They called Boo after they made their exit out of the Holland Tunnel to confirm the address.

Boo got his self a banging Condo downtown over looking the West Side Highway. I was surprised when I walked inside. Everything in the condo had 18kt gold trimmings. Boo wanted to break in his new place, and what better way to do it then with your niggas and some sexy females. It was 7 o'clock when they arrived. When they walked in our mouths hit the floor, cause they were off the hook, Seven of God's gift to the earth. It was like we were doing a video shoot. All of them were fine. My eyes were stuck on this one in there that had my full attention from the moment she walked in. she was 5'5, 165 pounds, Dominican, and half black shaped like a hour glass her name was "Anna." They all were from New Jersey." Anna asked me about the bandages she saw under my New York jersey. I told her it was nothing but some minor scrapes. Anna started telling me about herself. She was 20 years old, she was still in College studying to get her Masters because she wanted to become a doctor one day. She didn't have any kids and she wasn't ready to have any no time soon either. Anna wanted to reach her goals first before she started thinking about a family, and as far right now she was enjoying herself. She definitely had her head-pointed in the right direction. Rob walked in carrying a large black duffle bag that he had picked up from his cousin Blinky. He went and dropped it in one of the many rooms in Boo's Condo, then he joined the party.

Me and Anna, decided to slide into one of the rooms to get a little closer. I was feeding her bullshit, I was telling Anna that I was a real estate broker, but she wasn't buying, but she played along like she was. Anna noticed the blood stains that was coming through the bandages.

"I think you need to change those bandages, cause you don't wanna catch any infections."

"I don't have any extra bandages with me, I left them downstairs in my car in the back seat, but I don't feel like going down to get them."

"Oh, I'll go get them for you if you want me to, trust me I won't steal your car.

Believe me I ain't worried about you doing that, here its parked out front, it's the white SL 500 Benz. When Anna returned from retrieving the bandages she complimented me about, my Benz. Then she went into doctor mode. Anna removed my New York Jersey I was wearing."

"I thought it was nothing major, cause I do know what these are." She said. Looking at the bullet wounds on my body my inner shoulder, chest, stomach and arm.

"Shit happens, I'm alright though, I got you to take care of me, you the one gonna be a doctor."

"Well, let me guess, what you sold somebody a fucked up house, and they wanted they money back and you didn't wanna give it back."

"I'm still here right?"

"That's a good thing, cause we wouldn't be here now." Anna said.

Admiring my tattoos, and my chiseled body as I laid flat on my back while she took care of my wounds. "He's finer than a mother fucka. Anna thought to her herself. Biting her bottom lip. The music was loud that was coming from the front of the Condo, but we could hear the girls in the next room screaming out in pleasure. Anna looked at me after hearing the sexual sounds made, and exhaled feeling her emotions rising as she was licking her lips with lust in her eyes. She put her hand on my dick seeing my erection growing in my jeans.

"What is this? Anna said. Massaging my 10 inch dick.

That's just my little friend."

Little friend. She mumbled

Anna leaned over towards me and kissed me on my neck, that gave me freedom to explore her body. I grabbed her by her hair and started doing the same, fondling all over her big titties, then our tongues met for the first time. We was all over the bed like we was wrestling.

"Stop! Wait a minute, let's do this the right way." Anna said. Taking off her skin tight Christian Dior jeans, then she removed her tank top.

Her breasts were nice, and firm the way they stood at attention.

Anna's body was a work of art, God really blessed this girl. I then slipped off my jeans, Anna pulled my boxers off while I ripped off her thong.

She grabbed my over sized fat dick, and kissed it. Then she started licking up and down on my shaft. She laid down on the bed, I placed my fingers in her pussy, she began pulling on the sheets. I then crawled on top of her in the 69 position. My tongue was moving around all in her pussy. Everything was moving fast, sweat dripping off our bodies. Then the bed room door slowly opened. It was one of Anna's friends standing in the door way looking amazed at the sight of my dick in Anna's mouth, and my tongue in her pussy.

"Oh my God, um um look at that shit. She said.

Then she closed the door, and walked over to join us. We now were having a threesome. I was taking turns fucking the shit out of them.

Anna rode my dick like a champ. while one of them had their tongue in the other ones pussy, I had my dick buried in their ass. Tits and ass was everywhere. I stacked Anna and her friend on top of each other like pancakes, sliding dick in and out of them. When we were done, all three of us took a shower together. Then they gave me head again until I nutted in both of their faces. "Whoa." I thought to myself.

I ran through two packs of Condoms. When it was time for them to leave Anna put my number in her phone, and said, "I'm gonna keep your number on speed dial so when I'm feeling horny, you only a button away."

Anna said.

After they left we split the money up that Rob had got from Blinky.

"Yo Dice man, I can't believe we ran through all that work already, we gotta find another Connect, or catch another jukes, cause the way shit is moving we don't wanna get caught in a drought, we'll start loosing money. Rob Said

"Shit!" Fuck that, ain't nothing stopping my money, fuck what ya heard, because if that happens we going out putting that gun game to work and take what we need. E. B. said.

"Word dog", cause my people outta state are killing' em out there, nah mean. We gotta keep hitting them with them joints, cause I don't wanna put no speed bumps in our flow." Boo said.

What we need to do, is find a new connect that can hit us with what we need, with a good price. Once they see that we are serious it would be no way they could deny us what we want plus we putting up that cash. We can't keep robbing everybody their ain't gonna be anybody else left to fuck with, but if we have to we robbing them too. I said.

We all were making valid points, and the point we all were making was that we needed work. But we also had some unfinished business that we needed to handle first.

It was now Midnight. We were in front of Twins brother building. He lived in the Bronx in Morris Projects off of the Grand

Concourse. We knew we had to be quick about it because the D's (Detectives) patrolled these projects hard. And we didn't want to get into no bang out with them unless we had to. 12:45am is when our prey arrived. He was walking with some chick heading towards his building in the projects 345. We could of jumped out on his ass right there and pushed his shit back, but we chilled cause we wanted to minimize the noise. We waited for him to walk in the building then we walked in behind him dressed like two old ladies. When we got by the elevator we made our move.

"Yo, what up homie." I said to him with my .357 auto pointed right at him. I got his attention immediately. He turned around and was surprise to see me standing there with a gun wearing a dress. His eyes damn near popped out of his eye socket. He quickly grabbed the girl he was with, and pulled her in front of him. He tried to use her as a shield. But that didn't help him, cause the head shot that blew off half of her face made him realize that. He then darted into the staircase trying to make a run for it and we was right behind him. Before he could reach the top of the stairs a bullet was traveling at lightning speed ripped through the back of his head coming out between his eyes, then two more entered his spine killing him before he was able to take another step. We watched him come tumbling back down the stairs and landed at our feet, then I hit him one more time in the head to make sure the job was done. We made it back to the waiting car quickly just before the D's made it down the block we were gone with the wind into the darkness.

*   *   *

Chapter 7

"Drama"

Cookie and Shaniqua were back from shopping at the mall. Cookie was in her bedroom putting away the things that she had brought while she was shopping. Shaniqua treated herself to a nice diamond necklace that cost $4200. Shaniqua was in the living room watching T.V. Cookie walked out of the bedroom and entered the living room where Shaniqua was.

"How long have you been with my man". Cookie said.

What? Shaniqua replied.

"You heard," don't what me, how long have you been fucking Dice"

"Hold the fuck up, you better watch your tone, and I didn't even know about you first of all, for your information that's my man, and I been fucking with him for over a year now." Shaniqua said.

Standing up

Hum, look I don't give a fuck what you say Dice is my man and I love him and he's never gonna leave me to fuck with you, or any other bitch, so don't think you gonna come up in here, and try to break up a Happy home over here cause it ain't happening and I don't see what he wants from your ass anyway, I'm all that he needs and then some O.K., so let that be known to you, and any other bitch that thinks she could come, and take my man away from me, and get his money got another thing coming, cause its not happening." Cookie yelled

Snapping her fingers.

"If he was your so called man, and he loved your ass I wouldn't be standing here now with you pregnant. Second of all, I got my own money, so sorry miss know it all, I don't know what you talking about, I think that's probably why you with him, hanging around while he's outside fucking with other bitches. You got some nerve, its obvious you must not be doing something right for him if he keeps coming to me getting all up in my pussy like he always do."

"Wait a minute bitch, who the fuck you think you talking to like that?"

"You bitch", What?

Right before they was about to pop off I walked in.

"Oh," I see y'all getting along well, I don't see no bleeding or any bruises that's good. I said. As I was walking in the kitchen.

"Look let's not start no bullshit tonight, I'm tired it's been a long day for all of us, plus I need to get some rest before I past the fuck out, tomorrow is another day, whatever we need to talk about we'll talk about it tomorrow on our way to breakfast." I said. Heading to the bedroom.

"What you mean, we'll talk about it tomorrow, we need to talk about this shit now, this can't wait till tomorrow, I waited long enough cause this bitch needs to know who the fuck I am. Shaniqua said.

"I don't give a fuck who you think you are, cause you ain't shit to me "huh", I'll tell you that much home wrecker. Cookie said.

"Y'all better chill the fuck out, cause neither one of y'all doing shit to each other, so shut the fuck up, I told y'all already to cut the bullshit out, y'all already know that y'all both having my babies, we don't need to be in here calling each other names either, so lets just fall back and relax for the night." I said.

I knew I was dealing with two razor blades that was ready to cut, and any slight mistake or any sign of weakness they was gonna eat me alive.

I had to make sure I stood firm and held my ground. Cookie knew that I had little patience for bullshit. She seen the things I was capable of doing if my hand was forced. So Cookie was willing to do whatever it was to stay by my side, even under these circumstances she knew she had to play her position. It was Shaniqua that I was worried about. I didn't want to lose her like I lost my family. I needed her by my side and was gonna do anything to keep her there.

After we said what had to be said for the moment. We walked into the bedroom.

"I don't know what you was doing outside anyway, Dice you know you just got out the other day, and you still outside running like nothing happened, you need to stay home for awhile, at least until you get better". Cookie said. Sitting down on the bed.

I could see all the built up frustration in Shaniqua's face that she wasn't definitely feeling the situation.

"What's up with you? I said.

"I'm not sleeping here with her "Dice", this aint that type of party, you are really feeling yourself huh, you can't expect me to be happy with this like this shit is acceptable. Shaniqua said.

"You better get your ass here and lay down and cut the bullshit out, cause I already told you, I'm tired, and I don't have time for this shit now."

Shaniqua couldn't believe how I was talking to her at this point. So she stood there frozen thinking to herself, Is this nigga crazy or what? But she also knew I was very serious by the expression on my face. She looked at Cookie laying in the bed, and knew it must be a reason why she wasn't putting up any argument. So Shaniqua climbed in the bed, and prayed that the night would soon be over. I didn't want to treat Shaniqua the way I was, but I had to. It was my only way of dealing with the situation.

* * *

In the morning, Shaniqua was sitting up on the edge of the bed crying. I felt bad for her, I didn't want to see her like this.

"I wanna go home, please, just take me home Dice." Shaniqua said softly.

Cookie was still sleeping like a baby.

"Aight, you wanna go home, come on I'll take your ass home, because I don't have time for this." I said. Jumping out of the bed to grab my clothes and car keys from off the dresser.

Cookie woke up from hearing all the commotion going on. She sat up in the bed, and watched me steam out of the bedroom. Shaniqua was so paranoid that she didn't even bother to say another word until we got in the car.

"What the fuck is your problem! We already know, what's up with you and Cookie, the fact that both of y'all pregnant by me, I understand you being mad and all about the shit, but what's done is done. Shaniqua, I cant change that it is what it is, I'm sorry that it happened, the way it did, I never meant to hurt you in any way, Trust me. Believe me I know we belong together, I know I fucked up big time it ain't nothing I could do about it now, y'all both six months pregnant, and the babies are going to be born soon. That's why I need y'all to get along with each other, for the kids and I don't wanna have no baby mama drama with y'all, and don't even think for a second about trying to leave me cause that shit ain't happening, I would have to kill you before I let you do that to me, I already lost my family once before, my mother, my father, my brother, and my friend who was like a brother to me. I'm tired of losing the people that I care about and love that are close to me. I'm sorry Shaniqua . . . . But I can't let you go like that. I said. Gripping the steering wheel tight. Then tears slowly started coming down my face as I was letting all my emotions go. Thinking about everything that I was going through in my life. I never felt like this before about a woman.

I had feelings for Cookie but nothing compared to the way I felt about Shaniqua. I loved her with my mind, body, and soul."

Shaniqua turned towards me and stared at me. She never knew anything about my family being murdered, cause I never told her anything about them. I didn't like talking about it. But it was no escaping the pain, the reality of the pain I was feeling for all these years. This was the first time anybody ever saw this side of me. I was opening up my heart to Shaniqua just to give her an idea about the things I was going through. If anyone could understand what I was dealing with was Shaniqua cause we both shared similar things like pain and loneliness in our hearts. Once I explained everything to her about what I was going through in my life, she didn't understand everything, but she had sympathy for me. She knew that my past affected some of the choices that I made in life. Shaniqua placed her hand on top of mine and said, "Dice I'm sorry about your family, I never knew about them I always thought that you just didn't want to talk about them, that's why I never asked you about them, I'm really sorry but we can't keep making excuses for our mistakes, I'm glad that you let me know exactly how you feel about the whole situation . . . . You don't have to worry, I'm not leaving you, we need each other more than anything but you need to look at what you created and think about it. I know you sorry about what happened, remember it's not just you anymore it's us. Shaniqua said.

Shaniqua now understood that we shared a special bond between us. This in a mysterious way made us closer. When we arrived at Shaniqua's house in Queens, we parked in front of her house. Before she exited my Danali. She said.

"Dice, I love you baby, and I'm sorry for all your pain, but you don't have anything to worry about, I respect you for being honest with me, you brought me out to Cookies house to show me exactly how you felt open about it, and I love you for that, I'm not happy about it, but I understand if you say you have your reasons for keeping her around the way you do, I don't know what it is, but in my heart, I believe you I know you love me, Dice. I just don't want you to hurt me anymore. I couldn't stay there at Cookie's house like everything is gravy cause it's not, I have my own house and we gonna keep it like that, I don't need her hospitality, I'm fine right where I'm at baby. Then she kissed me and smiled at me.

"Thanks for being so understanding." I said. Feeling relief because it could of easily went the other way.

"Are you coming inside, I'll make you some breakfast." She said. "Nah baby, I'm good, I have to go now but I'll be back later". I said.

"Alright, I'll see you later when you get back." Shaniqua said. Closing the door on my Danali truck.

I waited until she was inside before I pulled off. They say what don't break you, can only make you stronger. That's exactly what was happening to us.

Chapter 8

"Life"

It was the beginning of a new year. I now had two beautiful children.

Shaniqua had a baby boy weighing 9 pounds and 5 ounces his name was Dyemere a.k.a. Dice Jr. Cookie had a baby girl her name was Dicecita she weighing 8 pounds 7 ounces. They were born a day apart from each other.

I was happy that I was now starting my own family. Shaniqua and Cookie were alright with each other for the most part. They both were excited that their babies were born so close to one another. Shaniqua and Cookie were starting to get to know each other better now. They were spending time together making their own plans whenever they were going out together with the kids. That made me proud as a new father because no one wants to deal with baby mama drama. It could be very stressful for everybody.

I set up trust funds for Dyemere and Dicecita each starting with 100,000 apiece. Just in case something ever happened to me they wouldn't have to worry or be forced to live the life I did. Dyemere and Dicecita were my new pride and joy. I had 975,000 stashed away, and I still had another 630,000 to stunt with. That wasn't including the money I was making. I was planning a future for us. I had surprised Shaniqua and Cookie when I opened up two hair salons for both of them. Shaniqua's place and Cookie's parlor. They were so happy when I brought it for them cause they didn't have to work to live comfortable. All they would have to do for the rest of their lives was run the business and collect money and I'll take care of the rest. I had got it for them to occupy their time to keep them busy and off my back while I was out doing me in the streets. Even though I was still doing my dirt and fucking with them hoes. I made sure I always took care of home like a real nigga should. For the streets and for my niggas I had nothing but love for them but that was my biggest mistake because the streets don't love nobody. Where there's love, hate is always around the corner lurking.

You gotta stay focused on what you doing, and keep your eyes opened for them fake niggas that live in this concrete jungle and your circle tight.

E.B., Boo, and Rob all got together and threw me a surprise party for me. My brother Jay was there he had come up from North Carolina to see me and to congratulate me about my two children that I recently just had. We all were pushing big boys, they rented a full sized cruise ship that had four docks. It was docked at the South Street Sea Port, downtown Manhattan. We sailed to the Bahamas for four days. They also had brought me a Hummer H2. It was in the middle of the ship on the top deck. Everybody that was there was stunned to see it. It was a show stopper with its Canary paint, two 17 inch T.V. that flip down in the middle row, a 10 inch T.V. that popped out of the dash, a 35 inch T.V. that flip up when you lifted up the back door, 30 inch Giovanni chrome rims, a custom built sound system, and it had Dice on the license plate. I was happy to see my niggas go all out for me like they did. They also got 50 of the finest ladies that live in New York. Anna and her crew was there. I was fully healed now, back in the swing of things. Everywhere I looked there were more bitches than a little bit. Some were wearing nothing, and others were wearing two piece bikinis. Bottles were popping, people dancing, talking doing what they do. I was feeling like Tony Montana from scarface the world is mine. I was wearing my True Religion shorts, a white beater, a pair of throwback Jordans, and a platinum Cuban chain with a crazy Jesus piece flooded with princess cut diamonds that was blinging hard. I took pictures with damn near every female that was there. Everywhere I went I had bitches behind me trying to find out who I was. The D.J. was shouting me out on the regular, making it known who all this was for.

"Yo what's up little brother", give me some love. Jay Said. Excited to see me

Aint nothing! Just out here enjoying myself.

I see.

"I'm glad to see you here with us, Wait a minute you knew the whole time about this, and you couldn't tell me, "huh". I said. Punching Jay in his arm playfully.

"Yea, I knew but if I would've told you, it wouldn't be a surprise, so it didn't make sense to tell you, plus I wanted to surprise you too. And with all these fine ladies I wouldn't miss this for the world, you know I'm fucking something tonight." Jay said. Then he chuckled.

Yea, thanks for coming man I needed that.

"Oh, congratulations, I see you made me a uncle twice in one week, how they doing."

"They doing good everybody's happy you know it was a little rocky in the beginning but we worked it out."

"That's good."

"When you gonna come by and see them?"

"When we get back we could stop by and let me see my nephew and niece."

"Alright, say no more."

"Looks like you doing real good for yourself now." Jay said.

"Yea, I'm doing aight, I wish mom and dad was here with us to see their new grandchildren that I gave them, I said."

"Don't worry Dice, I know they smiling down on us right now, I know this is how they would want it if they were still here with us now."

"You right Jay, I just miss them and I think about them so much that's all but I know they in a better place right now."

"Dice, I wanted to ask something."

"What?"

"When are you gonna leave all this behind, you know, leave the game alone and move down south, remember you promised me that you would.

Cause I think it's time for you to do something else you got your kids now to worry about, and you being there as a father for them, you could take some of that money you got and invest it into something positive, you smart and I know you'll be successful at anything you put your mind to." Jay said.

"I know when it's time for me to do that, I know what I'm doing out here, but right now it's time for you to grab some of these bitches up in here and get some ass before you start that preaching shit you be on. We got all day for that". I said. Shoving him. Gone now.

"Yea you right, you not 15 anymore, but think about what I said, when it's time Dice if you want, I can help you with it when you ready aight."

"Yea aight." I said.

Then Jay was off to catch himself one of them fly honeys that was there.

That was just like Jay always trying to look out for his little brother. Even though what Jay was saying was right. I wasn't ready to do that yet, not yet, life was too good for us right now to just leave it like that.

Anna and her home girls were posted up at the bar when she spotted me walking by.

"Dice," She yelled out to me to get my attention before making her way to me.

"Yo what's up baby girl." I said. Picking her up as she leaped into my arms.

You know, getting my drink on enjoying the beautiful view of the ocean.

I never seen water so blue or clear.

"Yea," "well that's only the beginning of things."

I hope we could get together today, that only if you don't have plans to be with somebody else. Anna said. Licking on the rim of her glass.

Anna was wearing a "Dolce Gabbanna" two piece bikini swim suit that was connected by spaghetti straps, and a pair of Dolce Gabbana sandals.

"Damn girl you just popping out everywhere you don't know what you doing to me, the last time I checked I was free." I said.

"Oh, you like it, I wore it just for you, Dice. Anna said. Spinning around so I could see her ass hanging out." She smiled at me and said.

"You look good your damn self."

"Come on ma, you know that's how a nigga keep it baby I gotta stay fly, it don't get no better than this. I said. Holding up a bottle of Moet and a blunt in my hand." In my mind I was thinking about how Anna and her home girl put it on a nigga the last time I saw her.

"You wanna go down to the lower deck and get one of the rooms down there now and say fuck later."

"Aight, let me go get my home girl Judy." Anna said.

Making her way back to the bar to get her friend Judy that was there having a conversation with her other friends.

When we got down to the lower deck we walked into one of the rooms that we thought were empty. We caught a sight for sore eyes E.B. and Boo were tag teaming on this bad red bone chick. One had their dick in her mouth the other had his dick in her ass blowing her back out, and she was loving every moment of it. I was gonna go inside to join them with Anna and Judy but I wanted to be stingy with the pussy that I had with me. Once we finally found a room that wasn't occupied. I rolled me up another blunt, lit it and watched the preview that Anna and Judy was giving me. I stood up and stripped down to my boxers. Judy walked over to me and kneeled down in front of me and started kissing on my stomach, her hands was rubbing on my legs. Anna was on the bed watching with her fingers playing in her pussy. Judy's hands slowly made its way up my legs and under my boxers till she had my dick in her hand. She then pulled the dick out and put it in her mouth. Judy was going all around the head of my dick making loud slurping sounds. It felt like she was taunting me casue if felt to good and I didn't want her to stop. She kept sucking it until she tasted pre-cum in her mouth then she pulled the dick out of her mouth and said. "I want you to put all this dick in me."

Judy grabbed one of the condoms from the pack I had on the end table opened it up and forced it on my dick. Anna walked over to me and put one of breast in my mouth her nipples were long and hard. I slid my fingers inside her wet pussy. Then I snatched Judy by her ankles and threw her legs over my shoulders and started drilling her pussy until it started talking to me. Then I folded her legs down towards her making' em touch her shoulders. I slid my dick between her vagina lips with long and deep strokes while I had my tongue in Anna's pussy making all her juices flow.

Oh Dice fuck me baby, oh my god please don't stop I'm cumming again.

Judy cried out.

After making Judy cum several times it was Annas turn to feel the raft of my dick. I made Anna stand on her hands while I wrapped her legs around my waist with the whole 10 inches of me inside of her until she couldn't take it no more. They were my type of freaks just the way I like' em. When I finished with them I took me a quick shower and got dressed. As I was leaving the room I peeped Anna and Judy both stretched out exhausted.

On my way down the corridor as I was heading back to the upper deck I was approached by another freak. That was wearing nothing but a thong she had some nice C cups, 5'8 and healthy. She stopped me in my path.

"What's up baby, ain't your Dice." She said.

Looking at me up and down.

"That depends on who wanna know."

"Oh' it's nothing I just heard a lot about you, all the ladies seem to have your name on there tongues that's all."

"Yea, like what?"

"It ain't nothing bad, it's all good trust me, ain't this party for you, what you doing down here all alone by yourself." She said. With lust written all over her face.

"I'm not alone anymore." I said. Then she smiled at me.

"I was on my way up to the upper deck until you stopped me." I said. "Well, I didn't mean to hold you up I just wanted to meet you cause I heard so much about you."

"That's what's up, did you find out what you was looking for?" I asked.

"Not quite yet, but I will." She said.

Then she got down on her knees and said to me.

"Congratulations!" and began giving me head. Life was great being me but this shit was wearing me the fuck out, despite of all the drama that happened in my life. I thought to myself.

Before I was about to cum, I stood her up spun her around, bent her over moved her thong to the side and shoved my dick in her. She was hitting high notes like "Pattie Labelle." I never even got her name I just took off the condom and bounced. But that's how it is when bitches know you that nigga they come out from everywhere trying to get a taste of the good life. When that episode was over I was now back on the upper deck with my niggas. We were all shooting some dice, and I had to crack the bank.

"What's in the bank?" I yelled.

"It's 20,000 in it, what you want? E.B. asked.

Shaking the dice in the palm of his hand.

I got 3. Rob said.

"I got 5'g's man you don't scare me." Boo said.

I got the rest stopped, "Shoot it." I said.

"Aight!" E.B. said. Shaking the dice. He rolled a 5 and yelled. "Ah shit, fever yeah I'm hot boy."

Rob rolled, then he aced out with 1,2,3.

"Ya'll niggas cant fuck with that It's too hot for yah!" E.B. said.

Nigga you crazy, watch this. Boo said. Then he rolled when his number came up it was a 5. But he lost cause you can't push with the dealer, you automatically lose when you do.

"Ha, ha yeah baby that's what I'm talking about." E.B. said. All hyped up.

"You know when I roll, I roll with that fire baby, I make it burn." I said. Then I rolled. 4,5,6. "Yeah nigga pay me, I want all of mine." I said.

When it was over I walked away with all the cash that they had and they still owed me. Then we sat down to chill.

"Good looking, y'all my dude's for real, only real niggas do shit like this,

I appreciate everything y'all did for me, without y'all I'm don't know where I would be, and I would also like to thank God for blessing me with two healthy children Dyemere and Dicecita, and to the many more blessings that's to come."

Then we all made a toast.

You know It's all love my nigga, stop getting all mushy nigga and enjoy yourself or you wanna be kind enough to give us back our money. E.B. said.

They all started laughing.

"Nah," nigga you know what the fuck I mean.

"I'm just fucking with you."

"How did you like your gift I sent you, Shorty with the thong on. Boo said.

"Shorty was proper, she was about her business. Even Jay made sure he got a piece of the action."

"Damn Dice, this is how y'all do it, I need to hang with y'all more often. Jay said.

We started laughing.

"I bet you never seen these many hoes running around naked all willing to fuck." "Did you? Rob said.

"Word! You ain't lying about that, cause I ain't have this much fun in a long time, ladies all over the boat doing what ever you want them to do, shit I ain't use to this." Jay said.

"This is how we do it up here, no worries, no stress, just living our lives." I said.

"I see why this lifestyle is so tempting." Jay said.

"Yeah, but everything ain't always what it seems. This game is not for everybody most niggas jump in this shit blind without a clue what the game is about because of some movie or what they heard somebody else did in the game but its rules to the shit you could make'em or break'em but you can't fake'em because this shit will eat you alive because when the FED'S come that's when you see the other side of this shit. I Said

Real talk. E.B Said.

So jay don't get caught up on what we doing, God got better plans for you." I Said.

Chapter 9

"Hustle Hard"

Shaniqua was home with Dyemere. "You look just like your crazy ass daddy boy, doesn't he." Shaniqua said. Talking to her friend Ebony.

"Gurl" it look's like he spit him out, or that's his twin you never knew about. Ebony said. Then she chuckled.

"Ebony was Shaniqua's friend, she known her since elementary school.

They were close ever since then. Ebony was from Jamaica, Queens she lived there her whole life.

"Shaniqua, I know your happy, you got everything you ever wanted, your own house, a good man that loves you and takes care of you, and a son what else could a woman want."

"Yeah, I'm happy it feels good to have my own family for a change after all these years of being by myself."

"You wasn't even looking for love, it found you, and I been looking hard for it, but all these guys that I'm finding only want one thing a piece of ass, or they already have a wife and kids already, and they want you to be that side chick to play with on the side, I ain't no side chick I'm that bitch."

See when you looking for it so hard sometimes you overlook it, or you end up making mistakes like getting pregnant by rushing into something that's not really there, then y'all end up breaking up and then you get stuck with a child that's forever, that's why you gotta take your time and let it come to you, that's the only way it's gonna happen, you'll know when you got it.

"I hope so."

"Trust me you will."

"I gotta give it to you though, you a good strong woman."

"Why you say that?"

"Because, if my man would've got another bitch pregnant, while I was with him, I would've left his ass in a heartbeat."

"Shaniqua thought about it before but she loved Dice and she knew that Dice loved her and he has his reasons for why it happened. Not knowing what was but maybe one day he would tell what it was. But she still trusted him. She thought to herself.

"First of all you don't even know what you talking about, yeah he got a baby on the side by another woman, but let me tell you something he loves me and I love him he know he made a mistake and that's a mistake he gotta live with, I'm not trying to be messing up something that I wanted so bad, what I'm suppose to do just throw it all away like it doesn't mean anything to me. A family, are you crazy. This is my family, I'm not know desperate chick or somebody with a low self esteem, I have confidence in myself I, make my own decisions in life so I don't care about what you think or what nobody else thinks about me.

Ebony had her point, but Shaniqua had hers too and she made it clear that she was sticking by her man. Ebony was shock to see that Shaniqua took it to the heart cause in her mind she was only trying to be a friend.

"I was just saying what I would do, if it was me that's all."

"I'm not leaving him for nobody he's my everything, and I know he loves me more than anything in this world."

"If he's right for you "Niqua" and he makes you happy than stay with him."

"That's what I been doing, and we plan on getting married soon, so if you don't have anything positive to say, don't say nothing, cause I don't wanna hear the bullshit."

I'm sorry Shaniqua I just thought . . . .

"You thought my ass, you shouldn't be thinking about mine, that's my man, this is my life so save all your negative energy for somebody else." Shaniqua said.

"That's right baby girl let that hoe know. Knowing if she was in Shaniqua's shoes she wouldn't be going anywhere, she just running her lips." "Not every woman are like that but some are, cause soon as she leave there be another 30 bitches willing to take her place."

Ebony always wanted a man like me to call her own. What woman wouldn't want a nigga like me.

* * *

Cookie was at the mall baby shopping again. She brought so much shit they had to deliver some of the stuff she brought. Cookie loved shopping it helped her deal with the stress that she had on her shoulders. Cookie wasn't too happy about what was happening between her and Dice. That someone was fucking her man and she knew about it and that someone was Shaniqua. Even though she wasn't happy she played along. She also noticed that Dice was spending all his time with Shaniqua and the streets. But she knew that it wasn't in her power to do anything about it. She knew that she had a lot of dirt on Dice something that could bury him if she really wanted to. But it wasn't in her mind to only if he forced her to she was willing to use her trump card. So for that she carried larceny in her heart.

Cookie was in love with Dice and the lavish life style that he provided.

Cookie knew that she received a lot more when she started fucking with Dice than she ever did fucking with Rock. She also remembered that she put herself in this position when she walked into Dice's life. She was the only one that could get herself out of it. For now she was gonna let it ride until the tables turned her way.

* * *

June 6, 2004 it was Shaniqua's Birthday I surprised Shaniqua with breakfast in the bed in the morning right before she woke up. She loved that, then I gave her a envelope fill with cash 20,000 than I gave her a kiss and told her that I had another surprise for her. She climbed out of bed grabbed her robe and put it on. Then I blindfolded her, walked her downstairs and escorted her outside to where the driveway was. I opened up the garage then told her to remove the blindfolds. When she did she was now looking at a brand new Cadillac Escalade 2004 model with T.V.'s in the head rest.

Shaniqua jumped for joy because she was overwhelmed.

"Oh my God, thank you Dice you did all this for me."

"Of course, anything for my baby, you deserve it, and a lot more."

"Ahhhh, you're sweet baby."

What really knocked her head over heels is when I dug in my pocket and pulled out a ten carrot platinum diamond ring and put it on her finger and asked her to be my wife.

"Yes, Dice yes I would love to be your wife." Shaniqua said. With tears in her eyes.

Shaniqua has been waiting for this day for a long time. Now her dream was becoming reality. Shaniqua finally knew how much I really love her.

Shaniqua had all the qualities a husband looks for in a wife. She was filled with happiness.

She grabbed me and gave me a big hug.

"I don't know what else to say, Oh my God you did all this for me."

"Don't say nothing, just be my wife."

"This is the happiest day of my life, Dice I love you." Shaniqua said.

The energy and emotions that was running through our bodies were crazy. I never wanted it to end, cause I really loved her and now that she was gonna be my wife nothing in this world meant more to me then Shaniqua. I was willing to give up everything to prove my love to her. All she had to do was ask. Shaniqua's birthday was interrupted when I got a phone call from Boo. I wasn't gonna answer cause I was with wifey and it was her birthday and I was trying to spend some quality time with here but I knew it must be important if he was calling me this early.

"Yo what's good my nigga." I said.

"Yo what up Dice, I don't mean to disturb you and wifey on her day, but we got a problem."

"Yeah like what?

"This nigga Rob got knocked with ten of them things and a burner on his way to see Blinky." Boo said.

"Get the fuck outta here." "Word!"

"Where you at?"

"I'm on my way to the court house downtown Brooklyn."

"Who was he with?

He was by himself.

"Aight, I'm a meet you there." (Click) the phone hung up.

What's wrong Dice? Shaniqua asked. Seeing my facial expression she knew something was wrong.

"Nothing baby, I'm sorry but I gotta go, and emergency came up."

Do you gotta go right now?

"Yeah baby, I'll be back soon." I said. Walking away.

"Wait!" wait wait She said. Giving me a kiss before I left.

"Don't worry I won't be long."

"Be careful baby."

"I will." I said. Getting in my Danali and sped off.

*   *   *

"Hey, how you doing." Detective Johnson said.

"I'm fine, what do we have here." Detective Honeytoon said.

"We got some asshole driving with some heavy shit, 10 keys of coke and a loaded fire arm, this is big and you won't believe this asshole had the nerve to be smoking weed while he was carrying all this shit, look at it, this might help me get my promotion that I been waiting for since I joined this unit, I also think we could get him to talk and tell us who his supplier is and who he's working with cause he's real scared because he know we got him by the balls." Detective Johnson said.

What kind of car was he driving?

He was driving a Lexus GS 400.

"These fucking guys always driving nice fucking cars making us look like we down with the wrong team."

"I wouldn't say that Honeytoon, because ain't no loyalty in those streets."

You right about that, did you send it to the lab to test it yet?

"No! but I know it's real cause I tasted it, it's 100% pure." "Okay let's give it a shot." Detective Honeytoon said.

As they were heading into the interrogation room where Rob was being held hand cuff to the chair that was bolted to the floor.

"How you doing, my name is Detective Johnson, and this is my partner Detective Honeytoon we already know who you are, so let's get right down to business." You know you facing some heavy charges here with all the shit you got, you might end up getting life in jail, cause they gonna throw the book at your ass, but we could help you with that, only if you help us." Detective Johnson said. "Look at it this way", you help us, help you cause if not your fucked your going up shits creek." Detective Honeytoon said.

"We could make all this go away, and you would only be charged for the gun, and with that we'll make sure you only get probation, but the choice is yours." Detective Johnson said.

"I know you probably think that you don't wanna do this cause you don't wanna be no "rat", but you gotta think about yourself here, cause if someone going down for this it's you, all by your fucking self." Detective Honeytoon said.

"We know you working with somebody, we know you aint moving this type of weight by yourself." Detective Johnson said.

"That's not mine, I didn't know that the was in the car." Rob said.

"Cut the fucking crap", you knew it was in the fucking car, do I look like I was born yesterday to you." Detective Johnson said.

"Believe me, I let this bitch hold my car that I met at the club the other night." Rob Said.

"That's bullshit, you expect me to buy that shit get the fuck outta here."

Detective Johnson said, tossing his cup of coffee on the floor.

"You better think about what I'm saying to you, or we'll just let the big boys come in and take over this case, I know you don't want them suits on your ass cause they will hit you with 848 and you'll never come home, we giving you the opportunity to save yourself now." Detective Honeytoon said.

Rob leaned back in the chair and started staring at the ceiling thinking to his self how the fuck this happened. What was he gonna do. He never been to jail before and he didn't want to go to jail now. Everything started flashing in his head. How him, and his boys were so tight with each other, from way back when they were about 5 years old when they use to sit around and play that's my car. He knew that his niggas would die for him if they had to. But like they say pressure bust pipes and he was under some serious pressure. But this comes with the game, you just never know when it's gonna happen. It also comes with a rule book, and this rule #1 "If you get knocked, You Don't 'Know Shit! But some niggas don't understand the meaning of that. It's all good when you pushing them big boys, robbing and getting money together. So under no circumstances do you "Snitch", but the game is fucked up now. In other words, Game Over. I can't believe they had this nigga shaking like a bitch. It was all good a week ago. Better them than me. Rob thought to his self. (sucka ass nigga.)

"We waiting for an answer boy", because we don't have all day some of us still have a life to live." Detective Honeytoon said.

Somebody going down for all this shit today I don't give a fuck who it is, I'm not losing sleep over it. Detective Johnson said.

"Listen to us kid be smart about it."

What do you wanna know? Rob Said. Mumbled under his breath holding his head down feeling ashamed.

This a stupid mother fucker, he didn't even ask to speak to his lawyer he so fucking paranoid. He probably would of beaten it on technicality if he just would of held his head and stuck to the script I don't know shit. What's wrong with niggas today, they don't respect the game, or their selves anymore.

*   *   *

A few hours went bye since Rob first got knocked. We were waiting at the court house for him to be arraigned in front of the judge. First we stopped at the precinct to see if he was still there, but they told us that they sent him to Central Bookings. I called in this Jewish lawyer that we had on stand by for situations like this his name was Peter Shecter. When he got in front of the judge they dismissed all the narcotics and only charged him with the gun. The District Attorney didn't even argue the case. We posted the bail and he was free to go.

"Yo what the fuck happened." I asked, as we was leaving the court house walking to the parking lot. "Man them niggas pulled me over talking about my tints were too dark, and I was smoking some weed."

"What the fuck you was smoking for and you know you had all that shit with you, nigga you crazy or what? Boo said.

"It was early in the morning, I thought it was nothing." T.T. said.

"You thought wrong what you did was a dumb move." I said.

My bad Dice.

"Well your ass lucky, they didn't charge you with that shit, cause your ass wouldn't be walking out here right now, you would have been sitting up with a crazy ass bail." Boo said.

"I know."

Where did you have the bricks stashed at. I asked.

In the trunk.

Who pulled you over, was it blue and whites? I asked.

"Nah", it was the D's." Rob said.

"They not suppose to search your trunk without a warrant, did they show you one?"

"No!"

"Damn, dog you hot, now we gotta lay off of you for a minute, and make sure ain't nobody plotting or scheming on us, cause you did get knocked with some heavy shit and they don't give up that easy unless they gotta plan in the making or they turned them big boys on to us (FED's). Boo said.

"That's a chance we can't afford to take now, we all gotta get new phones cause you had everybody number in your phone, we can't use the ones we got we gotta use blow up phones and change them every three days, that's how we gonna do it for now until this blows over, who knows how long it might take." I said.

"So what you saying that y'all ain't fucking with me no more." Rob said.

Nah, we just putting you on the burn for now until we find out what's good. I said.

After I finished talking to Rob and Boo, I dropped them off. I dropped Rob at his crib and Boo went and picked up his car to go to his girls house. I drove to E.B.'s crib to give him the news.

Yo, Dice man something sounds funny about that whole shit the way you said it went down. E.B. said.

"I know I feel the same way, we just gotta keep it clean for a minute until we know what's really good cause we came to far to fuck up now nah I mean, I worked too hard for mines."

"For real my nigga, you just let me know what you want me to do cause you know I'm with whatever, that's my man too, but I'll smoke his ass in a heartbeat if he trying to tear down what we built up here, just give me the word and his ass is outta here like last year." E.B. said. Examining his 9mm he had in his hand.

Let's watch him, and see what's up what before we jump the gun, cause if he slip up we burying him. I said.

That's not a problem with me, you just give me the word, this ain't personal this is business.

"Keep this between us for now."

"Aight, what you about to do now. I'm a go see my son.

That's what's up, so I'm a holla at you later aight. E.B. said. Then he hopped out of my Danali and got in his 528amg BMW.

I was heading for the Tri-borough bridge on my way to Shaniqua's house. When I arrived there at Shaniqua's house, Ebony pulled up behind me driving in her gold Nissan Altima 2001 model.

"Hey what's up Dice, how you doing? I haven't seen you in a while. Ebony said. Smiling at me like a kid at Mcdonald's.

I'm good Ebony, how you doing. I said. Checking my surroundings before I made my way to the house.

Oh, I'm great, thanks for asking and feeling good, I just came from the gym, you know a sista gotta keep her body tight and looking right. Ebony said. She was wearing a spandex body suit and some running sneakers.

Ebony was all that and then some. But she was off limits for me I didn't even look at her in a sexual way. I looked at her as my wifey's friend that's it. Plus I wouldn't even dare to try anything with none of her friends, even though they was all on my dick. I wasn't gonna disrespect my lady like that.

Shaniqua's inside she probably waiting for you. I said. Changing the subject making it clear I wasn't interested.

"Oh, yeah that's right I almost forgot why I came over here let me go see how my girl doing. Ebony said, making her way to the house.

"Yeah you do that."

When I walked in the house I gave Shaniqua a kiss on her mac covered lips. Then I took Dyemere out of her arms and started playing with him. He was laughing up a storm.

"Happy Birthday", gurl what's on the agenda for the day I know you got something planned. Ebony said.

"Thank you, you know I do, I'm going out with Dice, he got the whole day planned for us to do so much, I can't wait, Oh my God guess what Ebony?"

"What girl, don't do this to me."

Me and Dice are engaged now, girl we getting married.

Oh my God, y'all getting married, oh my God, I can't believe it. I'm so happy for you Niqua. I feel like crying girl. Ebony said. Examining her ring.

Damn! Look at her ring, shit you could blind somebody with that shit.

Ebony thought to herself after playing with Dyemere for about an hour we both fell asleep. When I woke up I went to turn on the T.V. I noticed a note laying on the dresser, that Shaniqua left, telling me that she went out to Roosevelt field Mall. To get something to wear for the night I put the note down and hopped in the shower. While I was in the shower I heard the door bell ringing. I jumped out the shower wrapped a towel around me and went downstairs to see who it was. I knew it wasn't Shaniqua cause she would of opened the door with her keys. Who could it be at my door. I thought to myself.

When I opened the door I was surprised to see who it was. It was Ebony.

Shaniqua not here she left, I thought you was with her. I said, standing behind the door.

I'm not here for her, I left my pocketbook on the chair. Ebony said.

"Oh, aight go ahead and get it, when you leave just close the door behind you on your way out. I said, as I was running back upstairs to finish my shower. When I was done in the shower I was in the bedroom drying myself off with my towel. I raised the towel up to my face exposing all of my human nature. Ebony crept upstairs and was peeping through the crack of the door. She was loving every moment of looking at my muscular chocolate body. Then I heard the door slowly opening. It was Ebony standing there naked.

"What the fuck", what you doing? I yelled out.

What you think I'm doing? Ebony said, walking towards me.

I grabbed the towel, and wrapped it around me quickly.

"No need for that Dice I already saw what I've been looking for standing right in front of me."

"Ebony you better get the fuck outta here before Shaniqua comes back, and she should be back any minute now." I said, trying to get her to leave. Don't worry Dice, this won't take long I promise. Ebony said, pushing me on the bed.

My dick was throbbing Ebony seen it rising underneath the towel she grabbed it and started massaging it then she dropped to her knees and started giving me head. Damn! Dice you got a big dick." She said. while she had it in her mouth.

I couldn't believe that she was doing this to me. She was up in my wifey crib sucking me off and it was fucking me up to the point that I was feeling weak. Then I finally got the strength to push her off me.

What's the matter Dice, what you don't like it. Ebony asked. Still reaching for my dick.

"No! I don't want it from you, now get the fuck outta here. I said.

I pushed her to the side and grabbed my shorts that I had on the bed and put them on.

"You ain't nothing but a hoe, trying some bullshit like that, while Shaniqua ain't here, I ain't with that shit".

"Dice I'm sorry" please forgive me I don't know what came over me."

"I don't wanna hear that shit just get the fuck outta here, I don't ever wanna see your face around here anymore." I said. Spazzing out on her.

She was so afraid thinking that I was going to do something to her that she ran out the house wearing nothing but a T-shirt.

I was pissed off when she left.

When Shaniqua returned from shopping at the mall. I was gonna tell her, but I chose not to cause I didn't want to spoil her birthday over no hoe.

We just went out and enjoyed ourselves for the rest of the night.

*   *   *

Chapter 10

"Hustle Hard"

Two weeks passed since Rob was arrested and released on bail. Today he got a surprise visit. Rob was on his way out to check his shorty when he walked out and spotted a black Chevy Impala with dark tints in front of his apartment building. He hesitated for a second comtemplating if he should continue to proceed to his car. He tried to turn around and go back inside of his building but it was too late cause Detective Johnson, and Detective Honeytoon already saw him.

"Hey, how you doing there Mr. Wilson going somewhere? Detective Johnson said. As he was rolling down the window from the driver side.

What the fuck y'all doing out here, y'all trying to get killed coming around her like that, like it's sweet. Rob said. Paranoid looking around before he rushed and jumped in the Impala with the detectives.

"We wanted to talk to you, and see what you got for us, you know why we here don't act stupid with us cause we'll wrap your ass up tight in so much shit you won't even know what the sun look like any more. Detective Johnson said. Giving Rob. the screw face.

"Look! Man like I told y'all, y'all gotta give me some time, but y'all can't be showing up at my crib like that, you never know who's watching. Rob said.

"You must have forgot, you work for us shit brains" we tell you what to do and when to do it, time is what you don't have asshole." Detective Johnson shouted.

"What the fuck you want me to do if it's nothing happening right now, they so fucking paranoid since I got knocked they ain't been doing shit, they won't even touch a fly, y'all just gotta lay back and wait, and let me see what I could come up with. Rob said.

"So give us something now a murder, a shooting, anything for us to go on with. Detective Johnson said. Getting inpatient.

"What murders?" I don't know nothing about no murders. I told y'all that shit already man, Damn! When something is popping I'll let you know, but like I told y'all, don't be showing up at my crib like we some motherfucking homeboys. Rob said.

"Call it what you want you still part of the home team." Detective Honeytoon said. With a chuckle Rob knew that he couldn't tell them nothing about any bodies. Cause he played a part in catching them bodies that we had and that would be shooting his self in the foot if he did.

"Your ass wasn't so fucking tuff, when we had your ass singing like a bird down at the precinct you fucking punk." Detective Johnson said. Staring at Rob eye to eye.

"Fuck you." Rob yelled back.

Where does your boy Dice live, we checked all our systems for Mug shots and fingerprints, and we still couldn't come up with anything on this guy, he's a fucking ghost." Detective Honeytoon Said.

That's because he's smart he never been arrested before plus I don't know where he lives, he never took none of us to any of his houses. Rob Said.

"Oh", so he got more than one house huh, who does he live with?'

Detective Honeytoon asked.

His girlfriend Cookie, and I don't know the other girl name. Rob said

"What is he some kind of playa or something like the guys in them rap videos? Detective Johnson asked.

If that's what you wanna call it. Rob Said.

"Don't be a smart ass." Detective Johnson Said.

"Look" I told y'all everything I know for right now, when something is going down I'll give you a call, until then leave me the fuck alone. Rob said.

Exiting the car slamming the door behind him.

"Why don't we get together and play some basketball one day. I'll show you that white men can jump. Detective Johnson said, being sarcastic."

Yeah how about next time I'll bring you some cheese and a wheel to run around in. Detective Honeytoon said. As Rob was walking away.

"Fuck you asshole" Rob sad. Mumbling underneath his breath.

I think he's going to be a problem soon. Detective Johnson said. As he watched Rob get in Lexus GS 430 and drive away.

Nah, I don't think so, he'll come around soon they always do. Right now he's just trying to get use to being in his own skin again. You know it ain't easy for him becoming an informant turning on his boys like that. Detective Honeytoon said.

I don't give a fuck how he feels because he always been a rat he just didn't know it.

*   *   *

I was on the Cross Island Expressway on my way to my house in Long Island coming from Harlem when Shaniqua called me on my cell phone.

Hello!

Hey baby.

What's good baby girl?"

Nothing I was just thinking about you where you at?"

I'm on the highway driving to the crib in Long Island I got some things I gotta pick up."

Are you coming here tonight Dice?

Yeah baby girl I'm coming, why? You got something planned for us tonight.

"You know I do, don't I always do?

Aight ma, where Dyemere at?

He's sleeping, finally cause I can't get nothing done with him up, he's just like you always wanting somebody to spoil him.

So what, you suppose to don't I spoil you?

You suppose to, I carried your child for nine months.

Aight, whatever ma I'll see you when I get there tonight, aight baby.

Alright, I'll be waiting for you, I love you Dice.

I love you too. I said. (Click)

When I made it to my house in L.I. parked the hummer in the garage and went into the house.

Dice baby how you doing. Cookie said. Giving me a kiss.

"Ummmm" that shit smells good Cookie, what you cooking up in here." I said. Looking in all the pots.

"I made some of your favorites, fried chicken breast, with some collard greens, baked macaroni, brown rice, candy yams, and some born on the cob, get your hands out of my pots wait until the food is done."

"Damn Cookie, that sounds good I can't wait to eat, where my baby girl Diceita. I said. Walking to my bar in the dining room.

She sleep, I just finished washing her up a little while ago before you came.

"I poured me a glass of henny and sparked me a blunt than sat down on my suede sofa waited for the food to be done.

Then I drifted into deep thoughts

All I need is another million and I'm good, yeah I'm a chill after that, I'll give the game to E.B. and them fall back and let them do them. I could invest a few hundred grand, and open up a few legit businesses and maybe some stocks and bonds, only a few more birds to fly and I'm good.

Dice come to the table, your plate is ready. Coolie yelled out from the dining room.

When we finished our dinner Cookie gave me a massage in the hot tub.

Dice, why you so tense baby, you had a hard day out there in them streets.

"Nah ma, I just got a lot of shit on my mind, I'm thinking about my next move, you know its like chess out there.

Well baby don't think about it too much Dice let it come to you it's always, does you ain't never have trouble figuring things out, just relax and let it come to you." Cookie said.

Then she kissed me on my forehead.

Cookie knew what I was dealing with in the street, and how stressful it could be for a nigga. I have to admit Cookie knew how to ease my mind to escape the things I was going through. She stood up and dropped her silk robe and climbed in the hot tub with me. My dick immediately stood up at attention. Cookie was smelling sweet. She slid over to me and our lips starting locking. We was making love in the hot tub. Cookie stood up in the hot tub and put both of her legs across my shoulders with her pussy all in my face. I began eating her pussy like it was dessert playing with her clitoris with my tongue making her body shiver like she had the chills. Then I bent her over the side of the hot tub slid behind her and clutched both sides of her waist with my hands giving me a firm grip on her. Ass up face down that's the way I like to fuck. Then I turned her sideways giving her all I got. She had her eyes closed and the expression on her face like she was in heaven biting and sucking on her bottom lip. Before it was all said and done Cookie rode my dick while I held her up in the air in my arms as I was standing up. All her pussy juice was running down my legs.

I had feelings for Cookie too but it was in a different way. She knew a lot about me, Cookie seen when I was at the bottom before I came up. She was there when I went from ashy to flashy. One thing I always gave Cookie credit for was that she always kept her word, and her loyalty and she was there then, and she there now. We could relate with each other on that level only, about certain things. Cause some things are meant to be left unknown. Still in the back of my mind I didn't really trust her. I had this strange gut feeling about her. But I felt that way about everybody except for my niggas. Maybe it was just my mind playing tricks on me. But one thing I always knew was that people are unpredictable. They will smile in your face like every goody, goody and be plotting to harm you behind your back.

*   *   *

Chapter 11

Ain't No Love Lost

It was 2am when I finally made it to Shaniqua's house in Queens. I parked my SL 500 Benz behind Shaniqua's Cadillac Escalade. I was tired as hell from running the streets all day taking care of some minor things I had to do. I went straight upstairs to the bedroom were Shaniqua was sleeping at and crawled under the satin sheets and did the same. I had left my duffle bag that I was carrying with me downstairs behind the sofa that was filled with cash and a burner. In the morning I woke up to breakfast in the bed.

Thank you baby girl. I said. Smiling at her.

You welcome. Shaniqua said. Then she kissed me on my cheek.

What time did you come in last night, I tried to wait up for you."

It was late when I got in. I said. Stuffing my mouth with one of her home made biscuits.

I found your bag downstairs that you put behind the sofa, what you doing with all that money Dice, it's over two-hundred thousand in there.

I picked it up last night from this small company that I started, I was too tired to bring it upstairs last night so I left it there.

Why do you have a gun in there, somebody's trying to hurt you Dice?

No, baby it's not like that, I had it with me because I was traveling with all that money, it was late and you never know when somebodies out to get you, I already got shot before it ain't gonna happen again.

Dice, whatever you are doing baby you need to stop it, because if you have to carry a gun with you, than you don't need to be doing what you are doing, you got us to worry about and we should be you first priority.

Don't worry Niqua, ain't nothing gonna happen to me, I aint going no where I promise you baby, now come over here and give your man somethat gushy stuff.

I'm not playing with you Dice.

I know.

* * *

I haven't seen my niggas since Rob got knocked. We put everything on pause since then to let things calm down for a minute. Just to make sure that we were in the clear. We spoke several times on the phone, but that was it. It was all personal when we did, not business everybody was playing the family role. But today me and Boo got together to discuss some business, after several weeks went by of doing nothing, just spending money. We were talking about the new connect that his peoples had got for us.

Boo's peoples were very useful to us they helped us find out about a lot of things. Like things that we needed to know like who's who, who got what, and with whatever else we needed. They also knew about us, and the deadly games that we play. They never wanted to meet us, they only wanted to deal with Boo. Under no circumstances did they want to meet anybody else and we had to respect it cause it was all business and we needed them. They lined us up with this Haitian nigga down in Florida. They called him Haitian Black. The biggest supplier on the east coast. On the day that we was leaving nobody knew that we were leaving except for Shaniqua and Cookie they didn't even know where we was going they just knew that I was leaving. I told them I was going to visit my brother Jay and my Grandmother. When we arrived at the airport in Florida we rented a Chrysler LHS and went to get something to eat from a local seafood restaurant. We called Haitian Black and told him that we was there in Florida. He already knew we was there and he was waiting for our call. Haitian Black shit was correct, he had everything on smash (under the wing). The DEA, Coast Guards, a couple of F.B.I agents and the President of Haiti. They were all on the payroll. It was no problem getting the shit that we needed. Haitian Black was a very valuable asset to have on our team. After the phone call with Haitian Black we paid for our food, and we were on our way to meet Haitian Black at his estate.

When we pulled up to the gate of Haitian Black's estate we heard a voice coming from the intercom that was positioned right before the gate.

"Hello", how may I help you?"

Yeah we here to see Haitian Black. Boo said. From the driver's side. "One moment please!"

Then, the gate slowly opened up. We drove through and followed the path that led us all the way up to the mansion that had a huge water fall in front of it. When we was in front of the mansion we got out the car and Boo handed the keys to the car to the guy that was doing valet parking. Then the two guys that was standing there wearing white suits in the front of the mansion approached us.

"He's inside, he's expecting you, this way please." The man said. We followed behind them through the mansion it was very elegant. It was laced with all kind of antique and imported furniture and fine art. When we entered this huge room that had two large doors at the end of it. The guys that was escorting us through the mansion asked if we were carrying any firearms. If we were we had to leave them there with them before we entered the room to see Haitian Black. At first I was a little hesitant to do it cause the last time I was caught without my hammer I got shot and I refuse to let it happen again. But I knew I was here to do business so we gave it to them. Boo gave up .45 auto, and I gave them a nickel-plated .44 Desert Eagle. Then we walked in the room where Haitian Black was waiting to meet us. He was sitting behind this huge table. There were two arm soldiers standing at each end of the room strapped with AR-15's. I immediately became uncomfortable but I didn't let my emotions show.

"Hello, welcome to my home." Haitian Black said. Standing up to greet us.

The pleasure is all mine. I said. Please have a seat. Haitian said. Thank you. I said.

"Let me see if I get this right, you must be Dice, and you must be Boo. Haitian Black said. Sitting back in his chair.

That's correct." I said.

Your people in New York speak highly of you they say that you good people and to take care of you, so please tell me how can I help you gentlemen here today. Haitian Black said, folding his hands together.

Haitian Black was a well groomed man in his mid-thirties that was well respected. Everything about him was spoken with confidence even his demeanor which could be mistaken for arrogance.

I looked over at his soldiers showing him that I was concerned about them being there hearing what we had to say.

Never mind them it's there duty to guard me with their lives or I will take their lives and their family's lives so it's okay they don't hear you, they only hear my commands. Haitian Black said. Giving us the nod letting us know that it was safe to speak freely

We are here today looking for a new supplier a reliable one that can give us a good mark on what we need and guarantee us quality on each shipment and with that we guarantee to purchase 200 keys a month. I said.

What happened to your last connect?

He's no longer with us, his time expired.

I heard all about it, how bout I give you 400 keys a month and give it to you for 8,000 a key if you pick it up, my product is based on quality nothing less, and if we can build a good relationship like you have with my people in New York I can set it at a better mark for you. Haitian Black said.

I would like it delivered to us up in New York. I said.

If we come as far as New York then the mark would be set at 11,000 a key but if you can pick it up in New Jersey I can give it to you for 10,000 a key. Haitian said.

Okay, that would be just perfect. I Said

You send me half, and when you pick it up in New Jersey you give them the rest.

We would like to pay for the first 200 now and for the other 200 on the end. I said.

Haitian Black looked at us and smiled because he was impressed by the way we was handling our business.

"I like your style, you are a true business man, I see why they speak Highly of you in New York.

"Thank you." I said.

"Great", then we have a deal, I will have my people get on it right away Haitian Black said. Shaking our hands.

We was glad that the meeting went well cause now we were gonna be doing it for real. And this was a perfect opportunity for us to build a strong relationship with a connect like Haitian Black that would take us straight to the top of our game. Just when I was thinking about leaving the game, the game got deeper. At 24,000 a joint we would be looking at 9.6 mil minus 4 mil we spent would leaves us with 5.6 mil to split. I knew that we had people in New Jersey that would be able to pick it up and bring it to us back in New York. Anna and her crew were perfect for the job. They were all young, gorgeous and innocent looking.

Before we left Miami we decided to turn in the Chrysler and get the Bentley to ball out New York Style. We were on our way to the club called the Lime Light. We was stunting down them Miami streets in the Bentley.

The Bentley attracted all kind of attention. Ladies were flagging us down at every stop light damn near pulling up next to us trying to see who we were.

It was like everything was at a standstill as we cruised through the city pumping that 2pac shit (all eyes on me). I had on a pair of Christian Dior shades with my seat all the way back on my gangsta lean feeling right like a nigga should. Thinking about all the good shit that was about to happen for us. Once we arrived at the Lime Light we did our two step and bagged a couple of freaks that wanted to chill with us for the night. We left there with our semi entourage following behind us on our way to another club called the Crow Bar. The parties in Miami were crazy, real freaky shit. It was almost 5:30am when we got back to the hotel to have the after party.

Me and Boo with eight bitches you could only imagine how that went down. Bitches were getting fucked everywhere on the wall, on the floor, in the air, on the table it was on and popping that night. Too bad it had to end.

* * *

Chapter 12

"Guess Who's Back"

When we made it back to New York after a successful trip, I called Anna and told her that it was important that I see her. She arrived a few hours after I spoke to her on the phone. Anna met up with me at the stash crib we had downtown Manhattan. She was looking good as always.

"What's up Dice, how's my boy doing?" She said. As she walked inside kissing me on the cheek.

"I'm good ma how you doing, you looking right in them jeans is there any room for me." I said. Palming her ass.

"Ha, ha, ha you stupid Dice that was cute, but I'm fine, I came to see what was up with you poppie you said that was wanted to see me right Anna said.

Rubbing on my chest licking her lips staring into my eyes.

Yeah I got some business that I need you to take care for me it's sort of like a business proposition for you.

Yeah go ahead, I'm listening.

My people are coming from down south with some shit, and they delivering some things for me, I wanna know if I can depend on you to pick it up for me and bring it to me here in New York, can you handle that for me?"

Yeah poppie, what is it?"

"Cocaine."

I thought you was into real estate.

Come on Anna you know what I do.

"Okay Daddy, I'll do that for you, now what's in it for me." Anna said. Twirling her hair looking me up and down.

Whatever you want.

Do you know what I want now?" She said. Getting closer to me.

What? I said. Like I didn't know what she wanted already.

I want you to fuck me. Anna said. Grabbing my dick.
That's nothing I'll do that with pleasure.

From that moment it was on I beat that pussy up like never before .With having money on my mind helped stimulate me even more. I knew exactly how to play the game to get what I needed to be done. I used my manhood to manipulate Anna in every which way and she loved it.

Now with everything established we was back in business taking it to another level. The streets were calling me. On August 13, 2004 we were back at it still gripping them automatics. Everything was up and moving again from the spots we were supplying to the niggas that was buying weight. We were still using them blow up phones staying on top of our job. E.B. and Boo still controlled everything as usual. We still had Rob on the bench because we wasn't ready to fuck with him yet we kept him on a short leash to watch him. Even though he wasn't doing shit we was still hitting him off with cash but as far as everything else he was off limits for now. Me and Rob got together later on that day we were sitting in my Hummer.

Yo Dice, what's good man, what y'all don't trust me no more huh, I know y'all getting them things, and y'all not putting me in the loop. I want to hit my people off to with some of those things, I got my cousin Blinky blowing up my phone. Rob Said.

"Nah homie ain't nothing happening right now plus if we was back on we wouldn't be giving you shit, cause we cant take no chances with anything right now, cause you got flagged already for some shit, that was to close to home you feel me, them niggas could be waiting on you to slip up, and get on some bullshit I know how them niggas play they sit back and wait and watch to they get enough to bring you down I'm not gonna give them what they want straight like that, right now you good you getting money just chilling just except that and the only reason why you getting that is because you my man and you helped us build what we got today, but we cant afford no mistakes, so breath easy and fall back, when the time is right we'll holla at you then about it, aight cause if they out there scheming, praying on my downfall. I'm a make them niggas wait till they turn old and gray, so it's nothing against you, its business. I said. Passing him the blunt.

You right Dice, man I'm just tripping I'm sorry man I didn't mean no harm.

"It's aight, now crack that bottle of yack so we can get our sip on.

The problem was that Rob was getting harassed by them pig ass niggas and he didn't have shit to give them. So they been following him around, and all kind of shit harassing him. Rob haven't been home in almost a week ducking and dodging them since their last encounter. Rob switched up his program and was driving his girlfriend's car while he had his car parked up in storage trying to buy his self some time.

* * *

Chapter 13

The Big "Pay Back"

September 2, 2004. Today was the day I been waiting for, for a longtime. I dreamed about this day many times, now it was finally here. Crazy Louie was being released from Clinton Penitentiary Prison. I made special arrangements just for him.

"It's about time you're sorry ass is leaving here cause I was tired of looking at your stupid face every day and every night." The C.O. said. As he was escorting him out of the prison.

"I bet you, your wife gonna love it when I'm giving it to her, cause while you're here doing dumb shit, and watching niggas jerk off every day, I'm a be in your house fucking your wife, then I'm a piss on your kids, and they gonna love it." Crazy Louie said. Then he started laughing.

"You think you funny huh you fucking bastard, I promise you Mother fucker that you will be back, oh yeah you'll be back and I'll be waiting for your punk ass when you do, if somebody don't kill your ass before I do, now get the fuck outta here you fucking scumbag. The C.O. said. Watching Crazy Louie walk through the gates sticking his middle finger up at him.

Crazy Louie was now free as he walked away from Clinton PenitentiaryPrison. As he was walking down the road with his net bag in his hand he noticed a pretty Caucasian female standing down at the end of the road.

Crazy Louie was heading in her direction as he got closer and closer he noticed she was standing there holding up a sign in her hand with a limousine waiting along with her. The sign said Welcome Home Louie.

He stopped, then read what the sign said. Then he smiled when he realized it was for him so he proceeded to walk towards her and the limousine that was waiting. Crazy Louie was excited because he thought to his self that his boys really looked out for him and sent the beauty of the week to escort home. Pussy gets a thirsty nigga all the time.

Louie? She asked him.

That's me. He said Examining her physique.

He wasn't even thinking about who the fuck was in the limousine because he was to busy worried about some ass like most niggas are.

She opened the door for him, he got in first then she followed him.

When he got in the limousine he was very surprised to see me and E.B. sitting there waiting for him. I had my gold .44 Desert Eagle in the palm of my hand and E.B. had a .357 auto aimed at Crazy Louie's chest.

"What the fuck is this? Some kind of a fucking game, do you know who the fuck I am. Crazy Louie said.

I don't give a fuck who you think you are, and do this look like a fucking game." I said. Then I cocked my gun back.

"His face turned pale as he was staring down the nozzle of my .44."

"Do you remember me?" I asked him.

He didn't answer. In his mind he was thinking that he did so much shit and now it was finally coming back to him. It could have been anyone.

"What's the matter you can't talk huh, the cat got your tongue or something, I'm a ask you one last time and never again, Do you remember me?" I asked. Aggressively as I was burning up on the inside ready to squeeze the trigger and let him have it. But I wanted to make him suffer the way I did.

No. He mumbled.

"Speak up I can't hear you."

No!

Well homeboy let me refresh your memory, let's do it this way, do you remember my mother or my father maybe you might remember my little homie Butta cause I do, did that spark anything yet in that stupid ass head of yours, cause I'm that same little nigga that lived on the block that you and your crew use to hustle on,

I know you remember my brother Wicked who shot your ass, he should've killed your ass, it would've saved me the trouble of killing you now, and my peoples would be here now, but they not, do you know why? Cause I do, let me tell you why, cause some asshole killed them and that asshole is you, you didn't give them a chance, and you knew that they didn't have nothing to do with what happened to you, did you care? No, you wanted him so bad, that you murdered them, "Bee are you Crazy", my fucking family, what the fuck is wrong with you, I know you probably didn't think that somebody was gonna find out about this huh, and come back to kill your ass, news flash nigga I'm here, and I promise you ain't walking up outta here. I know you heard what happened to your boys Mark and Raymond, while you was away they found their bodies chopped up in the basement like ground beef we put them niggas through the meat grinder, but I been waiting for you for a long time, maybe now after your dead I can finally get some sleep after all these years." I said.

The whole time while Crazy Louie was away in Prison he had nightmares about his day coming back to haunt him.

Everybody lives by a time clock, you just never know when your clock is gonna stop. I raised the desert eagle towards Crazy Louie's head he looked at me knowing he was about to die. The white female prostitute that we had with us started screaming.

"Oh my God", shit wait, please, let me leave my job here is done."

"Shut the fuck up bitch, you ain't going nowhere." E.B.said.

Man, I'm sorry do what you have to do. Crazy Louie said.

"Me too." Bang! Bang! Bang! Bang! Bang! Bang! I emptied the whole Clip in his chest, then from the small of my back I pulled out a .38snob nose got up close to him and stuck the .38 in his mouth and pulled the trigger until it was empty blowing his brains all over the backseat. Even then I kept squeezing. Click click click click click click . . . .

The prostitute started acting all frantic screaming and jumping around because Crazy Louie's blood splatted on her face. E.B. Then put two slugs in her head to calm her ass down.

I sat there looking at their life less bodies thinking about their family.

I finally got your bitch ass. I thought to myself."

E.B tapped me on the shoulder and said, Come on Dice let's get the fuck outta here he's gone. Then we got out of the limousine and torched it with their bodies in it. We watched as it went up in flames. Now my family can rest in peace, I thought to myself, thinking about my peoples that I lost staring down watching what just took place.

You aight? E.B. asked. Yeah I'm good.

* * *

It was Sept. 14, 2004 my mother and father's anniversary. I went to go visit them at their grave site in Long Island not to far from my house. I laid flowers and anniversary cards on each of their graves. I kneeled down to speak to them.

Please forgive me for all my wrong doings, it wasn't my choice to live this way, I was forced to do it this way, its an eye for eye, life for life what has been done had to be done. They took y'all away from me at an early age leaving me blind to life before I became a man. This world owes me everything that was due to y'all, is now due to me. All the things that happened to me in my life made me into a man before I was ready to become one and that the man I am today. I wish y'all was here with me today then maybe life for me would be different, but we can't change what's been done already. I know by me doing wrong don't make it right, but I gotta try to make it better.

I'm a father now with two beautiful children Dyemere and Diceita. I'll give them the life y'all always wanted for me. I know y'all watching over me out here in these streets, cause I can still hear your voices in my head, I'm doing my best out here I know y'all want me to hold my head and try not to end up where y'all at, but it's hard I'm only a man who can do so much. I also found my lady the woman I want to be my wife, if y'all was here y'all would love her the way I do every day I ask God why, why us, y'all never did anything but love us. I'm trying my best to do right, but I always find myself doing wrong, I will always remember y'all till the day I die.

Please forgive me for what must be done to anyone that caused any harm to y'all. They shall pay with their lives the way y'all did I will make sure of that if I gotta die trying.

I stayed there for a few more minutes to say a prayer. Why, O lord is it so hard for me to keep my heart directed toward you? Why do the many little things I want to do, and the many people I know keep crowding my mind, even during the hours that I am totally free to be with you and you alone? . . . Do I keep wondering in the center for my being whether you will give me all I need if I just keep my eyes on you? Please accept my distractions, my fatique, my irritations, and my faithless wanderings. You know me more deeply and fully than I know myself you love me with a greater love than I can love myself or another you even offer me more than I desire. Look at me! Look at me! See me in all my misery, pain and inner confusion, and let me sense your presence in the midst of my turmoil. "Amen." HappyAnniversary.

When I stood up and turned around about to leave I thought I was looking at a ghost cause I was surprise to see Jay standing there behind me with tears in his eyes. "How long have you been standing there listening to me." I asked him.

"The whole time I didn't want to interrupt you I wanted you to speak your mind plus I knew you would be here."

"What you doing here I thought you would be down south?

The same reason why you here, I always come to see them to pay my respect on every birthday and anniversary.

I just had a few things that I wanted to get off my chest, I feel alot better now."

That's good I know they heard you Dice believe me I know they understand and feel your pain. So you do what you gotta do but be careful.

I always do.

Chapter 14

"You Ain't Like Me"

What's up asshole, where you been you thought you could hide from Us. Huh, what you called yourself being slick we been coming by your apartment and you haven't been there, what's up with that, I know you ain't trying to skip out on us, or have a change a heart. Are you Roger?"

Detective Johnson said, calling him by his government name. Detective Johnson and Detective Honeytoon caught up with Rob when they was driving by the gas station on 96st and First Ave.

"Nah, I been around, y'all just wasn't doing your job. Rob said.

Oh so you wanna be a smart ass, you know what Honeytoon let's just charge his sorry ass with the drugs and fuck it with conspiracy of murder too. Detective Johnson said.

"Murda? Rob Said. Surprised

"That's right shit face "murder," we know you and your boy killed Crazy Louie you sick son of a bitch. Detective Johnson said, turning red in the face.

"What the fuck are you talking about' I don't know shit about no fucking

"murda". Rob Said.

"Yes you do", if we say you do, we the fucking cops here we make the rules remember we could say anything we want and we saying you did it, so if I say it's murder than its murder, you get it yet asshole. Detective Johnson said.

You can't do that. Rob Said.

"Why Not!!? I know y'all killed Crazy Louie, you fucking "cock sucka" you know that y'all did it, just admit it. Detective Johnson said.

"Hell no! I aint admitting to shit." Rob Said.

Cuff this motherfucker Honeytoon he's talking a ride with us downtown. Detective Johnson yelled.

Detective Honeytoon got out the car from the front passenger seat and opened up the back door where Rob was sitting.

"Wait a minute, wait a minute." Rob Said. Stalling them trying to buy himself some time.

"You don't have a minute cuff the bastard we don't need his help." Detective Johnson said.

"Shit", okay, damn . . . . What the fuck y'all always trying to wrap a nigga in some bullshit.

Look, I'm finished talking to you either you gonna do it our way or your ass is going to jail for a very, very long time, today. I'm through playing games with you. Detective Johnson Said.

Aight fuck it we'll do it your way then.

"You're wearing a wire." Detective Honeytoon said.

"Ah man," "I can't do that."

"You gonna do anything I tell you, you gonna eat shit if you have to, you wanna go to jail motherfucker cause I don't have problem locking your ass up, because I'll get your boy Dice later with or without you and take your ass down now."

"Alright, I'll wear the fucking wire."

* * *

Hey what's up Shaniqua. Cookie said.

Nothing girl just giving this boy a bath. Shaniqua said.

Just finish feeding Dicecita some turkey and green peas and she made a mess.

Yeah, I know how easy they get messy eating and playing everywhere getting into everything.

Shit, I keep Dicecita in the play pen, cause I be too tired chasing her Around.

"Um, hum"

You know it's gonna be nice outside today we should take the kids out and let them hang out together.

Okay that sounds good, I don't have nothing to do today plus I could use a little fresh air, where you wanna take them to?"

"We could take them to the amusement park or something or maybe we could take them to the park or the zoo, I don't know it really doesn't make a difference.

That's a good idea yeah let's take them to the zoo I know they will like that to see all the different animals.

How long would it take you to get ready.

I don't know.

I'll give you 2 hours to get ready.

Alright that's enough time for me to get everything ready and myself.

Alright so I'll call you then.

Alright later. (click)

When they arrived at the zoo the kids were enjoying themselves amazed by all the different types of animal's birds, snakes, lions, tigers, etc. While Shaniqua and Cookie was browsing around talking about how the kids were growing so fast.

Yeah I know he eat a lot right cause Dice could eat you out of a house and home. Cookie said. Then they both chuckled.

Um huh you know it.

How's the business going for you at the salon. Cookie said.

Oh it's great the shop is really starting to pick up now I hired two more beauticians and they could do some hair girl I'm telling you. Tesha did this.

You right cause that's nice I think I should get my hair done like that.

She'll do it for you, you just gotta call her and set an appointment.

I think I might do that, I'm glad business is going good for you, cause I love my salon, I never thought about me ever owning a salon before but ever since Dice got it for me I've been into it, I'm thinking about opening another one soon I'm a talk to Dice about it."

I hope he's alright, and not out there playing cowboys and Indians.

Shaniqua said.

Dice is a big boy, he knows how to take care of his self that's one thing you shouldn't worry about.

I know that he's a big boy and all, but I don't know what he's really doing out there anyway, that's what I'm worried about.

You shouldn't worry about that, Damn Shaniqua look at your ring girl, let me see it . . . . Oh my God it's beautiful. Where did you get it from? I know it must have cost you an arm and a leg that rock is "huge".

It didn't cost me a dime, Dice bought it for me, it's our engagement ring he gave it to me on my birthday. I was so surprised when he pulled it out of his pocket and placed it on my finger now I can barely fit my hand inside my purse, he didn't tell you about it?

Shaniqua asked. Seeing the expression on Cookie's face like it was breaking new to her.

"No." Cookie said. In a low tone of voice.

Yeah we been engaged for three months now, I'm just waiting for him to tell me when we going to make it official.

That's good, I'm happy for you. Cookie said. With jealousy written all over her face like she just swallowed a piece of shit.

Oh no this motherfucker didn't he's trying to play me for this bitch. Oh hell no who the fuck he think he is after what I did for him now he's going to do this me. All I ever did was love this nigga sorry ass and show him that I was loyal to him. And he going to do this to me. Oh hell no this time we went too far. Cookie thought to herself.

Cookie are you alright. Shaniqua asked. Seeing that she wasn't herself anymore.

"Huh", oh . . . . Yeah I'm fine. Cookie said. Trying to hold back all her emotions. I was just thinking about something I'm alright . . . . So when's the big day, did y'all make any arrangements yet.

No, we didn't talk about it yet he been too busy lately for us to talk about anything, but I know it's gonna be soon though.

Bitch you done signed your own death certificate with that one. Cookie thought to herself.

"Oh shit girl!" What time is it? Cookie said.

It's a quarter to four.

"Shit" Shaniqua, I forgot I had to pick up my mother from the doctor's office, I gotta be there to pick her up at 4'oclock so I'm a see you later.

I gotta go now, I'll call you. Cookies said. Grabbing Dicecita's baby stroller and rushing to her ML 430 Benz Jeep.

* * *

Boo was home in his condo relaxing counting some money when he heard the breaking news flash on his television screen.

We interrupt this program to bring you this breaking news update.

Hello! This is Robert Sanders reporting for the channel six news. I'm standing here with what use to be a limousine that was stolen yesterday from Big Apple Limousine Company that was found yesterday afternoon burned to a crisp there were also two body's recovered from the scene that were burned so bad their bodies couldn't be identified. Due to dental records they were able to identify one body as Crazy Louie all so known as Louie Pizzi. He was also shot several times and the other body is still unknown at this time, as more develops on this story we will inform the public, we now return you back to your original local programming, thank you this has been Robert Sanders for the channel six news.

A big smile suddenly came over Boo's face knowing his boy Dice had something to do with it.

* * *

Cookie was on her way back to her old neighborhood Amsterdam Projects. While Cookie was driving she was talking to herself. This Mother fucker must of fell and bumped his damn head trying to play me for that bitch, for that bitch oh no, no, no I'm not having that shit fuck that.

Who the fuck he thinks he playing? How the fuck he's going to get that bitch an engagement ring without giving me one when I'm that bitch. I helped his ass get where he at, I'm the reason why his ass is here today, and he gonna do me like this, after all the shit we been through together, he just gonna shit on me huh just like that. Oh no I don't think so I got something for that bitch watch Shaniqua. She thinks she all that cause she's fucking my man, watch I'm a fix her ass today. Cookie was pissed off.

Now it was about to get crazy. They say bitches are more grimy than niggas are. You seen what happened when that dude got his dick cut off. "Whoa."

I went by to check Boo at his condo.

What's good my Dice. Boo said. Letting me in the condo.

Ain't nothing, I just came from seeing my family having a lil talk with them, but what the hell you doing in here." I said.

I'm getting this money together in here cause I'm about to go cop me a truck and put some 28's on it with some T.V.'s and you know I gotta throw in a banging system that you could hear 10 blocks away.

That's what's up what you got in mind I know it's going to be something crazy to stunt in.

No doubt, I was thinking about an Escalade, Denali or the new 550 Benz Truck I need something chunky to accommodate the kid.

That's what's up, it's like we could do anything we want out here we got everything we got the cars, jewels, money, bitches, and power what's after all that, what you think you gonna be doing after all this is done cause you know we can't do this forever right. I said.

"Man I don't even think about that shit cause I'm a ride this till the wheels fall off until it's nothing left, why? what's up you thinking about giving up the street life

"Nah, not yet but in the future I will.

What you talking about, we just got a new connect that's giving us the work we need it's gonna get real crazy we about to make some real paper. He Said. With a grin on his face

I'm just saying I'm keeping my doors open for new opportunities to walk in because there's other ways to make money

I hear you man, but you are starting to sound like Nas did in belly wanting to go back to Africa and shit. He said. Laughing

Get the fuck outta here nigga, why you trying to my homie Nas like that.

Nah Nas my dude.

A yo what's up with that nigga Rob you heard from him lately?

I haven't seen him in a couple of days, but he's around some where probably our there chasing his bitch you know how that nigga do. Boo said. As he continued counting his money. What's up with him tho? You think that nigga is ready to get back at it with us.

I know that nigga thirsty for some action since the last time I seen him he was telling me that his people was blowing up his phone.

I know him and that nigga Blinky made a lot of paper for us, and their people been waiting for them to get some'em popping again for a minute now yeah . . . . I think he's ready to get back at it.

Aight, so when you ready holla at him and let him know what's good, but I want you to deal with him hands on and if any sign's of any funny business I want you to pop that nigga.

Aight, say no more I got you, yo . . . Did you catch the news today?"

"Nah, why? What's up?"

Somebody got to that nigga Crazy Louie and finished his ass for good, and fried that nigga like Chinese food ain't no coming back for that nigga it's a wrap that was some straight "Gangsta shit."

Did they say anything about who did it?

No! They ain't got a clue, they probably looking for tips. They killed him and the bitch he was with the only thing they said they found were their bodies in a stolen limousine. I know a lot of niggas are happy that his ass is dead.

I guess he got what he had coming to him running around murdering people like his ass was untouchable, that nigga stupid as hell that's why his ass dead now . . . . Did they say anything else?"

"Nah, they interrupted the T.V. program and all that for that cracker ass nigga like he a celebrity."

"Fuck that nigga", A yo Boo I'm a holla at you later don't forget to holla at Rob.

Aight Dice, I got you my nigga. Boo said. Giving me dap as I was walking out his condo on my way to the elevator.

* * *

When Cookie arrived at Amsterdam Projects in her old hood she ran into some cats that she knew from the Projects back in the days. They were some straight grimy ass niggas always looking for action. From the moment Cookie pulled up in her ML 430 Benz jeep they were scheming on her.

"Yo what's up Pooh and Buck?" Cookie said, As she was approaching them.

They were startled for a minute cause they didn't know who it was that was calling out their names. They did so much shit in the hood they didn't know what to think so they was on point for anything to jump off.

"A yo, who that?" Buck yelled out. Reaching for his gun as she was getting closer to them.

They were sitting on the bench in front of 2190.

"It's me Cookie, she said. Seeing that they were uncomfortable seeing a unfamiliar face.

As Cookie was close enough for them to get a good look they immediately recognized her.

"Oh shit, what's up shorty?" "I was about to blast your ass you know you can't be walking up on us like that what the fuck is wrong with you . . . . you must have forgot this is the hood. Buck said.

"Word!" Pooh said. Tucking his hammer away.

I see y'all guys still ain't change a bit huh, y'all look like y'all still up the same ole shit. What's up how's everybody doing around here? Cookie asked.

Do we look like we out here keeping tabs on mother fucka's, come on tell me, have you ever known me to be doing that unless I'm plotting on a mother fucka. Buck said.

No! . . . I was just wondering because y'all do live around here. Cookie said.

So fucking what, I care about what we do me and my nigga right here and we up to the same thing slinging crack, selling dope, bending bitches over, banging and jacking niggas all day that's what we up to. Ain't nothing change around in these projects. Buck said.

You know it ain't safe around here for a pretty thang like you especially not around us you know how we do. Pooh said.

Word, unless you about to hand us some cash . . . How much cash you got anyway what you got in that Gucci bag. Buck said.

"That's why I'm here".

Damn Buck niggas fear us that much now that they just bringing the money to us. Pooh said. With confused expression

No! . . . . I'm here to see if y'all wanna "make" some money cause I got a job for y'all if you're interested. Cookie said.

"Of course we wanna make some money what you think we out here for? Waiting for the birds to shit on us. Buck said.

Tell us who we gotta clap cause I know you ain't come here to give us no Mcdonald's job. Pooh said.

"Word", cause that would be some bullshit if you did come here with that sucker lame shit I fuck around and clap your ass. Buck said.

"No, I don't want nobody clapped", at least not yet, I just want somebody to disappear." Cookie said.

"What you mean? Buck said.

"You know, like disappear." Just for a little while, that's all. Cookie Said.

"Wait a minute, you just gonna drop out the sky with some shit like this, what you doing you trying to set us up, you working with the police now you wearing a wire or something bitch. Pooh Said.

"Noooo . . . . Y'all should know me better than that. Cookie said.

Aight so who is it a nigga or a bitch? Buck asked.

It's this "bitch" that I know. Cookie said.

"Oh shit! A bitch what she do? Fuck you man? Pooh asked.

Pooh and Buck started laughing they asses off. When they saw Cookie wasn't joking they stopped laughing.

"My bad shorty I see you dead ass serious about this shit huh. Buck said.

Does 50,000 sound's like I'm serious enough for you cause I didn't come here to laugh with y'all or to play fucking games. Cookie said. As she now had their full attention.

"Yeah I thought it would." She said.

All you gotta do shorty is let us know when and where and it's done. Pooh said.

Once I get the address, I'll give y'all a call to let y'all know everything. Cookie said.

You make sure we get our money shorty cause I'm telling you, I don't give a fuck how far we go back" I want my money." Buck said.

Don't worry about that part cause I'm a give y'all 10,000 now as a down payment to show y'all I mean business and y'all will get the rest when the job is done. Cookie said.

Then she gave them the money and then they exchanged numbers.

Aight, we'll be waiting for the call. Buck said.

Then Cookie walked to the parking lot and jumped in her ML 430 Benz Jeep with a smile on her face. As she was thinking that all her problems would soon be over and she would have Dice all to herself. "This is baby mama drama for real".

Chapter 15

"Switching Lanes"

Boo called Rob and told him to meet him at the dealership on Hillside Ave. in Jamaica Queens. Rob was now driving his Lexus GS again. When he arrived at the dealership he saw Boo talking to one of the salesman that was there. Before Boo approached him he continue to talk to the salesman about how they were going to work out the paper work.

Rob was walking around admiring all the different types of vehicles that the dealership had. Rob came upon a pearl white S 600 Benz 2005 model.

This shit is tight. Rob thought to himself.

Yo, Rob . . . . Boo yelled. Waving to get his attention.

Yo, what's up?

You like that one?

"Yeah dog, It's fully loaded I'm feeling this one, which one you getting?

"You looking at it right now it's banging right?

"Yeah this shit is crazy."

Since Boo was paying for it with cash the salesman gave him a good deal for it. 75,000 including tax and everything. Boo also gave the salesman an extra 10,000 to make sure all the paperwork was proper so he wouldn't have to worry about the I.R.S or the Feds.

Once all the paperwork was done and they put Boo's plateds and stickers on, Boo drove off in his brand new S 600 Benz Boo turned on his system popped in 50cents CD (Power of a Dollar) put it on track number 9 (Ghetto Koran) and played it mid-level.

Yo Boo, you came off with this one.

"I did right, now I gotta get some custom work done to personalize it.

"Fo sho my nigga, but the reason why I wanted you to meet up with me today was because I wanted to holla at you.

What's good?"

I wanted to know if you was ready to get it popping on your side of things with your people again.

"Nigga I'm more than ready." Rob said. Feeling like a major burden was lifted off his shoulder.

"Aight", so this is what we gonna do, we going to start moving them joints like you use and breaking them down, but this time my nigga don't get caught slipping make sure your program is tight. Boo said.

I know what I gotta do, so you aint gotta tell me shit like I'm a new jack at this shit I been doing this for too long, way before y'all even thought about hustling. Rob Said

"Yeah and you was the first one to get knocked too, so that shit you talking don't mean shit all I'm telling you is to be cautious about the way you do your thang do we have a problem.

Nah, but you know I will, I don't know why you giving me hustling 101.

"Just make sure you do your thang right. I'm a have them things delivered to you whenever you need them so it ain't no reason to call Dice, you call me and I'll set it up for you, you don't gotta go to the stash crib for nothing because we moved it.

Why y'all didn't let me know, I'm a part of this too, what is it what y'all don't trust me. Rob said. Raising his voice.

"A yo" I don't know what's with all the hostility about but you better check yourself this is for safety reasons mother fucka we ain't trying to go to jail. Boo said.

Staring at him trying to figure out where he was going with all the shit he was saying out his mouth.

Contact your people then call me tomorrow and let me know what you gonna do. Boo said. As he pulled up next to Rob car to drop him off

Aight. He said. Then he exited the S 600 Benz.

* * *

"Hello!"

What's up Dice? I'm on my way to drop off the groceries at the house are you there? Anna said. As she was driving on the 1 and 9 expressway in New Jersey.

Yeah ma, I'm here just come straight here. I said.

Okay, I'll call you when I'm downstairs daddy. Anna said.

Aight baby, I'll see you when you get home. I said. (click)

Anna was on her way with them birds. She always liked to drive by herself to attract less attention. The whole program was running smooth like this. Anna always picked up everything from Hatian Black's peoples on time. Haitian Black kept the deliveries coming and we kept sending the cash. Sometimes Haitian Black might send 5 extra keys for us just to see what would I do. Then on the next trip that Haitian Black peoples did I send them back with an extra 50,000 to cover the extra keys that we had got from him. This way I was building up trust and a good relationship with him. Now I was at a mark that I wanted to reach. I made the money that I wanted quicker than I thought. I was now ready to walk my last mile. All I needed was three more months and I was done. I was going to break the news to E.B. and Boo but they probably would think that I was just talking cause life was too good just to say fuck it. Where would I be if I wasn't hustling in these streets. I always thought cause hustling and the streets is all that I knew.

I was in the stash crib counting some money that I was putting away.

Nobody knew about the stash house except for E.B., Boo, and Anna. So I wasn't worried about nothing ever happening there. I had it hooked up like it was a regular crib. Anna arrived an hour and a half later from when I spoke to her on the phone. We carried everything inside than I put it away. I gave her a kiss then gave her an envelope with 20,000 for herself. I always took care of my people. You have to make them feel like they are a part of something.

Anna was looking good as always in her designer clothes, she was Prada down from head to toe.

How was the trip? I asked her.

It was alright, a little boring that's all but I'm fine now.

You know I like your style, you make a nigga wanna hold you and keep you on the passenger side, come over here and let me touch you with your sexy ass. I said. Then Anna came strutting over to me.

She tossed the envelope down on the table. Let her hair down from the pony tail she had it in, pulled the strings that connected her blouse around her shoulders slid it down to her waist. Now I was looking at her beautiful breast. I grabbed her by her waist and brought her close to me and started kissing on her neck soft and gentle all the way to her tongue was on her nipples while I was massaging her breast with one hand and the other hand palming her ass. Anna leaned her head back and started breathing heavily feeling herself getting sexually aroused. Anna's hands were going up and down on my back. She could feel my dick pressed against her body.

I slid her skirt down pass her ankles then she lifted one of her legs. I began kissing on her inner thigh I then laid her flat on the table. I sat down in the chair with her directly in front of me. I place both of her legs on the table than I slowly spread them apart and began eating her pussy like I was suppose to. When I was done with the appetizer Anna pulled off my shirt over her head then said.

"I want you now."

*   *   *

She pulled me on top of her I began teasing her with the dick rubbing it on her clit. Then I slowly entered her walls she started moaning feeling my pulse inside of her. Then I picked her up from off the table and put her legs over my shoulders holding her up in the air and began pumping her with all 10 inches of me. Anna whispered in my ear in the mix of it all and said.

"Dice, I love you baby, I love the way you make me cum."

Then I bent her over the top of the couch spread her big ass cheeks and buried my dick in her. When I was about to cum, I pulled out my dick and snatched off the condom and nutted in her mouth and watched her swallow it.

When Shaniqua got back home from the zoo she was still wondering why did Cookie breeze off the way she did. because she wasn't trying to hurt her feelings but she just wanted to let her know that she was number one in Dice's life. because it was clear as day. When Dyemere fell asleep she carried him into the bedroom and laid him in his crib. Shaniqua knew that Cookie was lying when she ran off talking about she had to go pick up her mother. Shaniqua was thinking about calling Cookie to see if she was alright but she changed her mind and said fuck it she gotta deal with it. Shaniqua went in the bathroom to wrap her hair like she do before gets ready for bed. When she finished wrapping her hair she went and sat down on the sofa in the living room. She started wondering why Dice didn't tell Cookie that they had got engaged as she thought to herself as she began watching her favorite T.V. program, "Law and Order."

Chapter 16

"Suicide"

E.B. was coming out of the Jamaican restaurant in Harlem on a 125th street when he got in his Cadillac Escalade. After he pulled off from in front of the restaurant he tried catching the light before it turned red but when he realized that he couldn't make it he came to a sudden stop causing his cell phone to slide off his lap and on to the floor by the gas pedal. He reached down and picked it up and put it in the console. When he lifted his head up from under the steering wheel the light now was green. He continued to drive down 125th street there wasn't any heavy traffic but he noticed a Black Lincoln Town car tailing him. When he pulled up to the corner of Second Avenue on a 125th the Lincoln Town car that was behind E.B.'s Escalade was now coming around on the driver side slowly. As the Lincoln Town car was now side by side with E.B.'s Escalade.

E.B. leaned over to see who it was that was tailing him. He couldn't see in the Lincoln Town car cause of the black limo tints it had all around.

Until E.B. saw the back window on the passenger side of the Lincoln Town car slowly come creeping down. Then E. B. noticed the barrel of a shot gun coming out of the window aimed at him. Before the armed assassin could pull the trigger E.B. had already stepped on the gas pedal and peeled around the corner on to Second Avenue. The first shot that was discharged from the shot gun knocked out the back seat passenger side window. The Town car turned the corner with E.B. on to Second Ave in high pursuit with the shot gun still brandishing out of the window. E.B. began weaving through traffic like it was nothing flying down Second Avenue trying to get away but the Lincoln kept getting closer. They took another shot as they was now a car length away. The shot penetrated the left side of the Escalade while E.B. was still maintaining control of the vehicle E.B. reached and grabbed his .45 auto from the glove department then he checked his side view mirror to locate the Lincoln Town Car that was giving chase. It was now directly behind him

E.B. stuck his arm out the window with the .45 in his hand and started squeezing off several rounds in the direction of the Lincoln Town Car causing it to swerve in traffic. The front window shield shattered and the front seat passenger got hit in the shoulder. He rolled down the passenger side window and started spraying the Escalade with a fully loaded UZI. When they heard the police sirens coming in their direction the Lincoln Town car broke off the high speed chase. E. B. quickly turned off Second Avenue heading for the West Side Highway downtown to his condo. He parked his Cadillac Escalade in the basement garage and pulled his truck cover over his Escalade to hide the damages. E.B. still had his .45 in his hand as he made his way to the elevator. Who the fuck was that? He thought to his self. He didn't even have a chance to see who it was that was trying to kill him but whoever it was didn't want to be seen. E.B. also knew that it was a hit. When E.B. finally made it up to his condo he didn't know what to do. He paced back and forth frustrated until he had decided to call Dice. When he called Dice he got his voicemail he looked over at the clock to see what time it was. It was only 8:30p.m. He tried again still no answer from Dice. Now E.B. started to worry about if the same people that was trying to kill him had gotten to Dice already. So he called Boo and told him what happened and that he haven't heard form Dice. Boo was shocked about what he heard from E.B. Boo told him that he haven't heard from Dice either since earlier today. Boo told him to calm down and not to go anywhere because he was on his way over there. Where the fuck is Dice?" E.B. thought to himself.

* * *

"Damn! I left my charger in the house . . . . I know somebody trying to call me cause my battery is dead. I was on my way to Shaniqua's house. It was about 9:30pm when I walked in the house.

Shaniqua was sitting on the sofa watching videos on BET and eating ice cream. Shaniqua looked at me like I killed her best friend.

"What's up baby?" I said. Then kissed her on her forehead. Attempting to ease the tension that filled the room. Why you didn't tell Cookie that we were engaged now?

Because that's none of her business, who is she that I have to report everything to her, she's only my baby mother not my mother."

"Well I was with Cookie today cause we took the kids to the zoo, you know to enjoy themselves, but when I told her that we were engaged now she came up with this excuse to leave, she said that she had to go pick up her mother from the doctor's office."

"She probably did", but I don't know cause I didn't speak to her yet. "Why you wasn't answering your phone, I was trying to call you for almost 2 hours now but I kept getting your voice mail."

"I didn't even know that my battery was dead, I forgot I left my charger here. I said.

Then I plug my charger in the wall pressed the power on button.

You need to get an extra battery for the future so it don't happen again, because it could have been an emergency why I was calling you and I needed to contact you right then and there."

"I know "don't worry baby girl I'm a get me another one! I hope you cooked baby cause a nigga sure is hungry.

No! cause I didn't feel like cooking when I got back from the zoo, we could order some pizza, or Chinese food or do what I'm doing eat some ice cream.' Shaniqua said. Then she chuckled.

"Nah I'm good" I don't want none of that and I don't feel like waiting to eat I'm hungry now. I'll just eat me some cereal and call it a night." I said.

Walking into the kitchen to get me a bowl of cereal. Then my phone started ringing I picked it up and looked at the caller ID. It was E.B.

"Yo what's up my nigga? I asked.

"Where you at man, I've been calling you for the longest now!

"I'm at the crib, why, what's up?

"Dice, man, come over to my crib now, hurry up and make sure you strapped too! Cause some crazy shit popped off today. I'll tell you about it when you get here. (Click) He hung up the phone in a hurry.

Damn! I exhaled. Cause I knew my nigga needed me and I knew some shit really jumped off cause he wanted me to be strapped."

"What's wrong baby?" Shaniqua asked.

"I don't know baby girl, but I'm a find out." I said. As I was heading upstairs.

"What's going on Dice", I know you ain't leaving out again." "Oh my god, here we go again." Shaniqua said. Following me upstairs to the bedroom.

I put on my level 2 bullet proof vest on that I had custom made for me along with my twin holsters and two .40 glocks.

"Baby where are you going with all that shit. Shaniqua said. Curious.

Don't worry baby, I'll be back, I gotta go make sure my peoples aight."

'What about me?

"What about you, you aight."

"No I'm not! . . . . Dice I need you to be here with me, when are you going to stop all this madness, I keep telling you that I don't wanna lose you, you got me Dyemere and Diceita to think about now It's not all about you anymore." Shaniqua said. Then she started crying.

"Baby calm down", it's all about to be over real soon trust me you gotta believe me Shaniqua but right now I gotta go do what I gotta do just trust me baby I promise you that, but now I gotta go and hold my man down I love you." I said. Then I kissed her.

As I rushed out of the house and hopped in my Denali I turned on my CD player and on came the LOX (We are the streets).

*   *   *

Chapter 17

"Who's that"

"Hey" look who it is, our M.V.P. the star of the show how you doing today" . . . "What's up you don't look so good today what's a matter you didn't get no pussy." Detective Johnson said.

"Look man" I'm not here for your sarcasm or your bullshit, here take what you wanted me to get for you we even after this Rob said, shoving him the tape.

"I see our boys finally coming around congratulations, I see you ain't a pea brain after all like I thought you was." Detective Johnson said.

"Let me pop this in and see what we have here." Detective Honeytoon said. As he took the tape from his partner Detective Johnson and popped it in.

"What the fuck is this some kind of a fucking joke you fucking asshole, I don't hear shit but some fucking garbage, who the fuck suppose to be here anyway, huh?" Detective Johnson said. Aggravated with a disgusted look on his face.

"That's me and Boo talking about our operation, just listen you might hear what we was talking about." Rob said.

We don't want him you" asshole", he a small fry in this operation and plus you can't hear shit any way because of all that damn garbage y'all be listening to you call music, read my lips I want Dice! That motherfucker is going down." Detective Johnson said.

"I haven't seen him, I don't even have his phone number cause he changes phone numbers the way you change under wears." Rob said.

Detective Honeytoon started laughing.

"What's that suppose to mean? Detective Johnson asked.

"He changes phone numbers every three days." Rob Said

Detective Honeytoon started laughing uncontrollably.

"Fuck you, you fucking rat bastard let's see if you wanna make jokes when one of your boys end up in a body bag in the morgue because it's gonna happen" Detective Johnson said. In a agitated tone of voice.

Why you say that? Rob said.

"Because that's what's gonna happen when I run into them." Detective Johnson said.

Well if that's the case, I don't wanna do this no more cause I ain't with that. Rob said.

"What you mean shit face", we'll tell you what you can or can't do, you work for us now, so get your monkey ass outta here and do what you suppose to do and chase the cheese you sack of shit." Detective Johnson said.

Rob got out of the Impala and got in his Lexus and drove away.

Detective Johnson wasn't worried about Rob doing or saying anything because if he did it would cost him his life.

Rob was now starting to have mixed feelings about what he was doing.

He knew his boys had nothing but love for him he knew that he wasn't giving them the same love back in return. Because he was going out like a sucka and he knew it." The game didn't change, the players did."

*   *   *

"Ah, Detective Honeytoon I need you to do me a favor can you drop me off I'm a go home to my wife early today. I got some things that I gotta take care of at the house." Detective Johnson said.

"Sure no problem, I'll cover for you for the rest of the day." Thanks pal.

"Anytime."

After Detective Honeytoon dropped off Detective Johnson. Detective Johnson faked like he was going in the house and waited until his partner was out of sight then got in his car, and headed uptown to 115th on the eastside of Harlem.

*   *   *

"What! Who the fuck would try some shit like that, Did you get a chance to see who it was." I said, gritting my teeth together.

"Nah," I couldn't see who it was cause I was trying to get away they had the drop and them motherfuckers was trying to kill me for real like they had a "hit on me." E.B. said.

"Where is your truck at now? I asked.

Down stairs in the basement garage that shit is fucked up Dice, I'm telling you I'm lucky I got away cause them niggas wasn't playing they were trying to air my ass out." E.B. said.

"Did you have your hammer with you? I asked.

"Of course, I was banging back at them, I think I might've touched one of them." E.B. said. Demonstrating his actions.

"This shit don't even seem right, I wonder who the fuck that was trying to clap you." I said.

"What kind of car you said it was? Boo said.

"It was a Black Lincoln Town car with limo tints so I couldn't see inside." E.B. said.

"That don't sound like no hood niggas to me, hood niggas would of used a hoopty or some other shit not no Town car to come at you . . . You wasn't fucking with nobody's bitch or nothing like that were you?" Boo said.

"Hell no!" E.B. said.

"If there was a hit on you they might be trying to get at all of us, we gotta be careful and watch our backs, cause we did make a few enemies along the way, I don't think they know where you rest at, cause if they did they wouldn't be going through all that trouble or risking getting caught in a shootout especially on Second Ave." I said.

"That's true." Boo said.

E.B. was standing there puzzled thinking who the fuck was that.

All we have do is drive around in different vehicles that nobody knows that they belong until we find out what the fuck is going on cause right now we all got a big bulls eye on our back and we don't even know it. I said.

"I just brought my Benz nobody ain't see it yet we could roll in that." Boo said.

"Good now all we gotta do is watch our backs and when I find out who's behind this because God can't even save them from the shit I'm a do to them and their family. I said.

"I'm chopping niggas heads off straight like that." E.B. said.

"What's up with Rob holla at him and make sure he's aight." I said.

"Aight, But yo Dice, what about that shit we did the other day, you think that got anything to do with this." E.B. said.

"Hell no!!! Don't nobody know about that but me and you." I said.

"But what if somebody knew all along about what happened to your family, and now Crazy Louie turns up dead somewhere without any warnings just like that day he was released from prison, people might think we did it, knowing that one day, you was gonna revenge your family death." E.B. said.

"He's right Dice, cause I knew y'all did it, without y'all even telling me.

I just put two and two together, that's why I brought it up to you, when I asked you about the news, I wasn't going to ask you about it if y'all wasn't going to tell me, cause I know nobody wanted him dead more than you did." Boo said.

"Aight, before we jump the gun and start shooting shit up, let's find out some facts before we start an all out war". I said.

"It already started." E.B. said. Making a Strong statement.

*   *   *

Thank's for coming here, please have a seat. I hope that you are right about these hoodlums that you said killed my nephew, and not using this to settle any personal "vendetta" that you may have against them.

"Yes", I'm positive about this, I been watching them for sometime now."

"What makes you so sure that these are the men that murdered him?

"I have my sources that are reliable."

What if your sources are wrong about this?

I have confidence in my sources, and if they are wrong I will take full responsibility.

"I bet you will, cause we don't need no unnecessary blood shed on our hands through out the streets of Harlem, it's bad for business."

"I understand that."

"Good" take this as a token of appreciation for the information that you provided for us."

"Thank you."

"Next time don't ever come here unannounced, we will contact you if we need you in the future."

I understand.

"Don't let it happen again."

It won't.

What about your partner, do you think that you can trust him.

He doesn't know anything about this.

"Hum . . . Okay we appreciate you coming here."

Anytime if I can be a good use to you. Then the men stood up and shook hands then the meeting was over.

*   *   *

Hey Shaniqua, I'm sorry about the other day but I had to rush and pick up my mother from the doctor. I almost didn't make it there on time. Cookie said.

Is she alright? Shaniqua asked.

"Yeah, she fine now she takes chemo therapy for her cancer every week, but thank God she's fine now." Cookie said.

"That's good, I know that cancer can be very serious if it's not treated properly." Shaniqua said.

"I know, that's why I have to make sure she keep's up with her appointments, they also give her medication for it. But the reason why I called you is to apologize to you for my rudeness the other day and I wanted to know if I could make it up to you tomorrow, if you want to, we could take the kids to the mall and take some pictures of them. Cookie said.

"That sounds alright, but you not going to run off and leave us again are you? Shaniqua said.

"No I promise."

Alright, yeah why not, they need some pictures together that would be nice. I thought you was mad at me the other day.

"Girl Please! For what, for you being engaged to Dice, nah I ain't mad I was just a little surprised that's all. I'm not worrying about nothing cause Dice is going to be Dice.

"Yeah I guess you right."

"So what time you want me to pick you up tomorrow? Cookie asked.

Yeah it don't make sense for the both of us to drive, you could pick me up at around 12 o'clock is that good. Shaniqua said.

"Yes, I'll see you tomorrow, hold up Shaniqua, I don't have your address. They both chuckled.

"Oh, I'm sorry, I forgot you never been here."

"It's alright.'

"Ok, ready."

"Yeah, I got pen and paper."

"Okay, it's 233-03 133rd Avenue that's in Queens."

All right I know where you at, you over by "Merrick Blvd".

"Yeah, I'ma few blocks away from there".

Okay, I'll call you tomorrow before I pick you up."

"Alright, Bye Cookie."

"Later girl". (Click)

Hello Buck. Cookie said.

*   *   *

We were out all night riding around in Boo's S 600 Benz looking for answers all through Harlem. Nobody heard anything as of yet about the shooting that took place earlier. It was like we were trying to solve a unsolved mystery. We ran down on local drug dealer's rivals that could've been a potential candidate. But to be honest they weren't that stupid to try something like this knowing the consequences. They already knew that we knocking down buildings when the drama came with the shit we got. Whoever it was, was keeping a low profile because the streets wasn't talking but what's in the dark always come into light. We were getting very frustrated as we rode around in silence with murder on our minds.

I started zoning out thinking about all my future plans. Why was this happening now when I was ready for a change as I sat there thinking about Shaniqua, Dyemere, Cookie and Diceita. I was ready to live a different life, and invest money in some property, stocks, barber shops, beauty salons and Laundromats. And be a full time father and a husband. But my niggas needed me now and I wasn't going walk out on them now and turn my back when they needed me. Not after all we been through together. My niggas were there when I needed them, they were with me before I had anything and they were still here riding with me. I sat there and made myself a promise. That when all this was over, I'll tell them that I was finished and I will be there for them whenever they needed me for anything. But right now we had some personal drama to handle. We contacted Boo's people to find out if they had heard something yet. Everywhere we turned was a dead end. I started to think about what E.B. and Boo was saying. What if they did know something, why would they come after E.B. instead of me. It wasn't adding up. There was still pieces that was missing that would of connected something to the person or people that was trying to kill E.B. We decided to check out every possibility that there was. We was now back In our old hood cruising up and down Lenox, Madison, Park, Lexington, Third, Second, First and Pleasant Avenues. Looking for a black Lincoln Town Car.

But we had no luck with that, because that was a common car around here we must have saw maybe fifteen-twenty black Lincoln Town Cars that resembled the one we were looking for It was now getting late. We decided to continue our search another day. We headed to a Strip Club in "New Rochelle called Sue's Rendezvous. The strip club was packed with female strippers and niggas that thought they was balling in the club throwing away their re-up money. We headed in and posted up in the VIP section and was watching all the females get freaky as our bottles came. The strippers immediately came to our section when they saw us and started putting on a show for us. Chicks started shooting quarters out their pussies and shoving Heineken bottles in and out their bodies. We brought a couple more bottles and rolled up some weed to get right and take our minds off things. We were still strapped up like Taliban's. Bitches kept coming over asking us did we want a lap dance or some head. I turned down every chick that approached me. Rob grabbed one and slid off to the back with. Me, Boo, and E.B. were still in VIP. No matter how much we drank or weed smoked we still couldn't get what happened to E.B. off our mind. We were looking and thinking that anybody as a suspect. So we kept our eyes open, and ready for anything to pop off at any time. As I was scanning through the crowd the action at the bar caught my attention. There were a couple of strippers surrounding these two guys. I couldn't see them too good cause the strippers that was surrounding them were blocking my view. One of the guys spoke with a strong Jamaican accent. The voice sounded very familiar to me. I must have played this voice over a million times in my head but I wasn't to sure if I really knew this voice because he was talking loud. I put my drink down and started to proceed to the bar to see if my mind was playing tricks on me or was it the liquor. E.B. and Boo followed behind me. We were now standing behind the strippers that were chilling with these two Jamaica guys. I stepped closer to get next to the bar.

"Dice, what's good." E.B. said. Tapping on my shoulder.

"Hold up, chill right here I'm a check something out." I said.

As I was now heading directly for the Jamaican guys. Boo and E.B. looked at each other cause they knew I was up to something by my facial expression said it all, and my body movement. They stood there and watched to see what was going on. There was only one stripper now that separated me and the guys as I made my way through the other strippers. I leaned on the bar and ordered a bottle of Crystal. I looked over to see who was this man with the familiar voice. When I turned and saw who it was I couldn't believe it. My blood shot straight to my head. Excuse me the Bartender said to me here's your Crystal. I paid for it and told her to pass it to the gentleman that was sitting next to me the I gave her a tip. It was my brother Wicked. As the bartender passed him the bottle of Crystal he told her that he didn't order any Crystal. She said if came from the man sitting right next to you. She pointed at me. He looked at me and stared for a minute cause he didn't recognize me because of the dim lights that was inside the club or because he was drinking too much. Whatever it was he wasn't on point. I tapped the stripper on her shoulder and told her that she had to excuse herself cause me and the dudes that was entertaining had some personal business to discuss. She looked at me and knew that I was serious about what I said and got to stepping. Now that we were face to face with each other it was no problem for him to recognize me.

"Rasclod, what's up my youth, wha gwon, you alright every ting crisp. Wicked said. Like he was happy to see me.

"Where you been? I said stern. With the mean ice grill.

"Boy, you know me day bout, me live a Queens now with me girlfriend Yah dun know." Wicked said.

"Ah wha him a qwon so, ah who that Wicked a puff up him chest like say him a bad mon. The guy that was with Wicked whispered in Wicked's ear.

A nah nothing that, a mi lickle brother still." Wicked said.

"Oh yeah, then wha gwon lickle brother. The guy that was with Wicked said. Extending his hand to give me dap.

I just looked at him like he was stupid ass fuck and kept talking to Wicked.

Did you hear what happened to my mother and daddy. I said.

Nah my youth wah happen to dem. Wicked said.

"What didn't happen to them . . . . They were murdered a years ago, you mean to tell me that you didn't hear nothing about it. I said.

"Nah mon, mi nah ear nothing bout that mi youth trust mi, mi ah tell yah ah the first mi ah ear it now." Wicked said. Sitting his drink on the bar.

Do you know why they were murdered. I asked him.

No mon. Wicked said.

"They were killed because somebody came to Harlem and fucked with them drug dealers that hustled on my block". I said.

"Ah lie yah ah tell." Wicked said. Remembering the day he shot Crazy Louie. In his mind he thought he killed him.

"Why did you and Tony come way up to Harlem and do some shit like that, there's so many spots and other drug dealers, that y'all could've robbed, y'all didn't have to come around where we live and do some shit like that."

"Boy . . . . mi sorry mon, mi never mean fi do something like that mi youth, mi think say him dead when mi come and juke the boy, trust me Jah know mi sorry."

"I been waiting to see you so I could ask you that for a long time, you don't even know how much pain you caused me. I didn't have anybody, cause you took all that away from me with that bullshit you did and left me with nothing. The fucked up part about it is that y'all shot and robbed the nigga but y'all didn't even kill'em y'all could at least made sure that y'all did that right, you didn't even come back to hold us down and make sure that we were alright y'all just left us for dead, we was just little niggas and you did all this to us."

"Boy mi nah no what fi say, but mi sorry trust mi.

I could see that he really didn't care about what happened to my family so why should I care about him.

"You know what Wicked, I'm not even mad at you, you did what you had to do, to get that paper, I can respect that cause it's all good shit like that happened, I just had to tell you that cause I had to get it off my chest because I've been carrying it for to long now." I said.

Then I gave Wicked dap and a hug to show him that It was all love between us.

So go ahead and enjoy yourself and don't worry the next bottle is on me also. I said.

"Yeah mon, mi day ah zeen". Wicked said.

Then I spun off to walk away when I got a few steps away from Wicked

I stopped and turned around pulled out my twin .40glocks. Wicked looked at it for his last time.

Before I go take this with you I'll see you in hell "motherfucka". I said. Bang! Bang! Bang! Bang! Bang! Bang! Bang! I let off both of the clips till they were empty on him and the guy he was with.

Everybody that was in the strip club was running for their lives trying to get the fuck outta there. Rob came flying out from the back of the club from where he was getting head at making his way for the exit with his dick hanging out. E.B. and Boo pulled me away from where I was standing over Wicked's body with my gun still pointed at him and rushed me out the club.

The next day it was all over the news. Everybody was talking about what happened at the strip club. It was on hip-hop radio stations people were calling in saying that it was fucked up that people can't even go out and have a good time anymore without someone fucking it even the hip hop police were there.

Hello once again this is Robert Sanders for the Channel Six News, I'm here live at Sue's Rendezvous strip club up in New Rochelle where several bodies were found dead. Many of them were trampled to death form the mayhem that broke out inside the night club last night around 2am. Two men were also found dead with multiple gun shot wounds. Instead of it being a party it turned into a blood bath, the question that many people are going to be asking is how did the guns get inside the club who was in charge of the security how does incidents like this one here keeps happening in the Urban Night Clubs. When the security was tight Secret Service Style. There will be a lot of questions that need to be answered by the local police. This has been Robert Sanders bringing you this breaking story for the Channel Six News."

* * *

Chapter 18

"Shit Happens"

Cookie picked up Shaniqua and Dyemere around 12:30pm. There were on their way to take some pictures at Green Acres mall off of Sunrise highway. When they arrived at the mall it was crowded. The pictures that they took at the studio in the mall came out beautiful. They took many different poses. When they were finished taking pictures they went and got something to eat from the food court in the mall. Shaniqua was munching down on some Japanese food and Cookie had some Italian food. While they were eating Shaniqua noticed Ebony walking in the mall with one of her friends. When Shaniqua called her, Ebony was surprised to see who it was.

"What's up Ebony?" Shaniqua said. Giving her a hug.

"Hi, how you doing Shaniqua, oh my god look at Dyemere, he got so big from the last time I saw him, how old is he now?" Ebony asked. Playing with Dyemere in the stroller.

"He's 10 months now, and this is his sister Diceita and her mother Cookie. Shaniqua said.

"Hi, how you doing, nice to meet you." Ebony said. Waving.

Hello . . . . Nice to meet you also, so this is Ebony the girl you always telling me about. Cookie said.

"Yeah, but I haven't seen her in a while, girl where have you been? I've been calling you, what you changed your number without calling me to let me know something, you don't even come by the house anymore what happened cause I'm curious now, I thought we suppose to be friends. Shaniqua said.

We are friends Shaniqua, I'm sorry but I been so busy lately, I got a new job, and they been killing me with overtime and I'm working

7 days a week that's why I haven't had a chance to call nobody at all, I'm sorry Shaniqua. Ebony said. Looking around paranoid.

"Sorry about what" I was worried sick about you, I miss you. Shaniqua said. Trying to figure out why she been missing in action.

"I missed you too" Shaniqua but I promise I'll call you when I get a chance, I swear." Ebony said. Keeping the conversation short.

Then Ebony gave her a hug and walked away fast before Shaniqua said another word or asked for her phone number.

"Damn!" She's in a hurry. Cookie said.

"I know." Shaniqua said. Watching Ebony speed off walking. Ebony was afraid that Dice was there with Shaniqua and he would see her talking to her and flip out. Plus Ebony didn't know if Dice told Shaniqua what had happened while she was at the mall on her birthday. And she wasn't woman enough to apologize to Shaniqua. And she wasn't going stick around to find out.

Shaniqua got out of Cookie's ML 430 Benz Jeep. As she parked in the driveway and she had also noticed a green Dodge Intrepid parked across the street with two niggas in it. She couldn't see their faces all she saw were their shadows. She never seen them around before so she hurried to the house opened the front door and closed it fast. Once Cookie seen her make it in safely she drove off. Shaniqua carried Dyemere upstairs to his room and laid him in his crib. Then she went back downstairs to peep out the window to see if they were still sitting there. When she looked they were gone so Shaniqua brushed it off like it wasn't nothing. Now Shaniqua was thinking about Ebony. Because she wasn't acting like her usual self. So she suspected that something was wrong with Ebony. But Shaniqua had no clue as to what that was. So she decided that she was going to wait until she called to find out what that was. I was upstairs sleeping when Shaniqua walked into the bedroom. She saw me in the bed passed out then she smiled. Glad to see that I made it home safe cause I wasn't there when she left. She woke me up with a warm passionate kiss on my cheek. I turned around and knew it was her because of her sweet fresh scent and smiled at her.

"What's up beautiful, ahh, where you was at?" I asked. Stretching. "Me and Cookie took the kids out to take some pictures today at the mall, why you was looking for me."

"Yeah, you know I was." I said. Wiping the cold out my eyes.

"Why you didn't call my phone?

I thought about it, but I was tired so I said fuck it.

You wanna see the pictures they took together, they look so cute."

"Yeah, let me see them." I said. Sitting up in the bed.

Shaniqua went down stairs to the living room to get the pictures of the kids. When she came back into the room she showed them to me.

"Oh, look at them they look beautiful just like Daddy." We both chuckled.

"Please Dice, you know and I know Dyemere look just like me, he only got your chincky eyes.

"Whatever baby girl, you beautiful too. She smiled at me, I grabbed her and pulled her close to me and kissed her. As I was in the mood for some love making.

"Wait baby, that's your dessert, you can have some of that after I make you something special to eat."

"You already got something special for me to eat, now give it to me." I said. Pulling on her clothes.

"Wait baby, wait please I want do this for you first then I'm all yours.

Why I can't have some now and later. I said. Kissing on her neck.

Cause I got to run out and get what I need to cook for you, and I don't want to have to jump in the shower after we get finished doing our thang, if that's the case, I just wanna lay next to you, and get comfortable with your arms around me baby, so don't worry baby it's all yours, soon as I get back, you can eat it up, beat it up anyway you want, okay baby." Shaniqua said.

Slow and Seductive, rubbing on my face.

"Aight baby you win, where you going?

"I'm going to Jamaica Avenue, I should be back in about one hour the most, you gotta listen out for Dyemere cause he's sleeping in his crib right now, alright make sure you don't forget he in the room okay, I'll see you when I get back." Shaniqua said. Then she kissed me on my lips and said I love you.

When she left I went right back to sleep.

When Shaniqua left she went to the fish Market on Jamaica Avenue.

She picked up some shrimps, Lobster, snow crabs, clams, and scallops.

Shaniqua was feeling good bout herself on this beautiful day. She also stopped at the super market to pick up a few more things for the special meal that she was making for Dice. The whole time she was driving since she left the house. Shaniqua's Escalade was smelling like raw fish cause of the seafood she had picked up. So she rolled her window's down to let some fresh air in. Shaniqua put on her Christian Dior shades and started singing along with Mary J Blige's CD (No More Drama) cause that's how she was feeling at that moment. Everything in her life was going her way despite dealing with Cookie and the lost of her family members she was alright. When Shaniqua made it back to the house she was taking out the groceries that she picked up while she was on Jamaica Avenue. She laid the bags on the ground to make sure she locked the doors on her Escalade then she noticed a car speeding coming in her direction then it came to a screeching halt. Then one of the men that was in the car jumped out of the car with a .9mm pointed directly in Shaniqua's face.

"Scream bitch and I'm a leave your ass right here, with your brains on the pavement bitch!"

Shaniqua was so scared that she didn't move an inch. She couldn't even scream if she wanted to cause she was in a state of shock. Shaniqua dropped the bags that she had in her hands. Buck snatched her up, threw her in the backseat then he jumped in the back seat with her. Then they went flying off the block before anybody knew what happened.

* * *

Boo was trying to get in contact with Rob for two days. Everytime he called his phone it rang three times then his voicemail would pick up. Boo haven't seen Rob since he first gave him them 20 birds (keys). He wasn't really too concerned about him cause after all that was his boy and he would turn up soon. So Boo decided to fall back and give him them a few more days. Boo was also still trying to figure out who was behind the attempt on E.B.'s life. Boo had his ears to the streets cause the streets talk you just gotta listen when it do. But they wasn't talking as of yet.

*   *   *

Chapter 19

"Somebody Gonna Die Da Night"

Hello, can I speak to Shaniqua. The lady said. Waking me up outta my sleep.

"She not here, you gotta call back in about in about twenty minutes." I said.

Then I quickly looked at the clock, seeing that Shaniqua was gone all most two hours now. Then I got up out the bed. And said to myself. She said that she would be back in an hour. May be she stopped at the mall or something.

"Who's calling? I said.

The lady hesitated for a few seconds before she answered.

Ah, it's me Ebony.

"Didn't I tell you, don't ever call here no more?"

"Yes you did Dice."

"So what the fuck you doing calling here?

Please Dice, let me talk.

"I don't have to hear this shit."

"No please Dice", I'm sorry for what happened, I couldn't control myself, cause I always had strong feelings for you, from the first time I met you, but that's the past now, I'm over that, I never meant no harm or was trying to come between you and Shaniqua."

"So why would you do some shit like that?

I don't know . . . . I just saw your body standing in front of me, and I forgot about everything else, I just wanted you at that moment so I went for mines thinking that I had a chance but I was wrong, I'm a woman so I'm able to admit that I was wrong for doing that.

"Hold on a second Ebony." I said. Wondering where was Shaniqua. I went downstairs to see if Shaniqua was back yet from

Jamaica Ave., but there was no sign of her. Dyemere was still sleeping in his crib.

"Hello Ebony. "Yes."
"Where you at right now I'm at home.
Then I looked out the window I saw Shaniqua's Escalade in front of the house.
"Hold on Ebony I think she just pulled up. I said. As I watched through the window to see if she was coming in, but it still wasn't no sign of her yet. I put the phone down, opened the house door and walked out towards the Escalade to see if she was inside. I went around on the driver side and noticed the grocery bags that was spilled over in the street. At first I didn't think nothing of it. Then it hit me like a brick. Shaniqua said she was going to make me something. Then I looked it was seafood on the ground in the middle of the street. I touched the hood of Shaniqua's Escalade to see if it was warm and it was. Then I ran back into the house and picked up the phone.
"Hello Ebony"
Yes Dice, I'm still here.
"Did you speak to Shaniqua today?
"Yeah, why what's wrong?
"Nothing, how long ago did you speak to her."
When she was at the mall with Dyemere, Cookie, and your daughter.
Aight, well she's not here right now.
"Alright."
Hang up Ebony, I'm a call her cell phone, then I'm a call you back.
"Alright."
Then I dialed Shaniqua's number to see if she would pick up.
Hello, you have reached Shaniqua I am unable to answer my phone right now, so please leave your name and number and a brief message and I will return your call as soon as possible, thank you.

After calling her phone three times and getting her voicemail, I called Ebony back.
Hello.

"Yeah Ebony it's me Dice, did you hear from her yet?
"No."
"Damn! I uttered. Getting frustrated
"Is everything alright Dice?
I don't know, but I need you to come over here.
Alright, just give me a minute and I'll be there.
"Aight." (click)

Then I started thinking where is Shaniqua. Why she wasn't answering her phone. I tried my best not to worry about it too much. Because maybe her phone was dead or something of that nature. I was doing my best to keep myself thinking positive hoping that Shaniqua would call or walk through the door. My thoughts was interrupted when I heard Dyemere crying. I went upstairs to his room and brought him down stairs with me. Another hour went pass and it still was no sign of my baby girl Shaniqua. When I opened up the door, it was Ebony she came inside then I closed the door behind her.

"Is Shaniqua here yet." Ebony asked.

"No!" Did she call you?

"No, I told you, the last time I spoke to her is when I saw her at the mall, and I told her that I was going to call her later today that's why I called earlier."

"What the fuck is going on? I mumbled.

Ebony looked at me seeing that I was getting frustrated.

"Did you try to call her again?

"Yeah", but I got her voicemail again, I ain't never get her voicemail before, that's what makes me think that something is wrong.

Let me call her from my cell phone and see if she answers now. Ebony said. Then she dialed her number.

Yeah Dice it's still going to her voicemail.

I pray that nothing happened to my baby girl, I'll go crazy without her.

Dice you can't think negative, you gotta think positive because I know she's alright she should be here soon watch you'll see.

"I hope so."

* * *

"Yo!" "Shut that bitch the fuck up before I pop her ass". Buck said.

"Please', let me go I didn't do anything to you, or nobody else, please just let me go. Shaniqua said. Pleading for her life. On her ride to hell.

Like I told you, this will be over real soon if you shut the fuck up, but if I gotta keep telling you to shut up, I'm just going put two slugs in your head and bury your ass. Pooh said. As he was now sitting in the back with Shaniqua and his gun pressed against her forehead.

"Just chill the fuck out ma, we see you pushing that big boy truck, we know you got money and you badder than a motherfucker, so don't worry girl we ain't gonna rape you, we ain't on that rape shit, but I'll kill your ass if we have to without a problem. Buck said.

Shit . . . . she got a fat ass, I might wanna hit that I know she got some good pussy to go along with that. Pooh said.

"Nigga fuck that shit! . . . . like I told you, you don't have anything to worry about as long as you know how to follow directions, now put that bitch in the trunk. Buck said. As he pulled the car over.

Shaniqua did as she was told and got in the trunk. She was relieved to hear that they wasn't gonna rape her but she was worried about making it out alive. Soon as the trunk closed Shaniqua started praying for her life.

Please God all mighty, please help me don't let these men kill me here today, I have a son that needs me please lord can you spare my life on the strength of my son let me live for him and show him life, please lord I need you to help me, Dice where you at baby, I need you to help me, Dice where you at baby, please come and get me I need you.

Once Buck and Pooh had Shaniqua tuck away in the trunk they called Cookie.

Yo man, make that call and call that bitch. Pooh said.

"What the fuck it look like I'm doing? Buck said.

"Hello." Cookie answered.

"Yeah it's done, we got her now, what's up with that cash. Buck said.

"Okay, I'll call you back." Cookie said (click)

* * *

Yo Dice, what's up you aight? E.B. said.

Yeah I'm good, I'm just waiting on wifey to come back man, she been gone all day damn near and that shit getting me tight man.

"She probably out shopping or something out here spending some of that money you got.

"I don't know, but I hope so cause I don't like waiting around like no bird in a pigeon coup."

"I feel you Dice, but what can you do?

"You right my nigga, I'm just gonna chill til she call, nah I mean."

Yeah.

So when I'm about to bounce I'm a holla at you, soon as I find out where she at, so we can handle our shit.

Aight Dice, be easy my nigga I know you been going through some shit these last couple of days.

Nah! I'm good fuck them "niggas."

Aight then call me when you ready, I'm a be up in Boo crib til later.

"Aight. One!" (click)

E.B. knew that I was stressing over Shaniqua because he heard it all in my voice when I spoke to him.

Don't worry Dice, Shaniqua is going to be alright, trust me." Ebony said, while she was holding Dyemere patting his back.

"I just wish I knew where she was at or just let me know something, because why she didn't call me yet this is not like her she got me stressing now.

Baby girl if you could hear me I'm coming for you, just call me, why you not here, why your truck still here, where you at? God please make sure my lady is alright. I don't need this type of shit in my life right now. I been through too much already, I need her with me. I thought to myself.

Dice are you alright?

"Yeah." I said in a low tone of voice staring at my phone.

She going to call watch you'll see. Ebony said, rubbing my back.

I knew it wasn't much I could do, but wait until she come home or call.

There's so much shit I wanted to tell. Ever since I been with Shaniqua she never been away from me this long without me knowing where she was. It was a quarter to 10. 8 hours had passed now since I heard Shaniqua's voice. I was really getting impatient now. I was breaking down on the inside thinking about my lady and it was starting to show.

Dice, you gotta calm down, cause you starting to scare me. Ebony said, as she was feeding Dyemere.

"I'm sorry, but I can't help it."

I kept pacing back and forth looking through the window and checking the phones making sure that they were working. Then the phone rang I grabbed it on the first ring and answered it. It wasn't no one but one of her friends looking for her and that made me worry more. I knew something was wrong now because I could feel it.

Ebony put Dyemere to sleep and laid him in the crib. Even he tried waiting for his mommy to come home.

Dice what you want me to do, you want me to leave or you want me to stay with you because it's getting late.

Yeah you could stay if you want, just in case if she call and I gotta run and pick her up, you could watch Dyemere because I don't wanna have to wake him up.

I couldn't even think straight everything was happening too fast. I was use to controlling the situation now the situation was control me. It felt like My whole world was slowly crumbling at that point in front of my face and I couldn't do anything about it. So many thoughts started running through my mind. Flashes of everything that happened in my life and the things that was happening now. My mother, my father, Butta, Crazy Louie, Wicked, Shaniqua, Cookie, Rock, E.B. and a lot of dead people. But I didn't give a fuck about the niggas I murdered. They got what they had coming to them blood or no blood they all deserved to die. I guess it was God's plan for me to experience everything I was going through. I was ready to leave the life style alone. But in came the devil pulling me back in the fire. Soon as I get Shaniqua back in my arms I'm going to tell her I'm finished it's over.

Dice you hungry, I'm about to order some food do you want anything? Ebony said.

Nah I'm alright, I'm not hungry.

You gotta eat something Dice, she going to be alright.

What make you so sure?

I don't know, but I believe she will.

I was really getting tired of her saying that she was going to be alright but to be honest that was the only thing keeping me saine.

* * *

Rob took the drugs that he picked up from Boo and brought it Detective Johnson and Detective Honeytoon 2 days ago.

You doing real good son, what about the wire taps, did you get anything we want yet. Detective Johnson said.

Nothing yet I gotta make them feel like I got everything under control on my side of things, this way they feel comfortable enough to trust me. Rob said.

Well you better do what you gotta do, because it's either them or your sorry ass is gonna be somebody's bitch. Detective Johnson said. Then he chuckled.

Fuck you, you fucking pig ass nigga, you know what I think. Rob said.

What? Detective Johnson said.

You a fucking real asshole, you get a kick off shit like this huh? Rob said.

"You fucking right I do", watching y'all asshole's bring each other down like fucking dominoes y'all guys always talking about y'all some so called gangsta's in your rap songs, standing on the corner like y'all tuff, when y'all ain't nothing but a bunch of bitches, there ain't no honor between y'all, see that's y'all problem y'all cant deal with the pressure when it's on, but y'all wanna live that life like y'all built like that, when y'all ain't nothing but ice cream on a summer day melting when the heat is on, start telling on each other, that's why it's funny to me watching y'all, look what they did to Miz out in Brooklyn them cowards told on him. Now those were some real gangsta's. Detective Johnson said.

Yeah I heard about it, but I guess you haven't met the right nigga yet. Rob said.

Yet! Please . . . . They all some fagots to me.

Here take this shit, and let's do what we gotta do. Rob said. Tossing the duffle on the table.

Detective Honeytoon get that money cleared for us so we can get this maggot outta my face because he's making me sick. Detective Johnson said.

I already got it cleared. Detective Honeytoon said.

Great can you go and pick it up, while I sit here with this bastard.

Detective Johnson said.

Alright, I will be back in a few minutes. Detective Honeytoon said.

Before Detective Honeytoon left the room he placed a tape recorder underneath the table.

Yeah, now it's me and you, if it was up to me I would rather kill your rat ass, because I don't respect no fucking rats like you, people like you ain't worth shit you belong in the sewer with the other rats, besides that none of your boys are going to live in these streets these are their last days, because y'all really fucked up, oh yeah y'all really fucked up, but your boy Dice his ass is going down! Detective Johnson said.

"What you mean we really fucked up?"

"For murdering Crazy Louie I know y'all had something to do with it."

Detective Johnson said.

"What makes you so sure that we murdered Crazy Louie and if that's the case why ain't none of us being charged with murder. Rob said.

Cause I got other plans for your boys and you going help me do it, What you thought I wasn't going to know, come on don't play stupid with me shit face, you could play stupid with your boys but not with me, you think I don't know that Crazy Louie murdered Dice's family, why you think he didn't get charge for it, shit brains I was the first Detective on the scene, I removed all the evidence that could of got Crazy Louie arrested that's why they move me to this unit.

"So you a dirty cop, huh, so why don't you let me just pay you whatever you want instead of going through all this trouble, how much do you want?"

Read my lips, fuck you and your money."

"Why the fuck you telling me all this for, if you not trying to help me."

"I don't like you that's why you ain't nothing but a sack of shit, and a rat I want that motherfucker Dice."

* * *

Chapter 20

"Why ask Why"

"Yo!" Cookie what's good, shit it's 12 0'clock am, and we still here waiting on you, what's going on? "I told you don't play with my money, we did our part, now the rest is on you." Buck said.

Buck I know how y'all get down, I'm not playing no games with you, you just gotta give me a little time to get situated, then I'm on my way, believe me this shit is for real, I gave you my word, I'm waiting on somebody right now then I'll be there, but make sure she doesn't hear y'all say my name when y'all talking. Cookie said.

That bitch in the trunk she can't hear shit, so don't worry about her you just worry about my mother fuckin money, cause I don't have time for no games. I already told you that I don't give a fuck if I know you form yea high, don't play with my money! Buck said.

Take that bitch somewhere, and wait until I call you, don't worry Buck yall gonna get your money, but I can't just leave like that, somebody might suspect I had something to do with it, so wait til I call you, and don't call me no more. I'll call you. Cookie said. (click)

What she say? Pooh said.

That she gonna call us when she ready.

How long this bitch expect us to wait for her. I don't know, but my patients are running short, and that bitch better have my money when I see her. Buck said.

*   *   *

What's good my nigga?

Im still waiting on wifey to come, I don't know what the fuck is going on.

Get the fuck outta here. E.B. Said.

Word! She never was gone this long before without me knowing where she was, and she still didn't call yet, this shit got me mad like a mother fucka.

"Damn Dice," I hope she's aight man, what you want us to do, cause we could just shoot straight over there right now, it's nothing but a hop skip and a jump.

Nah, I need you to take care of something for me, I want you to meet up with Anna and pick up those things from her, she going come to your place for now until I hear something from wifey, then I'm a come over there so we can take care of business.

"Aight Dice if you need us we right here for you, just holla."

"No Doubt! My nigga that's what's up, call Anna and give her the directions to your condo, and when she get there tell her I'll be there soon."

"Aight, I got you." E.B. said. (CLICK)

*   *   *

When Anna arrived at E.B.'s condo she was looking sexy as she wanna be in her Versace dress. This time she brought her friend Judy with her for the trip. They both were wearing the same thing but opposite colors.

"Hey yall. Judy and Anna said as they walked inside the condo."

"I love the view you got from here, what's that the Hudson River right there?" Judy said. Looking through the terrace windows that was connected to the balcony.

"Yeah." E.B. said

What's up with Dice, is he coming? Anna asked.

Yeah, he should be joining us in a little while he had some business to take care first. E.B. said.

"Y'all ladies want anything to drink?" Boo asked.

"Yeah we will take whatever y'all got." Anna said.

What's up Boo? Judy asked.

Ain't nothing baby girl, what's up with you, I haven't seen you in a minute, what you don't got love for me no more. Boo said.

I just been chilling and going to school that's all but I'm here now with you right? Judy said.

"So come and give me some of that groupie love." Boo said.

*   *   *

When Detective Honeytoon made it back to the office with the mark money he gave it to Detective Johnson.

"Here you go, now get your sorry ass outta here and go do your job." Detective Johnson said, tossing Rob the duffle bag with the mark money in it.

Rob then walked out of the office with the duffle bag in his hand.

"I guess our work is done here today." Detective Honeytoon said. "Yeah . . . . well I guess I'm a leave now if you don't need me for nothing else.

Yeah, I can take care of the paperwork, you go out and enjoy the rest of the day.

I'll see you later than. Detective Johnson said.

He grabbed his blazer from the back of his chair then he left.

Detective Honeytoon checked to make sure that Detective Johnson was gone than he reached under the table and grabbed the tape recorder that he had planted. Once he retrieved the tape recorder that he had on record the whole time it was there. He rewind it back and he press play. After letting it play for two minutes he smiled, got him. He thought to himself.

*   *   *

Rob called Boo and told him that he was ready to see him. Boo told him to meet him at E.B.'s crib. When Rob arrived there he gave the duffle bag that had the money in it to E.B. he then placed it in his bedroom. Anna and Judy were feeling nice and tipsy. Boo was in the bathroom fucking the shit out of Judy on top of the sink. She was screaming his name.

"Yes, big daddy, beat that pussy up, oh my god, Booooo!"

Anna was sitting on the leather couch holding her drink in her hand thinking about Dice. Wondering where he was and what he was doing.

She had something to tell him that was very important that he needed to know. Anna had butterflies in her stomach just thinking about Dice. She couldn't wait until he showed up she kept looking at her watch checking the time. Anna was growing strong feelings for Dice. He never tried to shit on her, he always treated her with respect. Anna wasn't to sure how Dice felt about her. But she knew every day her feelings for him kept growing. From the first day she met Dice. She thought about how much fun they had every time they got together. Judy walked out of the bathroom, and saw Anna sitting on the couch by herself in a daze. Judy knew what Anna was thinking about, and she knew that it was Dice cause she talked about him all the time. Then Judy, E.B. and Boo went into the bedroom and got there freak on. Anna was still thinking about Dice, and what she had to tell him. She was hoping that Dice would walk through the door. Rob was on the terrace smoking a blunt and drinking some yack thinking about what he was doing to his people, and why was he doing it. His niggas were true to him they had love for him. Why was he shitting on them. Going out like a sucka on them. When he knew that he could've ended it all with one leap off of the terrace instead of serving his boys to the Fed's on a platter. Then he tossed the half of gallon of Hennessy in the Hudson River and watched it sink.

* * *

Chapter 21

"Day After Day"

Me and Ebony were still at the house waiting up for Shaniqua to show up at the house or call to let us know that she was ok. As hours went by me and Ebony both fell asleep on the sofa. When I woke up my head was in Ebony's lap. Ebony was rubbing on my head trying to comfort me at least I thought she was. I just laid there zoning out thinking about Shaniqua. I had so much that I wanted to say to her. I had everything planned for our future and it was slipping away from us slowly. I couldn't believe that this was happening to us. I didn't know if she ran out and left me or if something happened to her. Why everything that I love always gets taken from me. Was this god's plan maybe I wasn't put on this earth to love or to be loved. This had me confused about everything. I've been through enough pain and suffering to last 2 life times and I was still going through it. I was at a very vulnerable state in my life. And Ebony knew it so she played on my emotions. Ebony leaned forward and kissed me on my forehead then she kiss me again this time on my lips. At that moment I didn't know what to do so I went with the flow. Her tongue was touching my tongue. I was squeezing her breast. She was rubbing my chest. Ebony then lifted her shirt over her head then she unstrapped her bra exposing her hard nipples that stood out. I was licking and sucking on her nipples. She had a sweet smell on her body that smelled just like Shaniqua's. Maybe I was just missing her. I got up off the sofa stood up in front of her pulled out my dick. She put her lips around the head of my dick playing with it with her tongue ring. Then I started fucking her face until she swallowed my cum. Then she stood up and took off her skin tight Designer Jeans and her lace panties. Ebony turned around cocked her ass up in the air. I put a condom on and eased behind her to enter her wet pussy.

Once I had my dick all the way in her. Ebony started throwing her ass back she was loving every moment of it. I grabbed her by the back of her hair and started pulling it back with every stroke.

Her expressions said it all that I was fucking the shit out of her. "Yes Dice, yeah oh, oh, oh my god, yes Dice."

Ebony's body started shaking like a earthquake as she was having a orgasm. I was really tripping now because I was fucking my wifey's friend. But I was so worried about her that I didn't stop and think about what I was doing. I kept on fucking her for the rest of the night.

That was the bomb Dice." Ebony said, as she had my dick in her hand playing with it. I didn't respond to what she said I was too busy thinking about Shaniqua. Where could she be all this time, why she didn't come home yet? When I saw Shaniqua I was planning on telling her about the episode me and Ebony had. As long as I knew that she was alright it didn't matter is she wanted to kill me because I'd rather be dead then to be without her. I wasn't born in this world to love God wanted me to experience the pain I was going through and be the gangsta ass nigga that I am that was becoming a reality for me. Ebony grabbed my dick and put it back in her mouth. I leaned my head back and let her do her job because I needed something to ease my mind.

* * *

It was 12oclock in the afternoon the next day. Yesterday had come and gone. Anna still hadn't seen Dice. She knew that something very important must had come up that's why he didn't show up last night. But she also had something that was important that she wanted to share with him but it had to wait for now. She just hope whatever it was he was alright that was her main concern. She thought about how special Dice always made her feel when he was around that brought a smile to her face. Her and Judy were on their way back to New Jersey. Judy drove while Anna played the passenger seat in deep thoughts.

* * *

When I woke up I was upstairs laying in the bed with Dyemere sleeping next to me. Ebony was in the living room sleeping on the pull out bed. I got up hoping that Shaniqua made it home while I was sleeping. I went downstairs to see if she was here but she wasn't. I didn't know what else to do. All I knew was that Shaniqua was missing. She could of been laying dead in an alleyway somewhere shot or stabbed to death. The more I started to wonder the more angrier I got. Because it wasn't to many places that she could have gone. Especially not without her Escalade or without letting me know where she was. Then I started thinking that what if the same people that was out trying to kill E.B. the other day was the reason why Shaniqua was missing now, then my cell phone starting ringing.

Hello! I said. In an aggravated tone of voice.

"What's the matter with you baby? Cookie asked.

"Nothing! I'm pissed the fuck off right now."

"Why, Where you at?"

I'm at Shaniqua's house, did she call you, cause I haven't seen her since yesterday, after she came back from the mall with you."

"No . . . . the last time I spoke to her was yesterday when I dropped her off at her house."

"Shit!"

"You mean to tell me that you haven't heard from her or seen her since then?"

"That's what I said right . . . . Did she drive yesterday when y'all went to the mall?"

"No" she wanted me to pick her up, so we could ride together in my jeep.

"Damn . . . . I don't know where the fuck she at right now, I'm ready to hurt some'em.

"Calm down Dice."

"Where's Diceita?"

"She's right here crawling around the house trying to walk."

"Listen Cookie, if she calls you, tell her to call me immediately, because I'm looking for her, and I'm still here with Dyemere, and I got shit to do.

Why don't you bring Dyemere here to me, I'll watch him for you so you can go handle your business."

"Nah, that's aight, cause I'm a be here until she calls, but if I have to run out and go somewhere I'm a call you to come pick him up or I'll drop him off to you."

"O.K. baby."

"Aight so I'll see you in a little while." (click)

While Ebony was in the bathroom taking a shower I tried to call Shaniqua again but her cell phone was still going straight to voicemail. I slammed the house phone down and shouted.

"Shit, what the fuck!

Ebony was running out of the bathroom naked after hearing the commotion.

"Dice what's the matter, is everything alright?

"No . . . . I need you to put some clothes on cause I'm a need you to watch Dyemere for me while I go out and take care of a few things, if Shaniqua calls, find out where she's at, and tell her to call my cellphone."

"Alright, I'll do that for you."

I went upstairs and go my level 2 vest and my Desert Eagle. Then I put on my army fatiques cause it was time to get dirty and take the streets to war. I was tired of waiting around for answers. It was time to go out and find them. I got in Shaniqua's Escalade and hopped on the Van Wyck expressway on my way to E.B.'s Condo. Now it was time to get down to business a lot of heads gonna roll back for this.

As I was crossing the Tri-Borough Bridge I called Boo and told him to meet me at E.B.'s crib. I was doing 90 mph the whole way there without a care in the world. When I arrived I informed them about what was still going on.

"When did this happen? Boo said.

"This happened yesterday, and that's not like her to go out without calling me, that's how I know some'em had to happen to her, she was only going to Jamaica Avenue to get some'em to cook, ever since then she been missing, I'm telling you boy, this shit got me tighter than a motherfucka, and I think it might be them same niggas that tried to kill E.B. the other day."

"We still don't know who it was that tried to smoke him, we went all through Harlem looking for something to go on and our people's still didn't hear shit about what happened, you know how the streets talk and ain't nobody saying shit, it's like it never happened." Boo said.

We know somebody gotta know some'em about all this shit that's happening, people just don't get shot at like that and disappear everyday just like that.

I'm not buying that, niggas ain't gonna be riding up on me like some'em sweet, fuck that, I'm not having that shit, I got some'em for that ass, I'm ready to start bringing it to everybody. E.B. said.

"That's exactly what we gonna have to do if we want answers, leave no stone unturned. I said.

Dice man, listen to me . . . . I know you are upset right now and you want your shorty back and all, that's understandable, but we gotta think about the situation that we got at hand right now, let's just say that the same niggas that tried to assassinate E.B. the other day are the same niggas that got your shorty, and we go around tearing shit up, what you think is going to happen to her when they find out that it's us that's going around killing shit trying to get at them." Boo said.

"I'm not even trying to hear that shit right there you talking about, cause I don't give a fuck, what if they killed her already, then what, huh, none of that shit you talking is gonna bring her back is it? I'm not just gonna sit around with my fingers crossed waiting, fuck that I want answers now!" I said.

"Dice is right, fuck all that waiting around shit, we gotta go out, and bang on niggas, and ask questions later, we don't have time to be waisting with all this talking, we know what we gotta do from here on." E.B. said.

"I'm down with y'all 100% no matter what, but what I was saying was let's think about what we are doing here." Boo said.

"I did that last night, now it's time for some action." I said.

Then we all loaded up in Boo's S 600. E.B. was carrying a mac-11 with two 9mm under his armpits. Boo had two twin uzi's fully loaded. I had my .44 Desert Eagle and a Calico with a hundred shot clip. We were on our way uptown (Harlem).

*   *   *

"Son, I know that bitch is probably hungry by now cause I'm starving, we should get her something to eat." Pooh said.

"What happened you got a heart now, I thought you wanted to rape her? Buck said.

I was just fucking with her. Pooh said.

"Yeah whatever" why not she been quite, but I'm not going to get it though, you brought it up so you going to get it. Buck said.

"Aight!" Pooh said.

Then Pooh left to get something to eat.

Buck and Pooh were keeping Shaniqua hostage in a basement of a abandon building somewhere up in Harlem tied up to a radiator.

"Wake up shorty?" Buck said. Tapping her on the cheek.

Shaniqua slowly opened her eyes squinting them trying to gain her vision.

"You was sleeping for a while now." Buck said. As he grabbed a crate to sit on.

"Can I get something to drink please, like some water." Shaniqua said.

"My man went to get you some'em to eat, he should be back in a few minutes so be patient." Buck said, sitting directly across from her.

In Buck's mind he was thinking why would some body want to have her kidnapped. Then he shook the thought off cause he had a job to do.

"Why did y'all kidnap me, I didn't do anything to you or nobody else,

I'm a mother I have a little son that needs me home with him I shouldn't be here." Shaniqua said. Then she started to cry.

"You better wipe your tears away cause I'm not with that emotional shit." Buck said.

"Why! Why! Why me? Shaniqua said.

"I didn't say you that you could ask me any questions did I? . . . . No! So what the fuck make you think that I'm a tell you that, "huh."

"I'm sorry . . . . but I, I, was just asking you, cause I wanna go home to my family, you don't have to do this." Shaniqua pleaded.

"I can tell you this, whoever you did some'em to, you must have really pissed them off, for them to want this done to you."

Shaniqua couldn't think of anybody that didn't like her and would want something like this done to her and for what. Whoever it was must really hate her to go through all this trouble.

I know I don't deserve this type of punishment, I never did anything to nobody, oh my god why me!" Shaniqua yelled out.

"How old is your son?

He's ten months old.

You just had him not too long ago, you must really love him, don't you.

Yes I do with all my heart that's why I need to get back home to him.

What about his father yall still together?

Yeah, we getting married if I make it outta here alive.

I don't know about that shorty, it's up to the person that's paying us, they call the shots if they want you dead then you gotta go.

"You make it sound easy to take another person's life."

This won't be the first time nor the last I'm use to it now."

"Can you please let me go please, I never did anything to hurt nobody, why is this happening to me why, why? Shaniqua said then she started crying again.

"I'm sorry shorty but I can't do that for you, I know your family is missing you right now wondering what happened to you."

"I know they are, why me?

I don't know shorty, but it's a crazy world that we live in, some of us make it and some of us don't, that's just life there's nothing no one could do about that.

Then Pooh finally walked in the basement with Shaniqua's food and water.

"Thank you." Shaniqua said.

As Pooh and Buck was leaving the basement going upstairs Buck stopped and turned around and stared at Shaniqua thinking to himself that she shouldn't be here. Then he turned around to catch up to Pooh.

"Did that bitch call yet? Pooh said.

Nah, and we not gonna call her either, cause I'm telling you if we gotta call her again, she gonna make me kill her ass.

"Well, I think I'm a fuck that bitch in the basement, cause I'm not gonna be babysitting this bitch, without getting me some pussy from her fuck that."

"Shut the fuck up Pooh, you ain't doing shit."

"What, you catching feelings for this bitch already?"

"No! You just talking real stupid, that bitch you talking about is our fucking meal ticket you asshole, we didn't do this for no pussy nigga.

"You right man, so what we gonna do if this bitch Cookie don't come through with the paper like she suppose to."

"I don't know, but I'll think of something." I know Cookie ain't gonna go through all this trouble over no dick, duke must be eating that pussy right, or tossing her salad, cause whatever he's doing to her he turned that bitch out, she's a crazy ass bitch for real, I'm glad she not my bitch cause I would have to kill her ass.

Maybe she want shorty out of the way so she could have duke all to herself.

"Homeboy probably feeling shorty more than he's feeling Cookie ass, and now the bitch is mad."

"Man, fuck all that Jenny Jones and Ricki Lake shit, I want my money, that bitch better be getting that shit straight cause I want mine.

"Yo Buck . . . . you think shorty's man might be holding some cash."

"How the fuck I suppose to know."

"Think about it, shorty was pushing an Escalade sitting on chrome with T.V.'s all in it."

"Maybe he is and maybe he ain't, we don't know so why waste our time thinking about it, when we already got somebody that's giving us cash for this bitch."

"Nah Buck, it was just a thought, just in case this bitch Cookie try to stunt on us, we could call her man, and see how much he really loves this bitch."

* * *

Chapter 22

"It's a War going on"

The next day Detective Honeytoon took the tape recorder that he had with Detective Johnson voice on it and brought it straight to his supervisor's office downtown.

This might be enough that we need to bring him up on charges, and I also think that he's working with someone that's involved with heavy illegal street activity, because when you listen to the tape you will hear him talking about it with the (CI) how he reassures him that his friends will end up in a body bag, and how he brags about tampering with a crime scene, that which a family was murdered in, and that happens to be his prime suspects family that was murdered, now it seems like he is conspiring to have his prime suspect and his crew murdered. Detective Honeytoon said.

As he sat the recording device on his supervisor's desk.

"Well let's see what else we can gather up on him before we bring him in.

He's a disgrace to the department, people like him give the government a bad name. But you can't forget what side you on, these guys gotta go down, they flooding the streets with Drugs, Violence, and the murder rate has increased since these guys stepped on the scene, and that has to stop now, it looks bad on all of us if we allow them to continue." The Supervisor said.

"O.K. sir I'll keep you informed with anything else that develops you will be the first to know." Detective Honeytoon said, as he was leaving his supervisor's office.

"Agent Honeytoon." The supervisor said.

"Yes sir." Detective Honeytoon said.

Good Work, I'm very "impressed."

"Thank you sir, I'm just doing my job."

Then the supervisor picked up the recorder leaned back in his chair and pressed play.

* * *

Hello, is this DetectiveJohnson?"
Yes! Who is this?
The boss wants to see you.
Alright tell him I'm on my way over. (click)
"Hello, hello damn!" Detective Johnson said. Into the phone but it was to late cause the other person that was on the phone had already hung up.

Then he tossed his phone on the floor.

"Hurry up bitch! I got things to do, suck that dick and make me cum, you fucking whore, I know you not use to sucking little dicks like this but do your best bitch." Detective Johnson said.

"I want you to put your dick in my ass."

"Bitch! Are you out of your fucking mind, I wouldn't dare put my dick in your ass without a fucking condom. Don't ever ask me no shit like that, now finish sucking my dick."

"I don't know why you getting mad at me for, you already put your little dick in my pussy twice without a condom on, so what's the difference, what you scared to get a little shit on your dick."

"The difference is that I'm paying for the pussy, so I got a choice to do what I want do, if I want to piss on you then I will piss on you."

"I guess that explains why you put your cum in my pussy when we was doing it, your dick is good enough for my pussy but you don't want to put it in my ass, I need to be satisfied too, I can't feel that little shit in me anyway."

"Bitch shut the fuck up and make me cum already you wasting time bumping your gums."

"So you must don't want me to put the dildo in you no more than, huh, see you ain't right I could put something in your ass but you can't put your sorry little dick in my ass, fuck you I'll do it myself and you can suck your own dick cause I don't want your fucking money." The Prostitute said, getting up off her knees. Then she walked over to her clothes to put them on.

"What bitch" Detective Johnson said, jumping out of the bed charging in the prostitute's direction.

"SMACK!"

He slapped the shit out of the prostitute knocking her down to the floor.

Then he reached for this dillinger that was strapped to his ankle and shot her twice in the head. Then he quickly grabbed his clothes and left like nothing ever happened leaving her leaking out the side of her head in her apartment.

*   *   *

Aight, park right here so we could see everything coming and going from here. I said.

We were now in Harlem on 116st and Pleasant Avenue. We was watching the Italian Restaurant that was down the block from where we was parked at on the opposite corner.

"I swear to everything I love, if these niggas had anything to do with my shorty being missing, I'm killing everything in that bitch, that's my word. They don't know that they fucking with satin himself when it comes to the drama shit, but they about to find out if I see anything that looks funny to me I'm bringing it to them. I said. Staring through the front window shield with my eyes glued to the restaurant.

I'm with you all the way my nigga, don't worry we gonna get your shorty back, and find them niggas that tried to ride on me. E.B. said. Letting me know that he was going to ride to the end with me.

I gotta get Shaniqua back God please let her be alive if you don't have love for me at least have mercy on her because she doesn't deserve none of this that she's going through. I need her back in my life my son needs his mother please don't let nothing happen to her. You already took my family away from me that should be enough. My son shouldn't have to suffer the way I did through my life. Look at us god we are about to go on a killing spree to save one life, we going to take many you could prevent all that from happening just give me back Shaniqua please. At least do it for my son. If I have to die to spare their lives than fuck it you can take mines. If you could hear me I'm sorry for all the drama that I put you through. But hold on baby because I'm coming. I thought to myself.

Look Dice, it's a black Impala pulling up to the restaurant right now." Boo said.

"I think that's popo right there, he looks familiar to me, I swear, I seen him before, I just can't place his face right now, but I seen him before." I said. Watching Detective Johnson walk into the restaurant.

"Yeah, that's that Detective that be fucking with niggas all the time, he ain't nothing but a asshole he works for them Italian niggas, I got a bullet with his name on it, if he fucks with me." E.B. said.

"What the fuck is he doing there? I asked.

"He probably getting some'em to eat, or going to a meeting, but it really doesn't matter to me anyway cause I don't give a fuck about his ass." E.B. said.

"I wouldn't put it pass him, niggas like him be doing shit like that." I said.

Our conversation was interrupted when we spotted a black Lincoln Town Car coming around the corner and parked in front of the restaurant directly behind Detective Johnson's Chevy Impala.

"That's, that same motherfucking car right there that was banging at me the other day." E.B. said.

"How you know that's the same car? I asked.

"Shit, I'm sure that's the car right there, you won't forget shit, if a nigga was trying to kill your ass, I'm telling you that's them, I remember the license plate started with CJW, I should jump out on they ass right now." E.B. said.

When the three men got out of the Lincoln Town Car one of had his arm in a cast.

"If that's them, what the fuck is going on, and that cop still in there." I said.

"They might be having a meeting there." E.B. said.

There wasn't no sign of Shaniqua. Where the fuck is she at? Damn this shit is stressing me the fuck out. I thought to myself.

"Come on lets go up in there and see what's up. I'm tired of sitting around waiting." I said.

That Detective is still in there. Boo said.

"Fuck 'em he could get it too." I said.

We all hopped out of the Benz and began walking towards the restaurant. My adrenaline started pumping as the blood that was traveling through my veins felt like fire burning inside of me.

I entered the restaurant first waving the calico from the door. E.B. and Boo was right behind me with their guns aiming at everybody that was in the restaurant. Yelling.

"Move and your dead!"

"What the fuck is this?" One of them said.

"Don't even think about it, I'll blow your fucking face off. I said. Still waving the Calico.

"Wait a minute now! Before you do something that you don't mean to do, Do you know who the fuck I am. The fat Italian man said. That was sitting down eating at the table.

"I don't give a fuck, who you think you are, cause to me you ain't nobody to me, but one dead pizza eating mother fucka, that's about to get hit with fifty shots till your face explode." I said.

"Just relax, don't nobody move, seems like we got a loose one." The fat Italian man said.

"Did I tell you to talk motherfucker, we didn't come here to socialize with your fat ass or these motherfuckers." I said.

"The fat Italian man's face turned red as an apple.

You can't talk to me like that, nobody talks to me like that, I'm a made man, I'm a man with power and respect, you better give me some respect and watch your fucking mouth, before I cut your fucking balls off and feed'em to yah." The fat Italian man said. Knocking down everything that was on the table he was eating on.

Fuck you asshole, you a dead man anyway. I said.

"Let me smoke this fat motherfucker now." E.B. said, Pointing the mac-11 at the fat Italian man.

"Wait! This motherfucker is gonna tell me where my girl is at, and you better tell me quick, before we start killing mother fucka's in here, including that motherfucking cop." I said, staring eye to eye with Detective Johnson.

The fat Italian man looked into my eyes and saw the fire that was burning inside of me."

"What girl are you talking about, that's what this is about, a fucking broad, like I told you, I'm a man of respect, not no fucking rapist, so what girl are you fucking talking about." The fat Italian man said.

"Don't play stupid with me, if I gotta ask you one more time, niggas start dying in here." I said.

"Look, like I told you already, I don't know nothing about no girl!"

"Boom! The first shot from the Calico ripped through the guy skull that was sitting next to the fat Italian man spreading his brains all over the table.

You still don't know what I'm talking about? I asked.

"I don't give a fuck, how many of us you kill I still don't know nothing about no fucking girl, whoever you got your information from lied to you because it's like I told you before, the people that gave you this information is who you need to be questioning.

"You must really wanna die than, huh, what the fuck is this pig ass nigga doing here? I said.

"He's an associate of mine." The fat Italian man said.

Do you know who I am? I said.

Nobody responded. "Every one of them started looking at each other for the answer."

"My name is Dice and somebody been fucking with my family. They kidnapped my girl, and they shot up my man's truck trying to kill'em, we know y'all niggas had something to do with it." I said. The fat Italian man looked at Detective Johnson and spoke.

"Well you guys already know he's a cop, his name is Detective Johnson, he claims that you guys are the reason why my nephew is dead."

"Who the fuck is your nephew? E.B.said.

"Louie . . . . You probably know him as Crazy Louie." The fat Italian man said.

"Me and my boys looked at each other, knowing that we were in the right place."

"Yeah, we killed that mother fucka, and I'll do it again if his ass was here now." I said.

"Why did you kill him, and then y'all burned his body, we couldn't even give him a decent funeral because it was nothing left of him."

"That bastard murdered my mother, my father, and my little homie all cause of my brother who's now burning in hell, he didn't have to kill my family, he could of spared their lives, because they didn't have anything to do with it, so for him taking their lives I took his life." I said.

The fat Italian man immediately turned his attention towards Detective Johnson.

"You sick son of a bitch, you ain't worth shit!" Italian man said.

"Please! Let me explain. Detective Johnson said. Trying to justify for his bullshit."

"Fuck you, you mother fucker, you don't have shit to say to me, I never did trust your ass anyway, why didn't you tell me shit about this before, you been feeding me bullshit." The fat Italian man said.

"I wanted these bastards dead! That's why I didn't say anything, because they deserve to die, they killed Crazy Louie." Detective Johnson said. Pointing his finger at us."

"So you, the mother fucka that caused all this drama, I hate pig ass niggas like you. I said. Approaching him with the calico aimed for his face and my finger on the trigger."

"Leave him, he is my responsibility, I will handle him myself." The fat Italian man said.

Then I slapped the shit out of Detective Johnson with the back of the calico.

"You a disgrace to me, you caused all this to happen for your own personal reasons, you brought me and my family into this foolish game of yours, you fucking rat bastard, now the whole thing blew up in your face, do you remember when I asked you if your sources were wrong, you told me, that you would take full responsibility for their actions, now you have to be dealt with, I told you this kind of shit is bad for business, you disrespected me and my family . . . . you have to forgive me for all these problems I may have cost you, it wasn't my intentions as you can see, but what's done is done, I have to except my nephews death, the way you have to except your family's death, by you telling me this about your family, I understand your reasons for you coming here today, but you have to excuse me now please, as I ask my nephew to pass me his gun." The fat Italian man said.

We gripped our weapons tight as I gave him the permission to do so. We kept our guns on him the whole time as his nephew passed him a .38 snob nose revolver. He took the gun from his nephew and pointed it at Detective Johnson.

"You humiliated all of us here today for your own personal reasons, I thank these gentlemen for coming here today clearing things up for me, and also for getting rid of Gorgieo for me because he was the one that vouch for you, then he spit on his dead body. You ain't shit you fucking bastard." Then the fat Italian man stood up from behind the table and started approaching Detective Johnson.

"Please! Is it any way you can forgive me, I'm sorry, I know I fucked up big time, I don't know what made me do this." Detective Johnson said, walking backwards.

The fat Italian man raised the .38 to his face and shot him in the middle of his forehead and two more in the chest then he passed the gun back to his nephew and wiped his hands with a handkerchief and tossed it on Detective Johnson's lifeless body.

That still don't solve anything for me, my girl is still missing." I said.

"I'm sorry Dice about your girlfriend, but I can't help you with that, it's probably someone that's close to you, that's trying to take her from you or they want something from you."

"What about them niggas that was trying to kill my man, they fucked up his truck." I said.

"I'm sorry about that, I'm responsible for that I gave those orders for my men to do that, because of the false information that I received from a unreliable source which is no longer with us, but I will compensate you for all the damages . . . . Then his nephew passed him a brief case."

"I can't change the pass, but I'm a man of respect and I have mutual respect for you gentlemen, so I hope you can take this as an apology from me to you." The fat man said. Then he slid the brief case across the table towards me.

"What is that? I said.

"That's 250,000 for your troubles, and the damages I may have caused you for your friend's truck."

Boo grabbed the brief case popped it open and saw it was filled with money then he closed it back and held it at his side.

"That's cool and all but for the record, I still wanna know who it was that was trying to kill me, cause they almost did." E.B. said.

The fat Italian man looked at the man that was standing up with the cast on his arm, and the man that was stretched out on the floor.

He was shot by you, that day, and him well you already know, and Detective Johnson was the driver and he's dead also, so I hope you are satisfied with the result's. The fat Italian said.

"Yeah, I'm good, just don't let It happen again. E.B. said. So what's it's gonna be, we gonna go to war over this." I said.

You don't have to worry about no retaliation, it's over now, we all have enough blood on our hands and we don't need anymore. The fat Italian man said.

Then we walked out of the restaurant backwards with our guns still on cock until we was all outside.

"Uncle should I call in Pauly for this" The nephew said. "No Tommy, let them be, just call in the clean-up crew to get rid of this trash."

***

"Dice man . . . . I'm sorry you didn't find your shorty, but whatever it takes we gonna find her, and I don't think it's as bad as it seems, cause if they didn't have something to do with it, it's a strong chance that she could be still alive." E.B. said.

"Word Dice! We here for you till the end, we got your back your pain, is our pain." Boo said.

As they were speaking to me I heard them but I drifted into deep thoughts.

What if what that fat motherfucker was saying was right when he said it could be someone close to you. But who and why?

"Yo Dice, you heard us." E.B. said.

"Oh yeah, no doubt that's what's up, I'm a call y'all niggas later if I hear something from her, but I pray to god that she's alright man, I really need her." I said. as I was getting out of the S600.

"Don't worry my nigga, keep your head up and holla at us if you need us." E.B. said. Then I gave him dap.

"Aight, one I'm out. I said. Then I got in Shaniqua's Escalade. I turned on her system to hear what she was listening to before all this started."

Mary J Blige's vocals filled the speakers.

I was on my way back to Shaniqua's house to check on Dyemere and to see how thing were going there. I opened up my phone and called Cookie.

"What's up Dice, did you hear anything from Shaniqua yet?"

"No! Not yet, I hope she's alright."

"My women is missing, and I don't know what else to do, you, Shaniqua, and the kids made my life complete, now with her gone I feel like I lost everything."

"Don't say that baby, I'm still here for you, I know you miss her, and Shaniqua miss you too, but you gotta think positive, baby everything is going to work out just fine."

"That's what everybody keep telling me, but when is it going to be alright, when? She suppose to be here now.

"Why don't you just call the police?

"Fuck the police, I don't fuck with them pig ass niggas.

Dice calm down, come home please, you shouldn't be outside, just come home to me please Dice . . . . (click) I hung the phone up on her.

When I arrived back at Shaniqua's house Ebony was watching TV Dyemere was I'm his crib. I picked him up and hugged him real tight. I could tell that Dyemere sensed something was wrong by the way he was rubbing my face.

"Ring, ... Ring . . . . Ring . . . . My cell phone started ringing." "Hello."

"What's up Dice, this is Anna."

Hey what's up girl.

You alright Dice?, it sound like something is bothering you."

"Yeah I'm aight, why what's up?

"Nothing! . . . I just called cause, I was worried about you, I haven't spoken to you in days, and when I came up there to see you, I didn't get a chance to so I was checking on you, to make sure you alright cause you did have a girl a little concerned about you."

"Ha, ha, ha yeah I'm alright ma, What about you? How you doing?

I'm alright . . . . Dice I wanna come up tomorrow to see you, I have something that I want to tell you."

"What is it about, is some'em wrong with the package."

"No silly, are you going to be around tomorrow, so I can come and see you."

"Aight, any time after 4 o'clock would be good aight."

"Alright poppie, I'll see you tomorrow, after 4."

"Aight ma."

"Bye Dice, I see you manana." (click)

Ebony was standing there being nosy listening to the whole conversation.

"Dice any luck yet with Shaniqua?" Ebony asked.

"No, not yet but it should be soon though, I can feel her presence around me."

"I hope so, I know Shaniqua's a good person and she probably worrying herself half to death, over this shit, she doesn't deserve none of this that she is going through, I known Shaniqua my whole life almost, and she never changed while everybody else did, it hurt me to know that she's going through this now."

"Shaniqua is a strong person cause you gotta be to be dealing with my bullshit every day."

"You right about that." Ebony Mumbled.

When I was walking away going upstairs into the bedroom with Dyemere in my arms. Me and Dyemere crawled in the bed and went to sleep. The next morning I woke up and made all of us breakfast. I was doing everything that Shaniqua was doing for me when she was home.

Now with the drama settled with us and the Italians. All I needed was finished with everything, That was a promise I made to myself that I would do when I had her back. I was ready to break the news to E.B., Boo and Rob.

That they would control everything that we built up I was done with all the shit the streets had to offer. I just wanted to live a normal life and enjoy myself with my family. I did my share of hustling, robbing, killing, and a whole bunch of other shit. Soon as I had Shaniqua in my arms, I was gonna tell her everything. I was done with everything.

* * *

Chapter 23

"The Life we Live"

This is the channel Six news, my name is Robert Sanders, we are once again reporting live from yet another crime scene, we are here at the East River right off of the FDR Drive where a body was found decomposed stuff in a can, sort of like one of them chemical type containers floating here in the East River, the body was identified as Detective Frank Johnson from the 20th precinct up in Harlem, Detective Johnson had been on the force for 12 years prior to this tragedy discovered here today, he was also believed to be involved in with Criminal activities, that connected him to the "Italian Crime Family," no evidence has been produced as of yet, but our sources say that they have evidence, they just hasn't presented it as of yet, but it's sure to come in the future, Detective Johnson was shot in the head and twice in the chest, his tongue was also removed from his mouth, this will go on talk about amongst the ranks for some time, we will bring you more on this story as it develops, this has been Robert Sanders of the Channel Six news, reporting live, we now send you back to the studios with the rest of the cast.

The next day I met up with Anna at the stash crib.

"Hey, what's up my Dominican mommy." I said.

Hi Dice, how you doing? she said. Kissing me as she walked in.

"Ah baby, you don't know how bad I wanted to see you the other day, I waited until the next morning for you to come, but you didn't show up, what happened?" Anna said.

"Some'em important came up, that's why I couldn't make it there, I had to handle that first, you know I wouldn't have you waiting around for nothing, you know that ain't my style, but we here now, you said you had some'em that you wanted to talk to me about." I said. Then I grabbed her by the waist pulling her close to me.

"Yeah, ok, Dice you know I would do anything for you right?"
"Yeah" .... and.
"And I really enjoy everything that you do for me, I thought about this over a million times In my head how I was going to tell you this."
"What ma! Let me know what's up."
"O.K. I'm just so nervous right now, and I don't know how to tell you this, but I'm just gonna come out with it and tell you Dice .... I love you!"
Before I responded I thought about what she said to me for a minute.
Anna be delivering them packages for me without a problem so I would say anything to keep her happy. I couldn't just shut her down like that because I needed her it was all about business.
"I love you too baby." I said. Then I kissed her forehead.
"And I'm pregnant!
"What! How the fuck that happened?" I asked. Pushing her away from me.
"What you mean, how did it happen, how you think it happened, by you fucking me, that's how it happened."
"When did this happen?
"I don't know, I think the last time I was up here with you since then I haven't had my period, so I went to the doctor to take a pregnancy test, and it came back positive, I was shocked myself, that's why I had to see you, cause I had to let you know about it."
Now this was some bullshit that I didn't need in my life. What the fuck am I going to do? This can't be happening to me. We was just fucking I wasn't trying to get her pregnant. She's a nice girl and all but come on I got enough problems to deal with already. Plus she could be fucking with other niggas too. That might be somebody else baby that she trying to blame me for. This is fucked up why did this have to happen to us now. We have everything working good for us just the way it is.

When it rains it pours. What was I going to say next? Anna played a major part in my operation without her I would have to change a lot. She was putting me in a tight spot. I thought to myself.

"You sure it's mine Anna, cause I don't know."

"Of course, I'm sure it's yours, who else would it be, you the only one I been fucking since I started fucking with you, Dice don't even try to play me like no groupie or no hoe, cause I don't get down like that, ain't nobody else going up in this pussy, I'm not that type of bitch that get down like that, just because I gave you the ass on the first day don't mean shit, I really like you form the first day I met you, and I really enjoy your company, so what if I wanted to have fun with you, I didn't plan this or do this on purpose to trap you off, cause it aint that serious Dice, How you think I feel, I'm still in college getting my degree, I only got a few more months to go to get my Masters certificate, you think I just want throw all that away for a nigga, no poppie, it took a lot for me to come here and tell you this, I never been through this before I didn't know what to do, my friends don't even know that I'm pregnant, you're the first person, that I wanted to tell.

"Anna listen to me, I'm not ready for this I'm involved in too much shit already as it is, I like you and all Ma but this is not what I'm ready for, I can't deal with this right now in my life, you still got goals that you need to reach, you can't let this slow you down cause I sure ain't, you really need to think about what I'm saying to you, now's not the time for this in none of our lives.

"So what you want me to do, you saying that you want me to get rid of it then?"

"Yes!"

"OMG I don't think so, I'm not doing that, this is my body it's not that easy for me to just up and do that, What's wrong with you? I'm sorry but, I can't do that. This is my first pregnancy and you want me to get rid of it just like that, I can't believe this, Dice I love you, This is our child that I'm carrying inside of me, I know I said that I wasn't ready for any kids right now at this point in my life, but shit happens, this happened, I didn't plan this, the only thing I could do now is have this baby that I'm carrying, Dice I love you, and I would do anything for you, but I can't do this what you asking me to do, it wouldn't be right if I did Dice. I thought you would be happy about the whole situation, I didn't think you would act like this."

"It's not that Anna, I have a family at home, I have a son and a daughter already that I take care of, Anna you are a lovely girl, maybe if I didn't have any kids already, or a family at home that I go to every night things probably would be different, but that's why I can't have this baby with you, we are co-workers, we make money together, and we have sex together that's it nothing more than that."

"I don't care about none of that shit Dice, I'm having this baby no matter what, whether you like it or not, I thought you really liked me, but I see it was all business for you huh? Well if you don't wanna be a part of this baby's life, then we don't have much to do with each other, no more, cause Dice I'm having my baby, so if you ever feel you ready to be a part of this baby's life, you more than welcome, the door will always be opened for you. I wouldn't shut you down the way you doing me, whenever you want to become a family, you know how to find me, all you gotta do is call me." Anna said. Then she steamed out of the apartment slamming the door behind her.

That bitch must be crazy as hell telling me that shit like I was suppose to be happy. I got enough problems as it is already I don't need anymore. What would Shaniqua say if she knew about this shit? What me and Anna had was about business nothing more than that. It wasn't suppose to get personal between us. I enjoy fucking Anna but I wasn't ready to have a baby with her not in this lifetime. Especially if it wasn't by Shaniqua. Hell no that wasn't about to happen. Who know what Anna was gonna do after this. I didn't know if she was serious about having the baby without me. She sounded like she was serious to me. I couldn't believe that this was happening to me.

* * *

Cookie was home wondering what she was going to do next. She knew that she already went to far and her plan wasn't exactly working the way she wanted it to. Cookie thought by her having Shaniqua kidnapped It would make Dice closer to her with Shaniqua being out of the picture it would be just her and she would be the only one he thought about. But it worked out to be the opposite way it made them more distant, from each other. Dice hasn't been home at Cookie's house ever since Shaniqua been missing. Shaniqua was the only thing that Dice was worried about. Dice didn't really want to be bothered by Cookie or by nobody else unless it was something serious dealing with the kids. Cookie's world was turning upside down everything that was good for her was now fucked up. It was better for Cookie when Shaniqua was around cause now Cookie was feeling the pain also and the distance between her and Dice. Cookie was thinking that she should she tell Buck and Pooh to forget the whole thing, and let Shaniqua go. But why when she went through the trouble in the first place to have it done. Cookie couldn't just call them and say that she was sorry about the whole thing. That wasn't an option for Cookie she had to ride it out all the way through till the very end. Hoping maybe that Dice would run back to her for comfort and support. Only time would tell but time is always against you because it keeps moving even when you don't want it to. It was too late for her to change her mind now.

* * *

I can't believe that Dice tried to play me like that. After all that was doing for him. I was going way out of my way just to make him happy by bringing him drugs back and forth. He know that he was the only one that was fucking me the whole time. Nobody else but him nobody told him to fuck me without a condom because I sure didn't. Dice could of said to me that he was going to think about it, before he started with all that off the wall shit he was saying to me. I have feelings too, he didn't even think about that. I haven't been messing with nobody else but him and this is the thanks I get from him. Maybe he'll call me later to apologize to me about everything. I know he will, he's not just gonna dis me like that and forget about it like it ain't nothing. He needs me. "Anna thought to herself. While driving on the 1-9 in New Jersey.

* * *

I sat in my Hummer thinking about my life and everything that was going on in it. I sparked up a blunt to ease my mind as I laid back with my seat reclined then my cell phone started ringing. At first I wasn't going to answer it but I did.

"Hello!"

"Dice, where you at, please come and get me please." Shaniqua pleaded.

My heart damn near jumped out of my chest because I was so excited to hear her voice.

"Shaniqua baby, I'm coming for you, tell me where you at."

I yelled back into the phone.

Then a strange male voice spoke.

"If you ever wanna see this bitch alive again you better listen good to what I tell you, if you fuck up the bitch is dead, do you understand me mother fucka."

"Yeah I heard you, just don't hurt her. I Said. In a calm tone.

"Make sure you know how to listen then, I'll call you back in an hour, make sure you answer your fucking phone, if I get your voicemail, the bitch dies, if you call the police your bitch dies, did you get that?

Yeah aight . . . .

"Now wait till I call you back."

(click)

"Shit it's a blocked number damn". I said out loud then I punched the steering wheel.

Calling police was not even an option for me. I wouldn't call them if I had to I was going to handle this on my own. Then I got on the highway on my way to EB's condo speeding through traffic on the F.D.R. Drive. When I got to EB's condo I parked in the front of the building, and ran up the stairs.

"Shaniqua just called me a few minutes ago when I was on my way over here."

"Word! What did she say?"

"I didn't get a chance to speak to her much, but she wanted me to come and get her, but before she could finish what she was about to say, some nigga snatched the phone away from her, and told me to wait for his call cause they was gonna call back and to make sure I answered the phone or he was gonna kill her ass."

"Damn! . . . . That's fucked up, where's your phone at now?" E.B. said.

"I got it right here." I said. Showing him my cell phone that I had in my hand.

"What else did he say he wanted from you?"

"He didn't say shit but, wait till he calls back."

"Maybe he gonna want some money from you.

I don't give a fuck, what he wants from me, I'll give him anything to get my shorty back, I swear, he better not have hurt or touched my shorty, or I'm a kill 'em when I see 'em.

The only thing we could do Dice is, wait until they call back again.

"How much cash do you got here?

"I got about 180,000 right here if you need it."

"Good! . . . . I'm a need it but I'm telling you E.B. I feel like killing some'em right now man, niggas don't even know who they playing with."

"Did the voice sound familiar or anything to you?

"Nah! . . . . I wasn't really paying attention to the voice, I just wanted to know if my shorty was aight, that was the first time I had spoke to her since this shit happened man."

"Do you have any more money on you besides the money I have here already?"

All I got on me is 2,000.

"Dice what if they want more money than what we got here with us now, we should go pick some more up."

Yeah you right come on, let's go get some more cash from the stash crib."

I pulled out my SL 500 Benz from the underground garage in E.B.'s building and tossed E.B. the keys to the Hummer. And drove down 8th Avenue to the stash crib.

When we arrived at the stash crib we counted out another 500,000. That brought our total up to 682,000 with the extra change I had and we still had a lot of cash left in case we needed it. All we had to do now was wait till they call back.

Dice man . . . . I'm glad that she's aight more than anything, cause I know how you feel about your shorty cause I would feel the same way."

I can't wait to see her, I will murder that niggas unborn child, if anything is wrong with Shaniqua, I won't stop until I know I killed his whole family."

"You got some hammers here right."

"Yeah! I got a few of them."

"Aight, cause I'm a pop all them niggas when we get there where ever they at, is where they gonna lay at."

"Niggas don't know they playing with fire, and they about to get burned.

I said. Loading up two .45's and a 9mm that we was about to use to put that work in on these nigga that took Shaniqua away from me."

I was glad to know she wasn't dead and to hear her voice again. Now I knew I really had a chance to get her back even if it cost me my life.

Ring . . . . Ring . . .

"Hello!"

"You already know who this is, if you want this bitch alive you better listen real good, cause I'm a only say this once, any tricks or any stunts and the bitch dies without any hesitation do you understand me."

"Yeah, is she aight."

"The bitch is fine, you'll see when you get her back that's if you follow orders I want a 100,000 in cash in exchange for your girl, I want you to bring the money to 137st and Morningside Ave."

"You'll see a big park in front of you, when you get there, I want you to walk into the park and walk up to the third garbage can that you see and drop the money in it then leave the same way you came in the park, make sure you come alone, I don't wanna see nobody with you or following you, cause if I see anything that looks suspicious to me, you already know what it is, the bitch is dead without a motherfucking problem, we will have eyes all around, so don't try and be no slick ass nigga cause we some trigger happy niggas you don't wanna play with, or it will cost you your lady's life, are we clear?

"Yeah aight, I got you, but let me ask you a question, y'all did this for money right, or somebody paid y'all and told y'all to do this to me.

"How do you know that I'm working with somebody else."

"Cause I know you ain't working alone someone told you to this."

"What difference does it make now, do you want your bitch alive or what, cause we could chop her ass up, and toss her in the river and call it a day."

"Yeah I want her alive, the point I'm getting at is that if somebody told you to do it, or paid you, I would like to put a price on that nigga's head, the same way that they did to my shorty, for more money than what you are asking for."

"Buck turned and looked at Pooh, and stared at him for a second then said, I'll call you back. (Click)

"What the fuck you doing Dice, are you Crazy playing with them niggas like that, fuck all that other shit get this shit over with these niggas money ain't shit, you don't know what them niggas might do to her if they think you playing with them with that cash."

"Who said I was playing with them, I know what I'm doing these niggas don't know who I really am or they don't know what money is, cause if they did, they would of wanted more money for my shorty, than what they asking me for."

"How much do they want?

100,000.

That's it?

"Yeah! That's how I know they don't know who I am cause they would of wanted more cash but now I'm going to offer them more cash than what they was expecting."

"But what if they don't call back now?"

They will, them niggas hungry just how we was right now they trying to figure out what they gonna do next, cause I fucked up their plans, I'm not gonna let the niggas that caused all this shit to happen, just walk away like that, so he could try this shit again, fuck that I'm a end all this now, money is everything to these niggas.

By the phone conversation that Dice had with Buck he felt like Buck reminded him of himself when he was coming up in the game running the streets trying to get that paper. And Dice knew how to draw him in and turn this whole shit around.

What happened Buck. Pooh ask him.

"That nigga must be crazy or some'em cause he just offered us some extra cash to smoke the person that set the whole shit up."

"Word, What did you say?
I told him that I was gonna call'em back.
That mean he want us to smoke Cookie.
"I know."

"I think we should, if he's willing to throw in some extra cash like another 100,000 that's way more than what we expected Buck think about it."

"Yeah I know, but I don't know what kind of games he's trying to play."

"He can't be playing to many games we got his bitch, and she lucky I didn't put my dick in her ass by now."

You still thinking about pussy nigga, when we trying to get this money."

"My bad, Buck, but I still say fuck that bitch Cookie."

"You right about that, plus that bitch was playing with our money anyway, it would be a pleasure for me to do it."

"Well call that nigga back and let him know what's up."

"It better be worth it."

Ring . . . . Ring . . . .

"Yo!" I said Answering the phone.

"Yo what's up, how much more are you talking about here." Buck said.

"I got 250,000 for you to put that nigga in a body bag, I'll drop it in the park the same way you wanted me to without any problems, I just want my shorty back and that nigga that caused all this to happen dead, and we could forget the whole thing ever happened, you let my girl go after y'all pick up the cash and then tell me where I can pick my shorty up at, then we all could go our separate ways."

"I hope you not trying to pull a fast one, cause we still have your shorty with us, so do the right thing."

"Do it sounds like I'm trying to pull a fast one on you, I just want my shorty back, and that nigga dead!"

"Aight, go ahead and go do that, how long would it take for you to get there."

Twenty five minutes.

"Aight, I'll call you back then."(click)

"I now had control of the situation once again."

"You ready Dice, come on let's go smoke these niggas. E.B. said. Picking up the 9mm that was on the table."

I gotta go alone on this one, that's how they want it.

"What you mean, fuck that, them niggas might be trying to set you up, over this shit son, come on you I gotta take me with you."

"I can't . . . . They said if someone comes with me or even follows me, they gonna kill her, and I don't wanna take that chance with her life, I just want this to go smooth, and get my shorty back safe, and get this over with."

"You sure man, cause I don't know, it just doesn't feel right to let you go out there by yourself."

"Yeah I'm positive, it shouldn't take long for me to get back, if anything happens and I don't make it back, here's the location where I'm a be at, and remember no matter what happens you my nigga, and I love you aight."

"Aight! I got love for you too, but I still think you should let me come with you to be on the safe side cause if we gonna die, we gonna die together, we been through to much for you to do this alone, I could be your other set of eyes that you need when you out there."

"No! . . . . I need you here, just in case anything goes wrong I don't want you getting caught up in my shit, I can't let you get involved any further, I gotta do this alone you my nigga thanks for everything."

"I understand. E.B.said. Hearing the sincerity in my voice. Then I grabbed the bag with the money in it and my .45 gave him a hug and walked out the door."

"Be safe my nigga" E.B. said. With tears in his eyes that he was trying to hold back.

I really wanted to take E.B. with me but I didn't want to jeopardize Shaniqua's life any more than what I already did. I was glad that all this world be over soon, I couldn't wait. When I arrived at 137th and Morningside. I parked my Benz got out and walked into the park and dropped the money in the third garbage can and turned around and headed out the park. As I made my way back to the car I scanned the area to see if I spotted someone watching me. Everything appeared to be normal kids were playing on the swing, people riding bikes and jogging everywhere I looked. Once I was back in my SL500 Benz I was sitting waiting for the call. I kept my eyes glued to the third garbage can to see if anyone was approaching it to retrieve the money I had dropped in it.

I was only moments away from seeing Shaniqua. I sat there excited with butterflies in my stomach like it was the first day of school. Because I couldn't wait I had my .45 in the palm of my hand. I knew Shaniqua would be happy again when she was back home with me where she belongs. It was only a matter of time now.

Ring . . . . Ring . . . .

"Hello." I said.

"Yeah, how we looking?"

"It's there, you can go pick it up now, my part is done, now tell me where my shorty at.

"She's right here in safe keepings."

Let me speak to her then."

"Dice", Shaniqua yelled into the phone.

"Shaniqua you alright?"

"Baby please, give them what they want!" Shaniqua pleaded. I could hear the fear in her voice.

"Calm down baby, Shaniqua it's over now don't worry I'm coming to get you it's all over . . . .

Hello

"Yeah I'm here."

Once we collect the money, and everything is there, we gonna call you, and let you know where you can pick her up at. Buck said.

"Aight."

(click)

I sat there waiting on a 137st and Morningside Ave to see who it was.

A all tinted out green Dodge Intrepid pulled up and stop at the entrance of the park then two men jumped out strapped and walked towards the park, and went and got the money from the third garbage can. They got back in the car, and peeled off. Now with Everything in motion the person that caused all this drama with my shorty was about to swim in his own blood, and I was gonna get Shaniqua back. That brought a smile to my face.

E.B. was still at the stash crib waiting for Dice to return with Shaniqua.

He was debating if he should call Dice to see if everything was alright with him. Dice had been gone more that an hour already so he started to worry a little. E.B. didn't like the fact that Dice left him behind and went alone knowing that anything could of popped off out there. But he understood Dice's reason for not letting him go with him. E.B. lit a blunt to give him a change of thought. Then he heard a knock on the front door. E.B. jumped up quick and ran to the door and open it. When he opened it he thought it was Dice because he wasn't expecting no one else but to his surprise it wasn't him. It was three ski masked niggas standing there with semi-automatic weapons with silencers on them. E.B. turned and tried to make a run for it to grab his gun that was laying on the table not to far from where he was standing. But when he did he didn't make it too far because they was right behind him. Then one of the masked men let his Uzi rip the bullets that was traveling in the air landed in E.B.'s back sending him crashing to the floor.

"What the fuck . . . Yall doing. E.B. struggled to say as he tried to turn around and see who his killers were.

Then he started spitting up blood as he laid on his chest. He tried to get back to his feet but he couldn't cause he was in to much pain.

He tried to get back up on his feet but stumbled because he was in to much pain. They picked him up off the floor and strapped him down in a chair that was in the living room. They used duct tape to retrain him around his legs, waist, arms, and chest. Blood was oozing out from his chest and back so much that it made trail from where the door was all the way to the living room showing where they dragged him from. While one of the mask men was torturing E.B. the other two searched the crib. E.B. tried his best to endure all the pain that he was feeling cause in his mind, he was dead already. The mask man started using E.B.'s body as target practice. He shot him in both of his knees when the bullets entered his knees you could hear the bullets breaking his bones. Then he shot him twice in each one of his shoulders.

Ahhhhhhhhhhhhhhhhhhh! E.B. screamed out in excruciating pain.

E.B. wanted it to end but it felt like it was gonna last forever.

When the masked men finally found what they were looking for they had 85 keys and 765,000 in cash. E.B. was losing consciousness due to the pain and the amount of blood he was losing every second. Before he had a chance to pass out all three of the masked men opened fire on him with multiple gun shots all over his body. They left him there slump sitting in the chair dead than placed a note on his lap then the ski masked men left.

Meanwhile on the other side of things the exchange was going down.

"I see you are a true business man, I wish we didn't have to meet this way, but I will live up to my part of the bargain and do what you paid me to do you can find your shorty on 125st and Park by the Metro North where she's waiting for you."

"You didn't harm her in anyway did you?

"Nah . . . . I left her as the way we got her, take care of your lady." (click) I peeled off flying to go get Shaniqua. I been waiting for this to happen since the last time she walked out of the house. It felt like months went by without me seeing her face and holding her in my arms. When I picked her up Shaniqua couldn't stop crying. She was glad that her nightmare was over and she was back where she belongs. She grabbed me and held me tight until she felt it was safe for her to let me go. I hugged and kissed her told her how sorry I was that this had happened to her. I could see all in her face that she was still worrying herself. And she wasn't going to feel better until she made it home. Where she would feel safe again. Before heading to Shaniqua's house we drove back to the stash crib.

"Dice, where are we going? Shaniqua asked.

Oh don't worry baby, I just gotta make a stop and let my man know that everything's alright, I know he probably worried by now, about why I didn't call him yet, it's only gonna be for a hot minute."

"Well hurry up, I gotta get home to see my son, I know he misses his mommy."

"Aight baby, I promise not to take long."

Then I parked outside the stash crib left Shaniqua in the Benz with the car still running and went inside to let E.B. know the news. It was all over now. When I opened the door I was shocked to find E.B. tied up with duct tape in the chair dead. He was shot so many times in his face it was damn near gone. I stood there looking at his lifeless body wondering what the fuck happened. I was fucked up standing there looking at him like that but it was nothing I could do because he was already dead and the people that did this was long gone. The whole crib was fucked up I notice the 9mm that I left E.B. with still sitting on the table in the same place. I immediately grabbed the 9mm from the table and ran to get the money that I has stashed in the crib. They had only found the money we had laying around. I went into the bedroom and pulled the bed away from the wall and kicked the wall in until it caved in. Then I pulled out the main stash that was inside the wall. It was 4.5 million dollars in hard cash. I grabbed my keys to my Hummer and the two large duffle bags with the money in it and started heading for the door. Before I left out I turned around to look at E.B. one last time that's when I noticed a note laying on his lap. I grabbed it and hurried out of the apartment. I through everything in the back seat of the Hummer and told Shaniqua to follow behind me in the Benz because I was gonna drive the Hummer back to her house. Then we drove away on our way to Queens. I couldn't believe that when all the smoke cleared it was E.B. the whole time who had set this whole thing up for my shorty to get kidnapped. But why we were tighter than brothers. It never came across my mind that he would do something like this for what it didn't make sense he didn't need the cash he had a lot of that. In my heart I knew that this couldn't be true. When we arrived at the house Shaniqua was happy to be home again and so was Ebony and Dyemere. It felt good to have her back home where she belongs. After getting Shaniqua settled in, Ebony finally went home. Me and Shaniqua had a lot to talk about.

Shaniqua I'm sorry that all this happened to you.

Baby it's not your fault, it was nothing that you could of done to prevent it.

"Nah, it was my fault, if I wasn't living the life I was living none of this shit would've happened to you."

"But it could've happened to anybody Dice!

"That's the point!" . . . . It happened to you because of me, If I was thinking about the more important things in life, instead of thinking about myself and the streets, none of this would've happened.

"I know Dice, I'm glad you know that too."

I was doing a lot of thinking while you was gone, I made up my mind to change my life, I'm finished with everything, it's all over for me now, fuck all the cars, money, jewels, and everything else that comes with it, I just wanna be a family, and be happy, I have more people to worry about now then to just think about myself, I have to put my family first, that's by doing the right thing from now on, being a father, and the man you always wanted me to be, I just want leave all this behind us, and move on to better things.

"It's gonna be alright Dice, only if you really mean what you saying, we could get past all this together, but you have to be truthful with yourself."

"I am being truthful, that's why I'm telling you this now, cause I want all this behind us now, I seen to many people die and suffer, then I came close to losing you, I got everything that I need, I don't need nothing else, there's a lot of things that I could do.

I'm glad that you are finally understanding what I was saying to you no matter what you do, you can always be you."

"But Shaniqua . . . . I also gotta tell you some'em else that happened while you was gone between me and . . . .

Before I was able to tell her about me and Ebony my phone started "ringing."

Hello. I said. Answering the phone.

"Hello! Is this Dice? The lady said in a raspy tone of voice.

"Yes it is, who is this? I said looking at the phone strange hearing a strange voice on the other end.

This is Miss Lovely from next door.

"Oh Hi, Miss Lovely, how you doing?

"Well" I'm doing fine son, thanks for asking, the reason why I called you is cause Cookie gave me your number to call you if I couldn't get in contact with her, when she left here a couple of hours ago, she said she had to handle something, and it was an emergency, so she asked me could I watch the baby for her only for a hour, and it wouldn't be longer than that. Now it has been more than four hours ago since I heard from her now. I don't mind watching the baby for a little while, but now I'm getting tired, and I want to get some rest, that's why I'm calling you, I'm not as young as I use to be, I called that girl phone and I didn't get no answer from her phone, so I called you."

"O.K. Miss Lovely, I understand, I'll be right over to pick her up, thank you for calling me Miss Lovely."

"Ok I'll be waiting for you, don't take long now." (Click)

I had to go pick up Dicecita from Miss Lovely's house I buried the 4.5 million along with the note that I got from E.B.'s lap in Shaniqua's Backyard.

Cookie had went Uptown (Harlem) to go meet up with Buck and Pooh at the same abandon building that they were keeping Shaniqua at when they had her. Buck and Pooh was standing outside waiting for Cookie.

When she got there she pulled up in front of the building where they were at then they jump in with her. Pooh was sitting in the front passenger seat while Buck was sitting behind Cookie. She came to tell Buck and Pooh to forget the whole thing she didn't want to go through with it anymore the deal was off. She was also giving them 15,000 more for all the trouble they went through to get it done. That would give them a total of 25,000 they have received from Cookie. And she thought that would make them happy. But she was too late. Pooh and Buck already let Shaniqua go earlier that day. Cookie felt relieved to hear that Shaniqua was free and not dead. Cookie didn't think that it would be this easy. The sad thing about it was that Cookie wasn't as lucky as Shaniqua was cause she wasn't leaving there at least not alive. Dice had made sure of that for anyone who caused this to happen to Shaniqua would swim in their own blood. As Cookie was telling Pooh how happy she was that Shaniqua was alright, Buck pulled out his 9mm that he was carrying on his waist and put it right behind Cookie's headrest then pulled the trigger. Boom!

Then he reached over from the back and hit her one more time in the head. Boom!

Her brains were blown all over the dashboard and on the steering wheel. Then Buck and Pooh got out of Cookie's Benz Jeep and hopped in their Dodge Intrepid and drove away. They were never seen after that. What goes around comes around karma is a bitch and I love her.

"Thank you Miss Lovely for calling me."

"You welcome Dice, have a good and blessed day." Miss Lovely said After leaving Miss Lovely's house picking up Dicecita I drove back to Shaniqua's house. When I got there I told Shaniqua to watch Dicecita while I go, and grab a few things from my house in Long Island. She asked me why didn't I pick up the things that I wanted to get when I was out there. I told her that I didn't want to drive dirty with Dicecita in the car with me. Then I left and went back to Long Island. When I pulled into the driveway and got out of my SL500 Benz I noticed that there was more cars than usual parked on the block. But it wasn't nothing out of the ordinary so I went straight inside the house to get the other money that I had stashed away. Cookie still was nowhere in sight I tried not to think about that cause I already had a lot on my mind and I was already going through enough for one day. E.B. was dead and that was still fucking with me. I had to call Boo and Rob to let them know what happened to E.B. Plus I was running with a mean headache. I wanted to get back soon as possible to get what I came for and bounce. While I was in the room bagging all the money that I had in the safe I heard the doors busting open from the front and back. Everything started moving in slow motion like the matrix. I went to grab my twin .40 glocks that was laying on the bed and bang out with them but I thought about it. I got a family that needs me to live for them now.

"ATF, FBI, DEA get the fuck down on the floor now, get down, get down, or we going to shoot." The Agents yelled all at once.

I stared at my two .40 glocks one last time all I could hear was the devil in my head saying do it do it don't be a coward now. I gave you everything and now you want to leave the streets. You can't just walk away I gave you this life that you live. I put you on your feet brought bread into your house. I ignored the voice in my head and said fuck it laid down on the floor and then they cuffed me.

All they found was two .40 glocks and 475,000 in cash. I closed my eyes and thought about Shaniqua, Dyemere, Dicecita, Cookie, and E.B. running through my head at the same time. As they walked me out my house with my hand cuffed behind my back the whole block was shut down, and flooded with agents. All the neighbors were outside watching like it was a live show of Cops. On my way down to Federal Plaza I was thinking to myself when was it gonna end. The streets don't love nobody I fell victim of it like many others did before me. The sad thing about it was that I was really ready for a change.

* * *

Chapter 24

"When It all Falls Down"

When I arrived at the County Jail intake it was me, Boo, and Rob's Cousin Blinky all sitting in the bull pins waiting to get stripped of our personal belongings. We were all facing heavy charges. They were trying to scare us by telling us that we were all looking at life in Federal Prison.

848(c), 924 (c), 922 (g), 924(a),1512 (a), 1951 (a), and 3551, were all our charges and Murder. None of us got any bail. When we were in the court room Boo wild out and threw the chair at the judge and told him to suck his dick. They quickly restrained him and rushed us out of the court building and back to the county jail. That was some bullshit cause I never had any criminal history and I still couldn't get a fucking bail. It was a lot of people out there doing a lot worse shit than I was doing and they got a fucking bail. I was very frustrated so much shit kept happening to me like someone put a hex on me. After they housed us in different parts of jail. We were allowed to make phone calls from our cell block areas. When I called Shaniqua she couldn't believe what I was saying to her that I was locked up. The feds confiscated my SL500 Benz, Yukon Denali, and put a lean on my house that I had in Long Island. Shaniqua still had Dicecita there wasn't no sign of Cookie nobody heard anything from her yet. Even the Fed's were looking for her to take care of some paper work because everything was in her name. The next day when I was in the dayroom I was reading the newspaper the section that had the city news. It was an article about a woman being found dead in her ML430 Benz jeep shot in the back of the head. When I saw who it was a cold chill ran through my body then I got up and threw the paper in the garbage. Damn it was Cookie now my head was really fucked up. I didn't know what the fuck was going on. People were dropping dead all around me except for me. I was thinking that maybe somebody car jacked her or tried to rob her and they killed her instead. Later that day they called me for a visit.

"Dyemere Washington cell #12 you got a visit."

When I got down on the dance floor (visiting area) it was Shaniqua.

What's up baby girl. I said. Giving her a big hug and a kiss. I can't believe that you in here oh my god.

I can't believe I'm in here either, I went to get some things from the house and then they just rushed the crib, they were all over.

The Feds and the ATF agents were waiting for me to come home for a few days now. But I wasn't showing up because I was at Shaniqua's house.

They didn't know no where else to look so they waited. And then I finally showed up walking right into their trap.

"I hope they let you go baby, cause this is crazy Dice, this madness has to end.

I know babygirl, it's gonna be ayight.

Your lawyer told me that, if you blow trial you might get life in jail.

Yeah, that's true, but I aint worried about that they full of shit, I'm a be home soon but it's gonna take a good fight. I've been fighting my whole life for what I wanted. I'm a need you to do me a favor I need you to take care of Dicecita for me while I'm in here.

"Why . . . . Where's Cookie at?

"She's dead", I saw her in the newspaper today.

What! Oh my God.

Shaniqua said grabbing her face in shock."

"Yeah I know this shit is crazy, they got me locked up in this bitch like I'm a fucking criminal, I don't even have a fucking record that should keep me here, they got a nigga like me in here, while the real enemies out there doing crazy shit, like knocking down buildings and they still out there, but it's all good ma."

"Dice, I'm sorry, I don't know why this keep happening to you, Oh my God." Shaniqua said. Then she started to cry.

At his point in my life I was use to people dying that was close to me so it was hard for me to shed any tears over Cookie's death.

Because I didn't have any more left. Only God himself had all the answers to what I was going through in my life. Many nights I wish that God would come down and touch me and take me away from all the drama and the pain I had endured over the years. Chasing me my whole life because it seemed like it wasn't no escaping it. I knew I had become a changed man cause the way I looked at everything now. There had to be a better life for me to live I just needed God's tears to wash away all my sins. My whole life I felt like I was living in hell doing Satins dirty work. This must was the cross roads for me to make it to the other side to live as righteous man. This must have been a test of faith.

Shaniqua, all I want you to do for me is, keep in contact with my lawyer, and take care of Dyemere and Dicecita, til I come home, I don't want you by my side no more, just leave me alone, and let me handle this by myself, because all the bullshit and the drama I brought into your life already is enough, I don't want to worry about you, what you doing, where you at, that's some'em, that I don't need to deal with, bad enough I'm here behind these walls, I really don't need no more stress, so please Shaniqua leave me alone . . . .

"What! . . . .

What you mean?

"I mean, I want you to leave me alone!

"No! . . . . Why would I do that, I'll never leave you alone I'll always be by your side, and love you the way you always loved me when you was home,

I'm not going to leave you when you need me the most you must be crazy."

"Nah baby, please do this for me, I don't want that kind of stress on my head now, I did a lot of bullshit in my life Shaniqua, I haven't always been faithful and true to you, you don't need me now."

"Dice, what did I tell you? I will never leave you, I know what kind of person you are, and I know you ain't perfect, but I love you, and that's not going to stop me from being on your side, I see it in your eyes every day I look at you, I know what kind of person you could be and I'm willing to wait until that day come around, maybe this is his time to shine and uplift you from the Devil's grip.

Shaniqua said. As she held my hand.

"I don't want you to leave Shaniqua, but I never been through this before, this is all new to me, by me telling you to leave me, is so that I can focus and fight to get back home to you and the kids."

"So what you want me to do, just walk away like It don't mean nothing to me, what about us, we need you too, I'm not gonna let you shut us out of your life like that, cause I ain't going nowhere, I'm not trying to hear none of that what you saying right now Dice. I'm a always be here for you until you walk out of these doors a free man again, I'll be at all your court dates and all your visits."

"Dyemere Washington visit is now over. The loud speaker said.

We stood up hugged and kissed.

"Shaniqua, I need you to do this for me please."

"No . . . . I can't." Shaniqua said with tears in her eyes.

Then I walked back to my cell block area.

Shaniqua didn't understand why I didn't want her around anymore. It wasn't like she was the type of lady that would shit on her man cause he was locked up. Hanging out fucking around partying while her man was in jail fighting to get his life back like most females do. I've seen it happen to a lot of niggas when they get locked up. I'm a man I can hold my own and I know that If you love someone and you let them go and if it comes back to you that means that their yours and they here to stay. After everything I been through in my life I would rather let her go than to lose her down the line like I lost everyone that stayed around me. I didn't want anything to happen to her or the kids because everyone that was ever close to me died. Shaniqua knew I was from the streets when she met me. She saw my flashy life style and she also knew that when you that nigga bitches always trying to fuck with you. Shaniqua knew I always took care of mine and I treated her like the queen she was. Night after Night I laid in a small ass cell thinking about my family I had now and the turn my life was taking. When Shaniqua sent me pictures, and letters I sent them all back. Since the first time she came to see me in the County Jail I made it her last one cause I refused all of her visits. When she come to court to see me I didn't even acknowledge her. Shaniqua always tried to get my attention using hand gestures but I didn't respond. I didn't want to treat Shaniqua like this but I wasn't happy with myself and all the things that happened in my life that lead to this point. All the things I was doing when I was home hanging out with my peoples and things I never told her about me. In my heart I really wanted to see her, communicate with her, and let her know how exactly how I felt. My biggest fears wouldn't let me express myself the way I wanted to. I was afraid of losing Shaniqua the way I lost everything else that I ever loved. Now they were trying to take my freedom away from me. Shaniqua didn't have to worry about money cause I always took care of her and if worst came to worst she had enough money to last her and the kids for the rest of their lives. I wasn't too worried about Dyemere and Dicecita because I knew they were in good hands with Shaniqua. No matter how many times I sent her a letters and packages back she kept sending them back to me. Shaniqua made sure that she stayed in contact with my lawyer just like I told her to. He would relate messages from her to tell me that she misses and loves me and the kids were doing fine. Shaniqua was still there by my side even when I told her not to be. She was going to wait until the day that I came home no matter how long that would take she was going to be there.

Chapter 25

"Heads Up"

I received a kite from Boo saying that he had found out the reason why we was locked up. It was Rob the whole time working with the Fed's. That's why he started moving funny and wasn't around like he use to and wasn't locked up with us now. I already had that thought when we first got arraigned in Federal Court and he wasn't there. I sent him a kite back to him telling him to meet me in the yard tomorrow by the weight pile. Rob was a bitch ass nigga I should've let E.B. smoke his ass a long time ago when he wanted to, damn I miss my nigga.

*   *   *

"what's good." I said to Boo giving him dap.

"Ain't shit good up in this mother fucka, they got that bitch ass nigga Rob running around ratting on niggas and shit, all day like he don't have any remorse about the shit he doing he don't give a fuck. That nigga even told on his cousin what kind of sick shit is that man? Boo said as we was walking in the yard.

That shit touched us in the heart because we were like brothers. It's sad how your own people will destroy your family just to save their self's.

I don't know what kind of shit he on, but I know we ain't suppose to be here they could've gave us bail so that will could fight this from the street instead of being here like some fucking birds.

"They aint trying to do that shit while they got that nigga riding around pointing niggas out like a sucka ass nigga his day is coming tho.

That nigga don't have to much to say about me, cause he don't know shit about me."

"Didn't you say to me that they ran up in your crib in Long Island."

"Yeah!"

"How you think they know where you live?

"I don't know, and I don't give a fuck, cause they ain't find shit anyway but some hammers and cash.

Yeah, but that bitch ass nigga knows a lot about me, I was the one dealing with him, they only could try to get you on conspiracy charges, and fire arms, they can't prove that you had anything to do with shit.

They could only charge you with that and hope that you get stressed out and cop out to something.

I'm not trying to cop out to shit, I got a family to go home to, I'm not trying to be sitting in this mother fucka stress holding my dick, no more than I have to they need more than just what that nigga saying they need someone else corroborate his story.

Yeah you right that's why they might come at me to make me flip on you but them niggas could suck my dick I will never be a rat.

"Don't shit on me man, and go out like no sucka, cause you already know what it is and how we was doing it when we was in the town. If you gonna go out like a bitch let me know now. I said. As we now stood face to face with each other."

"Fuck that" I ain't no snitch, my name don't start with A and end with O I ain't like them other cats.

"That's what's up," that's how we gotta keep it official cause you know how I feel about that shit already them niggas die on sight."

"What's up with EB" what he do skip town on us without letting us know, if he did that's what's up cause we all don't need to be in this mother fucka anyway."

"Nah . . . . I found that nigga dead in the stash crib with his shit pushed back, somebody did him dirty."

Get the fuck outta here . . . . Not EB, when did this happen?"

"When I went to get my shorty back from the dudes that kidnapped her.

When I got back that's when I found strapped down in a chair with holes everywhere on his body, he got hit up so bad I couldn't even recognize him."

"Word!"

"Check the crazy shit out tho, when I offered the niggas that had my shorty a extra 150,000 to kill the nigga that told them to kidnap my shorty. This happened right before I left the stash crib then when I got back, that's when I found him dead."

"Word! . . . . So you think . . .

"I don't know."

"Get the fuck outta here, nah, I can't see that shit!"

"That's the same thing I was saying to myself, I still don't believe that he would do some'em like that to me, for what?"

"It don't make any sense to me either, not EB that was my nigga, he would rather die before he do anything crazy like that to you, it just doesn't add up to me."

"I also found a note on his body."

"Yeah, what did it say?

I don't know, I didn't get a chance to read it.

Damn I wish you knew what it said it might tell us who did it.

"You wanna hear some more crazy shit?

"What . . . . there's more?

The other day I was reading the newspaper, it had an article in it and it said they found a woman dead, shot in the back of her head in her ML430 Benz Jeep, when I saw the name it fucked me up cause it was Cookie."

"Oh shit! Get the fuck outta here Dice, ah man I'm sorry, where's the baby at?

"My shorty got her, she had her since the day I got knocked by the Fed's, that shit had me tripping cause all this shit is crazy."

"Damn Dice, that shit is crazy man, I'm surprised you didn't lose your mind yet, with all the shit you been through, damn I feel your pain."

"Yeah this shit be having a nigga on edge sometimes, but I just try to brush it off, and keep it moving, cause If I think about it, all the shit I've been through I'm a straight killing nigga in here, then I really won't be going home. That's why I gotta stay focus, and worry about getting out of this bitch."

"I feel you on that note Dice, but you know they might try to put my lights out behind all this shit, cause I was the one that was taking care of all the transaction the Fed's might come at me with football numbers, and when they do, I'm a tell 'em to suck my dick again, we going to trial with that shit, unless they come at me right."

"What's up with that nigga cousin Blinky, where he at in here cause I haven't seen him?

"I heard his bitch ass is down in H block, I got people over there with him."

"Word, so what that nigga over there talking about?"

"Nothing!" "That nigga don't be saying shit, he don't even be eating his food crying and shit stressing over the phone, and I heard that nigga went to court twice already."

"Twice", and we ain't been back to court since we first got arraigned, have your people talk to him, and find out what's up with that nigga Rob cause we need to see that man asap."

"Aight, I'll do that soon as I get back inside I'll send the word."

"I'm a make a few calls myself."

"On the go back." The voice said over the loud speaker. Letting us know that rec was over.

"Make sure you handle that soon as you get back." I said.

"I got you Dice, that's my word, don't worry I'm a do that right now."

*   *   *

The next day Jay came to see me.

"What's up little brother, how you holding up in here?

"I'm aight, it could be better though, what's up with you? I haven't seen you in a minute now, how did you find out that I was here."

"Shaniqua told me when I went by to check on you, and the kids, come to find out, you in here locked up, she also told me that you wasn't excepting any visit or mail from her Dice, what's going on with that?

"I don't even wanna talk about that, if you came here for that you might as well leave now, because I don't wanna hear shit about her, I got so much other shit to worry about as it is."

My bad Dice you right, the kids are looking beautiful, you know it makes me happy every time I see them, it brings a smile to my face all the time, it kind of reminds me of me and you when we were little."

"I bet it do, I can't even enjoy their smile's from here anymore, this shit really fucks with your mind and your family man."

"Yeah Dice but you can't let it get to you, remember you a strong man Dice, you been through a lot of shit in your lifetime, and you still here with all your marbles a lot of people would've lost it by now, only the strong survive."

"You right about that."

"God has plans for you Dice, and this ain't it, that's why you still here, through all the shit that happened around you, you still here."

"I wonder why It happened this way all a nigga was doing was trying to get some change to feed my family. Why do God make us suffer so much."

"We can't blame him for the life that we chose to live, we just gotta look at everything in a positive way, like now, I bet you are a different person, your whole way of thinking has changed I can tell by te way you speaking."

"Yeah I gave up all that excitement that comes with the fast life, I wanna do things in a different way. I got a lot of things planned that I'm a do when I get home."

"That's what I'm talking about Dice, I knew you had it in you, I was always waiting for it to come out, me and you was always two different people. I have a lot of mommy's ways, but you always had the brains and the heart to do anything you wanted to do and that's good to have that's a gift."

"You'll see when I get home."

"Keep that positive spirit alive, and you going be alright trust me Dice."

"I'm glad you came here today, to give me that breath of fresh air."

"That's what I'm here for."

Did you hear what happened to EB?

"Yeah, I heard all about it, it's a sad story that I don't wanna talk about."

I can respect that.

Thank you.

I need you to do me a favor, I want you to make a call for me.

Sure, who you want me to call.

A friend of mine his name is "Haitian Black."

* * *

The next time I saw Boo in the yard he was talking to some cats from Brooklyn. When he saw me approaching, he spun off on them and came to holla at me.

Did you have your people holla at that nigga Blinky?" I asked him.

"Yeah they put the squeeze on that nigga, and then he gave up a couple of addresses where that nigga Rob might be at."

"That's what's up", I got my people to contact Haitian Black down in Florida, I asked him to take care of some minor favors that I needed done a.s.a.p."

"Aight, what else do you want me to do next?

"I want you to cancel that nigga for good, cause we don't need nobody else running their mouths about shit, trying to get a deal with the U.S.

District Attorney we gonna beat them to the punch."

"No problem, I knew you was going to say that." Boo said with a smile on his face.

"Tie up all the loose ends."

Do you think we ever gonna get outta here Dice?

"Of course I do, you just gotta believe it yourself, and have faith Boo, we gonna be ayight, it's just me and you Boo all the way to the end."

Aight Dice, I believe you, you always find a way to make It happen, and you know I'm riding with you all the way out."

"I know you will Boo we cut from the same cloth."

What's up with you and that chick Anna

"Ah man, Anna?

"Yeah, what's up that bitch really feeling you huh?

"Man, that bitch is crazy, you won't believe the shit she tried to hit me with."

"What?"

"That she pregnant by me, and she wanna keep it."

"Oh shit man, what the fuck you trying to do man, have your shorty kill your ass?"

"Hell No! . . . . I told that bitch, she better get a abortion, cause I ain't trying to hear that shit, what we had was only business, that bitch got it twisted with that one."

Blinky was in his cell writing a letter to his girl telling her that he was stressed out because he was tired of being in jail and he wanted to come home. He also told her that he didn't know what else to do and he was thinking about snitching on the niggas that he was locked up with cause that was his only way of getting out. All because his girl said that she was leaving him cause she didn't have time for no jail bird and if he wanted to be with her he would have to find a way to get out of jail. What he didn't expect was what was about to happen to him. After he finished writing his letter he closed it and sat it on his desk that was next to his bed then he laid down to take a nap. Two blood niggas that was on his tier walked in his cell while he was laying down came in swinging bangers at him. Blinky tried to fight them off but he was no match for them. The first nigga stabbed Blinky in the stomach while the other one finished him off with stabs to his neck, chest, back until he was cut up like fresh bread out of the oven. Then they walked out of his cell one by one like nothing ever happened. When the CO's came around to do the standing count they realize that he wasn't standing up for the count so they walked in his cell when they did they noticed all the blood that his lifeless body was covered in. It was over for him before he even knew it.

Chapter 26

"The Clean Up"

The U.S. District Attorney that was on the case got a call from his wife while he was on his way to work. She told him that she needed him home cause it was an emergency and for him to make it fast. He really didn't want to turn around and go back to the house because he just left there a few minutes ago. But he also didn't want to get in an argument with his wife so he said fuck it and decided to go back to the house to see what the problem was. When he arrived back at the house he entered like he normally does opening the door and shouting out her name. He then closed the door behind him. When he did it was the last thing he would ever remember. There was a Haitian man standing right behind the door waiting for him with a machete in his hand. Before he even had a chance to turn around and notice him the Haitian man swung the machete with full force crashing down on the top of his skull splitting it down to the white meat damn near in half. His lifeless body collapsed on to the floor,. The machete went so deep in his head that the Haitian man had to yank it out to get it free. Then he started to hack away at his body until it was nothing left but pieces of him. Blood was everywhere. His wife got the same treatment after watching her husband die a horrific death. The Haitian men cut their bodies up into small body parts. They bagged up what was left their body parts and stuffed them in a card board box taped it up and addressed it to the Federal Court House in Central Islip.

Hello! This is Robert Sanders of the Channel Six News reporting live from the Federal Plaza, I'm standing here at the Federal Court House in Central Islip Suffix County area, where a horrible scene was discovered earlier today in the package room area of Court House. Oh my God, I can't believe what was discovered here today.

The entire building had to be evacuated due to the horrific tragedy that occurred here today. The US District Attorneys body was found here today, chopped up into minced body parts and was sent here by delivery from the Postal Service Company, along with his wife's body. They were both stuffed into a card board box and sent here with no return sender address. I can't believe this happened today, these people that committed this horrifying act are truly some savages, and needs to be brought to justice for this. No one deserves this type of a brutal death the Federal Plaza Building will be closed for investigators trying to find out what happened to this loving couple. I strongly advise anyone that has any information on this tragic death to please, I repeat please call, 1-300-444-TIPS, please it's for your own safety, you wouldn't want these type of people running through your backyard this has been Robert Sanders of the Channel Six News reporting live from Federal Plaza.

I was working out in the day room when I saw the top story come across the television. I smiled because that he was the head prosecutor on my case. The same way the Federal Government was taking actions against me I was taking actions against them. I knew Haitian Black and his peoples were on the job putting that work in. I was making sure that I was going home by any means necessary. I wanted to become a change man but somehow some way I was going back to my old ways. My whole life I was fighting to beat the odds against me and now once again my back was against the wall. I was a man and I wasn't going to lay down for nobody. This is how I had to react when the pressure was on never fold. I'm not one of them bitch ass niggas they was use to. They gonna have to take me out, with my gunz blazing because huh I'm going all out for mine. I was living with a vendetta anyone that prayed on my downfall and played a part of me being here had to pay the price of death. Pay back is a bitch but revenge is a motherfucker. Everybody was gonna get theirs one by one. Only a beast can run the jungle.

* * *

"I'm a Rider"

"Did you see the newspaper today? The supervisor said tossing the newspaper on his desk for Agent Honeytoon to see.

"Yes, I seen it already, I was in tremendous shock, when I read the news about the US District Attorney, he was the lead prosecutor on the Dyemere Washington case." Agent Honeytoon said.

"I know" . . . . This could be a major blow to this case, he was working on this for months now, he was still waiting for response from Washington DC. because he was trying to get the death penalty for this case."

"So, do they have any replacements for his position as of yet?

"No! It would take months to get someone else to fill his shoes, and that might be risky on our behalf.

"He did have people that was working under him on this case that may be capable enough, to come in and fill in for his position."

"Yeah, but they are not fully experienced for this type of case, if it falls in their hands, then i don't know if we would have such of a strong case, it would all be left on the (CI's) testimony, do you have him in a witness protection program as of yet."

"No sir he still refuses to take the Witness Protection program."

"Well you get him some type of protection, so we can monitor his every move, he is the key to this whole case, we got to pay close attention to him, and make sure nothing happens to him."

"I'll get on it as soon as possible, is there anything else that I can do for you sir."

No that would be it for today Agent Honeytoon.

O.K. you have a good day then sir. Agent Honeytoon said. Then he got up and walked out of the office.

*   *   *

Federal Agent Honeytoon A.K.A. Detective Honeytoon has been working undercover on this case for one year now. The FEDs also had information on Detective Johnson and his corruption and were on their way to bringing him down. The Federal Bureau of Investigators sent in a expert Agent right after Detective Johnson's X-partner came up missing without a trace and is still missing till this day. Dice AKA Dyemere Washington first came up on the FBI radar after Rock's death A.K.A. Robert Smith. The Fed's was already on to Rock back then when Dice first got started. The Fed's were about to shut down his operation until Rock became an informant. That's how the Fed's found out they had another major player on the rise Dice A.K.A. Dyemere Washington. The Feds has been looking for Dice ever since then. He fell off the radar along with one of the FBI special field agents Lucie Jones AKA Cookie. Due to the lack of information and the disappearance of one of their agents Lucie Jones AKA Cookie the Fed's didn't have any luck because Agent Lucie aka Cookie did everything in her power from keeping him from being apprehended by deleting files and tampering with evidence. Agent Lucie fell in love with Dice's ambition. That's why since Rock's death the Fed's wasn't able to find Dice until when Detective Johnson and Detective Honeytoon got lucky when they pulled over a GS 430 Lexus and the (CI) started spitting out names and Dice name rang a bell in Detective Honeytoon head. He was one of the few of them that got away from the Feds. Detective Honeytoon never reported it to his partner Detective Johnson because he was under investigation also. He reported everything back to his supervisor's office. When the Feds realized that Dice AKA Dyemere Washington was still around it became a whole new ball game. But the Federal Bureau of Investigations didn't expect to come across an intelligent, brutal, and vicious young man like Dice AKA Dyemere Washington. They would soon find out that he was there worst nightmare because they really under estimated the power Dice. To get him they had to come correct.

After meeting with his supervisors at the downtown office. Agent Honeytoon was coming out of the cafeteria at the downtown office then he got in his car and drove away. He was driving coming down Hudson street when he suddenly came to a complete stop at the busy intersection due to construction. As he accelerated his scorching hot cup of coffee spilled over on to his lap causing it to burn him. Agent Honeytoon pulled over into a gas station to clean himself up.

"Shit! Fuck." Agent Honeytoon said. Pissed the fuck off getting out of his car shaking his clothes off

That's when a cable van pulled into the same gas station that Agent Honeytoon was at. The driver of the cable van got out of the van and walked away exiting the gas station approaching a parked car that was waiting for him. As he entered the vehicle he stopped and turned around and waved bye to Agent Honeytoon. Then he got into the awaiting car that was parked by the curb waiting for him in front of the gas station and peeled off. At first he thought he knew him. Maybe it was one of his fellow agents he thought. When Agent Honeytoon realized what was going on it was too late for him he became a part of history. Agent Honeytoon tried to make a run for it but the cable van that was there was filled with enough C4 to take out a whole city block exploded. Detective AKA agent Honeytoon and thirteen people died in that explosion. The fuel from the gas station made the explosion more devastating causing it to feel like it was an earthquake that erupted because the vibration from it could be felt blocks away.

Rob decided not to take the stand against Dice after hearing what happened to his cousin Blinky in jail. He knew that Dice had something to do with it and he also knew that he would be next if he stuck around. Rob knew that was a sign of death coming his way he also knew the passion of revenge that burned inside Dice to get even with anyone ever crossed him. Dice would come after you until the day that he died and that was no time soon so Rob had a lot to be worried about. Rob wanted to contact Dice and try to explain the situation to him but he knew going to see him was out of the question because he was shitting in his pants and he had every right to. He said fuck it he'll just skip town and wait until everything was over or he would leave and say fuck it and just never come back again. Rob had enough of the hood life it was too much for him to handle. He knew like everybody else what to expect when you playing this game but he decided to take the bitch way out. Rob packed all his bags with all his clothes and money he had then called his girlfriend and told her to do the same because they were leaving. She didn't know why he wanted to leave in such of a hurry. She didn't have no idea that her man was a straight bitch ass nigga snitching on his mans and them like he was. Rob always had a bit of hate in his blood that money couldn't wash away. A nigga like him hates himself no matter where he's at or what he's doing hate will always be with him. Niggas like him are better off dead being envious towards your own people. Rob had no time to waste he had to move fast because time was against him. He could feel Dice's presence all around him like he was breathing on his neck that alone made him nervous to be in one place longer than he should. While Rob was driving on his way to pick up his girlfriend Gloria he kept his eyes moving in every direction like he heard footsteps coming behind him making it hard for him to concentrate on driving. Other drivers were blowing their car horns and throwing up hand gestures giving him the middle finger as he ran stop signs and red lights. When he finally made it to Gloria's house his face and body was drenched with sweat. He was so afraid to get out the car, when he did he ran up her steps like he was in a marathon.

"You ready yet? Rob said. Bursting in the door'

"Damn boy" . . . what happened to you, I need a few more minutes to grab some other things that I need. Gloria said. Walking in to the bathroom to fix her hair.

"Bitch . . . . You ain't ready yet", Oh my god, I called you an hour ago to make sure your slow ass was ready when I got here, and you still ain't ready yet this fucking girl damn, I should just leave your ass here. Rob said standing behind her in the bathroom.

"What the fuck is your problem, coming here acting all crazy, like the motherfucking police was chasing your ass, how you wanna rush me, boy . . . . you better calm your ass down.

Bitch just grab what the fuck you need and lets go Gloria, I don't have time for this shit right now, just grab your shit and come on." Rob said walking out of the bathroom to go look out the window to check his surroundings.

"Alright, damn! . . . . calm down, a bitch can't even fix her hair, without you screaming, come on, come on." Gloria said. Pushing Rob out of her way.

Then they grabbed their things and hurried out of the apartment and into Rob's Lexus and drove away.

Rob was happy that he made it this far so he started to calm down a little bit. Thinking that he was almost away from harms reach but he still felt Dice presence so he stayed on point.

"Can we at least stop, and get something to eat cause a bitch, sure is hungry, what you forgot that I'm carrying a little person inside of me now, why don't we stop at a restaurant and get some shrimps to eat, so we can relax, cause I ain't with all this rushing shit on no empty stomach, and I gotta use the bathroom."

"We don't have time for all that shit Gloria, we gotta keep it moving."

"What the fuck do you expect me to do, starve until we get where we going huh. Hell no, you must have lost your fucking mind now, if you think that, you better pull this motherfucking car over "now" before I slap the shit out of your ass, I bet if I told you I was going to give you some head you'll pull this motherfucker over."

"We ain't stopping at no restaurant, that's out of the fucking question, you better eat a burger and call it a day, until we get to where we going."

"Fine then stop at a drive thru since your ass is so fucking paranoid and shit, like somebody after you, what the fuck you do, steal somebody money or something, rob your friends cause something ain't right about your ass, I hope you not dragging me in some bullshit, cause I'm a fuck you up in this car."

Then they pulled into a Burgers "R" us drive thru to order something to eat. Gloria got out the car and went inside of Burgers "R" us to use the bathroom, while Rob. ordered the food for them through the drive thru. After getting the food Rob pulled over to park in the parking lot to wait for Gloria to come out of Burgers "R" us.

"Bitch what the fuck took so long?

"Shut the fuck up cry baby I just went in there, drive since you so damn scared."

"Watch when we get where we going I'ma show you some'em Rob said Snatching Gloria by her hair."

"You better get your fucking hands off me because you ain't gonna do shit."

Then right as they was about to pull out of Burgers "R" us parking lot two vans was approaching them from opposite directions to block them in. The side doors popped open and two wild looking Haitian niggas with dreads jumped out with two double pump Marshburg shot guns and on fire both sides of Rob Lexus. They pumped him and his bitch full with lead. Boom! . . . . Boom! . . . . Boom! . . . . Boom! . . . . Boom! . . . . Boom! . . . . that was all she wrote.

"Mayhem"

"Shit! I still can't believe this, we lost our US District Attorney, and our lead agent on the case, this shit smells funny to me, something's going on here."

"I don't understand how all this happened so fast under our noses."

"Agent Honeytoon is missing now, I gave him orders to give his (CI) some protection, and that was the last time I heard from him when he left my office."

"Do you have any information on the (CI) identification or his whereabouts?"

"No! Only Agent Honeytoon had that classified information, and there's no way that we can contact him right now, we tried every way possible, we even did a satellite trace on his car and cell phone, and we still didn't pick up anything."

"That's strange; it should've picked up something by now."

"I know."

Do you think he was a part of that explosion down on Dean street?

Anything's possible at this point, but I'll have a search team check it out.

"With all that's missing on the Dyemere Washington case, what options are we left with now?"

"I'm sorry to say Attorney General", that we are left with nothing at this point, only a fire arms charge and he could beat that alone on technicalities, the only option we have left is that we play the bluff game with him and his lawyer, we could tell them that we have a lot of evidence against him, and hope that he bites and don't wanna go to trial, because if he do we're fucked, excuse my language sir."

"You mean to tell me there's a strong possibility, of him getting away, if we don't have the (CI)'s testimony to testify against him?

"That is correct sir!"

"This is one of the biggest cases that our office has seen in a long time and we might loose it to some nigga from the hood do you know what that can do to our careers. Shit! . . . . We can't have this type of shit, do you know how much time and money we put into this case to let it slip away damn I can't" . . . .

(Click)

*   *   *

"Home Again"

Shaniqua was home praying every day that her man come home back into her life. She knew in her heart Dice really loved her and he was afraid of causing her anymore pain then he had already did. Dice was her soul mate and Shaniqua was his. Even though they had lost temporary communication with each other Shaniqua always felt Dice in her heart.

She had a lonely spot in her heart that only Dice could fill. Shaniqua never understood why he didn't want her to visit him or send him any letters. It wasn't like he was feeling guilty about the things he did. It was all about the pain he had surrounding his heart. Jay told Shaniqua when he went to see Dice that he was truly missing her more than anything because Jay could see the pain all in his brother's face when he spoke of her. Shaniqua just wanted to tell Dice that she loved him no matter what they were going through and that she was going to be there until the day he came home. Shaniqua was being a real true woman to her man. She took care of Dyemere and Dicecita very well. Ebony and friends would come by Shaniqua's beauty salon and by the house to see how she was doing.

Shaniqua also took over Cookie's salon so she had her hands full and Dice on her mind. Ebony and friends told Shaniqua that she needs to move on and forget about Dice because he was never coming home. But Shaniqua knew who she belonged to Dice and she was going to wait for her man. Only Dice could make her happy and the kids that's all that mattered to her. Now with Cookie gone she had to be the mother in Dicecita's life and Shaniqua was proud to do it. Shaniqua had finally received a letter from Dice she couldn't wait until she got inside to open it. It said.

"What's up Baby girl?"

How you doing? I'm sorry I haven't been calling you or been accepting any of your visits. I'm sorry but I couldn't live with myself if I let something happen to you or if I lost you. I never meant to put you through so much drama. Anything that I ever loved or cared about in my life always was taken away from me or died. Like the time you was missing I didn't know what to do cause I thought I lost you for good. Then when I got you back I was very happy to have you home again. I had to distance myself from you tho so that you would be alright. I never loved a woman in my life the way I love you. And I never had to many women in my life that I could say I love but my mother and I lost her and my biggest fear is losing you too. I only wanted you to be alright, I didn't wanna make you think that you did something wrong. It was me who did all the wrong things so I'm trying to handled all my mistakes the best way I can. Shaniqua I don't know what else to say to you but I'm sorry for anything I did to you and bringing you the drama I caused you. One day when I get home I will make it up to you, I promise you that I will do my best to make you happy. I got something put away for our future when I come home we won't ever have to worry about any of this ever happening again. I got everything planned out when I come if you are still there for me. I would love to finish what we started that's being together as a family again. I'm talking to a lot of O.G's in here and they schooling me on how to be a better person when I come home. All I ever wanted was the best for you from the first day I met you. You always been in my heart I want to send you my love and best wishes. I pray that you could forgive me for the way I've been treating you lately. I never meant any harm by it I only wanted to focus on one thing that's coming back home to my family. I know in my heart you will do the right thing I chose to live my life the way I did, I knew what could've happened if I slipped up this is all part of the game. I have to handle this on my own, I know it's hard and causing you pain by us not being together but it won't be like this forever. When they told me I might do life in Federal Prison you and the kids were the first thing that flashed across my mind. I was going to lose my family again before I let that happen I rather let y'all go this way. I will fight with everything I got to get back home to y'all. By me doing it this way gives me more to fight for because I know what's waiting for me outside these walls. I never lost any love for you no one or nothing can ever take that away from me. I only pray that you understand and feel my pain. I saw you there every time I go to court I might not smile when I see you but on the inside I'm smiling at you. I only wish that I would've told you certain things about me and did all the things I wanted to do sooner but everything happened for a reason. I don't know why this had to happen everyone deserves another chance to correct the mistakes they made in their life. You are a good person Shaniqua that's why I had to distance myself from you to protect you and the kids from any harm coming your way. You and my kids mean the world to me without y'all there's nothing else to live for. I would never forgive myself if I allowed y'all to get hurt in anyway. I know you Dyemere, and Dicecita will be fine I know this cause I feel it in my heart as of right now Shaniqua I gotta do this by myself my love and my best goes out to you and the kids. I'm looking forward to seeing you when I come home.

"I love you Always, Dice"

Chapter 27

"Ain't no Sunshine"

December 9, 2004. We were on our way to court being escorted by the U.S. Marshall's. I was getting sick and tired of wearing this bright orange clothing that the County Jail issued us. I felt like a big ass pumpkin the good thing about it was that it gave me a chance to see my Co-D. We were in the bull pins waiting to see the Judge. We had the worst Judge on the Eastern District and he was old as shit sitting in the Court room with an oxygen tank barely alive but destroying niggas families. Boo was happy how everything was working out for us. Boo didn't know that Haitian Black was behind everything that was happening but he was still worried about the evidence that they still had against him.

Son Don't even stress that shit, we gonna be alright, trust me, have I ever sold you bullshit we just gotta sit up for a minute and let all this blow over then we'll be going home when it's all said and done."

"I don't know about me Dice, they might come at the kid sideways with some other shit.

"Boo" we made it this far right, and they ain't come at us sideways yet because they don't got nothing they just want us to be stressed out in here over this bullshit, fuck that, they don't control our destiny them niggas don't move me, fuck them let me tell you how the FED's work they wait for people to provide them with information in other words do their work for them. That's why they offer niggas deals to sell their souls some niggas are so fucking desperate they take it. Not knowing if you don't say shit they don't got shit and that' a fact.

I hear you talking playboy, that's why I fucks with you, even when shit is against you and looking fucked up, you still believe you could make it happen, but whatever you got cooking under your sleeve, I hope it get us the fuck outta here maybe they might give us a bail today."

"Word . . . . My Lawyer said if they don't produce any evidence today against they have to give us a bail because he filed a 180 motion.

"Dyemere Washington" and "James Carl." The court marshall's said.

"Right here."

"O.K. this way, put your hands forward." The court marshall said. As they handcuffed and shackled us.

We were on our way to see the Judge.

"Excuse me your honor, I would like to present the Courts with a bail package for my clients Dyemere Washington and James Carl the US District Attorney had a 180 days to produce evidence against my clients, and they failed to do so, they haven't produced anything as of yet, it's clear that they don't have anything against my clients that should deny them bail."

"Bail is denied!" The judge said with a stern look on his face.

"What the fuck you mean, bail is denied, do you know who the fuck I am? I yelled out in court.

"Counsel! Please control your client, before I find him in contempt of court." The Judge said.

"Dice you gotta let me handle this for you, calm down." The lawyer said.

We are adjourning this case until Aug 12, 2005. The judge said.

"Get the fuck outta here", "that's bullshit." I yelled out in the court room.

"Guards! Please remove this man from my court room and I'm charging him in contempt of court."

"Fuck you!" I said. Then they rushed us out the court room.

I wanted to go crazy in that court room and slap the shit out of the Judge because that shit didn't make any sense. Their plan was to make us sit in jail and make us break.

My Lawyer came to the back to talk to me.

"Look Dyemere, it's obvious that they don't have anything against you, for some reason they want you to sit here with no bail."

"What the fuck you think I'm paying you for, to come here and talk to me, I need you to get in there ass, Man, and do your fucking job."

"Dyemere, this is not a court room battle that word came from the higher officails you gotta believe in me, and let me do my job for you, if we have to we going to push them to trail I'm going to get you out of here.

"You do what you gotta do, and get me the fuck outta here before I wild out in this motherfucker."

"I will."

*   *   *

On our way back to the County Jail. Boo was telling me how he met a new connect inside his block that he was talking too. He was from Colombia his people was still running his operation on the outside while he was inside doing him.

"Nah Boo, I ain't fucking with that I'm good."

"He's willing to give it to us for a better price than what Haitian Black was giving it to us for, and he's willing to have it delivered to New York."

"Nah son, I told you, I'm finished with that shit man, I'm serious."

Get the fuck outta here not the legendary Dice.

"You think I'm playing, I'm done with that whole shit I got better things to do when I get outta here, and I'm starting now."

"Like what?" . . . . Dice you know it ain't no money like this drug money, who you think you talking to, come on man I know you too long for that, what else would you wanna do besides hustle man, that's all you know how to do."

I got a lot more things I wanna do when I get back in the town like Real Estate, restaurants, barbershops, and mad other shit I was thinking about.

Well I'm a keep getting this money, the way I always been doing.

"More power to you, I got a family to worry about now they need me there with them, I did all that street shit already, it's time for me to step my game up."

"That's what's up Dice, I hear you, do you, you know I ain't no hater, maybe if I had a family like you to worry about than I would be thinking like you, so what about me, you think I should fuck with this Colombian cat?"

"Honestly speaking from me to you Boo, I think you shouldn't fuck with none of that, if you asking me, but it's up to you, what you wanna do, but be careful Boo, you gotta remember where you at."

"How the fuck can I forget that shit when I see shit all day that reminds me, all the time where the fuck I'm at?"

"You know niggas already moving shit in here, so you gotta worry about them, cause they gonna be tight if you start stepping on toes."

"What do you think I should be first then?

Take out the head and the body will follow, make sure you know what you doing son.

"Don't worry I got this."

"What's the Colombian nigga name?

"Jose Guzman."

Boo had his plan all mapped out and was ready to start pushing his shit.

That meant I had to watch his back. But I wasn't getting involved in his drug operation. Boo set up a meeting with the head nigga that was moving his product behind these walls his name was "Pito."

"Yo what's up Pito, I'm glad you took this time out to meet me here today and save me the trouble, you don't know me but I know you, and I've been watching how you operate your whole program, and I think that you getting a little too much money, than what you should be making." Boo said.

"What the fuck you saying to me bee, what you going to slow my money down? Pito asked.

"No! . . . . Not exactly, I'm saying that I'm gonna stop your money completely." Boo said. Giving him the mean grill.

"Ha, ha, ha, ha, ha, ha you sound like a fucking comedian, you should be on T.V., you are only one man, you couldn't stop shit if it hit you in the face, what makes you think you can stop me." Pito said. Him and his peoples started laughing at what Boo was saying. But Boo was dead serious only if he knew.

"You only have one week to finish off the packages, that you have left, whatever you have left after the end of the week, you gonna have to shove it up your ass."

Boo and Pito starting staring at each other with murder on their mind. "Fuck you mother fucka, I'm not stopping shit, you gotta make me stop, since you a fucking tuff guy, I should have one of my guys stop your fucking heart right now, for coming to me with this bullshit you talking to me, who the fuck you think you are bee, huh, do you know who you talking to?" Pito said. Standing up from where he was sitting down at.

Boo pulled out a big ass ice pick and gripped it tight in his hand ready to poke something showing him that he meant business.

"Well tell one of them to come on and stop it, if you think they can cause you still only have one week."

Pito didn't say another word and nobody didn't move an inch to make any attempt on Boo's life. Pito knew from that moment on he had a problem on his hands cause Boo meant every word.

Then Boo walked away after making his point.

"What the fuck was that you pulled out on them niggas cause you had them shook."

"Oh that's just my little friend I be keeping close to me."

"Damn boy!" "We in here and you still wilding out like we in the town."

"It's all hood Dice, you know how I do, I make it pop wherever I'm at, I don't give a fuck about none of these mother fuckers in here." Boo said. As we headed to the weight pile in the yard.

Now that Boo had started some shit between him and Pito I knew something was going to pop off. I spoke to my case manager and told her to move me from my block to J block where Boo was. Even though I wasn't involved with the drug war that was about to start between Pito and Boo I still had to hold my man down so that made me apart of it even if I didn't wanna be.

"What the fuck you doing over here Dice? Boo said. Seeing me walk in the dorm with all my shit.

They move me over here, it was getting real boring over there anyway. I said. Dropping my shit in my cell.

"Aight!" Boo said. With a slight smerk on his face.

Boo knew why I was there but he kept it to himself. He knew from the door that I was gonna hold him down no matter what cause that's how real niggas do it. Boo was starting to make moves throughout the jail with my guidance and brains he had a couple of C.O.'s under the wing niggas and females. Getting away from the hood life is hard to do it's like an addiction you trying to kick it but you can't especially if you deep in the streets. I don't care who you are you always find your coming back like you missing something. I was there every step of the way with Boo. Boo was now living the jail life bidding. In his mind he wasn't going home even when I tried to tell him different. To him this was reality and he was going to take it on head first. We lost a lot of people up until this point that we really cared about. It's funny how one minute you here and the next minute you gone just like that. If you blink to long life will pass you by you'll be either old and grey or deep in your grave. Through my life time I seen a lot and I been through a lot more than some people experience in a life time and there still was more to come in the future. Many nights I thought how it got to this point when I was doing my best to do everything right in my life. The only thing I learned in my life was how to deal with pain, I was surrounded by it. Pain is like a disease some of us get it and some of us don't. I never had it easy in my life but that's what made me a strong person inside and out. Even when I was younger I was suffering. I remember when it use to be all of us me, EB, Boo, Butta, and that bitch ass nigga Rob. We were all innocent back then look at us now. E.B. was murdered I still ain't sure why. Butta died for no reason at all before he even had a chance at life. Me and Boo were facing life in Federal Prison and Rob we all know what happened to his ass.

Everyone around me died except for Shaniqua, Dyemere, Dicecita, and my brother Jay. Sometimes I wonder why am I still here but only one person could answer that for me. I still didn't believe that E.B. had anything to do with Shaniqua being kidnapped. I wondered about the whole night and that note that I found on E.B.'s lap. If I knew what it said it might clear up everything for me. Then Cookie turning up dead somebody shot her in the back of the head that was a mystery in its self. There was no way I could find out the truth now behind these walls. There was a lot of questions that I needed answers to.

Chapter 28

"It Aint Over"

Haitian Black was there for me anytime I needed him. Haitian Black had sent in one of his people's to see me inside the County Jail not as a visitor but as a inmate. This nigga came in on the low just to see me and deliver a message from Haitian Black that was some shit cause It fucked my head up. He was proud to know how I was holding it down in there being a real nigga. Haitian Black knew that I wouldn't sell him out to the Fed's. We had built up a good relationship between us in a short period of time. I was glad I had him on my side. He was very reliable connect to have he also informed me how that I would have a new Judge when I went back to court because the last one I had went on a early retirement. Haitian Black knew how to get his point across. Haitian Blacks people were well connected in all the right places. The next morning when we woke up for chow Haitian Blacks messenger was gone like he was never there. People like me and Haitian Black are built to last. We knew what this game was about and we were playing to win and so far we was winning. The Federal Government didn't know what hit them but they knew that somebody was sending them a strong message and it was being felt without a doubt through the whole Federal System. I had only one mission that was to make it home.

As days went by I felt myself getting closer to going home day by day. It was only a matter of time before that happened for me and the way things were looking it wasn't far away for me. You always gotta believe and have faith in what you do no matter how rough it seems. Haitian Black had something else in the making I didn't know what that was. Whatever it was I was ready. I knew when I came home it was going to be hard for me to stay away from the street life especially with the love and support I was receiving from Haitian Black.

* * *

Chapter 29

"Stay Strap"

Boo recruited a wild young knuckle head ass nigga that was doing time for a body his name was Flip. Flip was from Brooklyn. That nigga cut more niggas in the county than the barber did. I like his style because he was a "G" 'ed up little nigga that was ready to bang on anybody at any given time even police. Boo was schooling young flip to the game. Me, Boo, and Flip spelled trouble for that ass with a Capital T.

One day we was getting our work out on in the day room on the pull up bar. When we saw this 6'5 350 pound mother fucker tried to phone check flip. Me and Boo watched to see how young Flip was gonna handle this nigga that was pressing him. Big man approached Flip on some gorilla shit.

"Yo . . . . What the fuck you doing on my phone little nigga?" "Did I tell you that you could use it, I should break your fucking neck for touching shit that don't belong to you motherfucker."

Flip turned around and looked at the big gorilla looking nigga and thought about it for a second that he couldn't just wild out on this big nigga like that cause he was ready to. Flip told the person that he was talking to on the phone that he was going to call 'em back. When he got off the phone he said.

"On my bad Homie, I didn't know that this was your phone.

This whole shit belongs to me, and everything that's in it to including you. Big Man said poking Flip in the chest. And everything you got, matter of fact, I want you to bring me all your commissary, and put it in my cell, or I'ma kill your little ass in here."

Flip did exactly as big man said to him. As big man was putting away the commissary that he just dee-bowed Flip for. I told boo that nigga Flip was a straight bitch cause how the fuck he just gonna let duke herb him like that I don't give a fuck how big he is cause big niggas get it too. Flip came out of big man cell for the last time bringing him all his commissary. Then he got back on the phone like it wasn't nothing. Me and Boo looked at each other and said "fuck that we aint letting Flip get played like that." Then we started approaching big mans cell we was about to do him dirty. But we was surprised to find big man laid out on the floor with his throat slit from ear to ear. We spun around quick before anybody noticed what happened. We turned and looked back at Flip and he smiled at us and kept talking on the phone. That little nigga was a problem

Dec, 20, 2004. The day was Pito's last day of the week that he had left. Boo was in the shower when he peeped everybody that was in the shower with him leaving except for the two men that was still taken a shower. So Boo slowly bent down to grab his towel cause he already knew what time it was. When he did both men that was in the shower started approaching him with long sharp metal objects. Boo immediately jump back and pulled out his ice pick that he had stashed in his towel. They were all ready to go gun to gun. The first Hispanic man rushed Boo swinging his metal object, Boo weaved it then swung his ice pick catching him in the cheek bone the man slid back and grabbed his face realizing he was cut by the blood on his hand then he looked up at Boo and Said.
"I'm a kill you motherfucker."
Then they rushed Boo at the same time. Boo was swinging his ice pick trying to keep them off of him. But he was out numbered while Boo was tussling and wrestling with one of them the other one took free shots at boo stabbing him in his back twice causing him to fall down on the shower floors. Blood was leaking out of his back. Boo grab one of the Hispanic mans that was the closet by the ankle and yank it causing him to slip and crack his fucking head on the wet shower floors. He was knocked out cold on the wet shower floors. The other attacker looked down at his partner on the floor then he jumped on top of Boo trying to stab him again. He had his knife aimed at Boo's chest trying to force it in him. Then I walked in and saw the nigga on top of Boo trying to stab him. I quickly grabbed the sharp metal object from the man that was laid out and stabbed the nigga that was on the top of Boo in the back of his neck

causing it to come straight through the front of his throat. I helped Boo up then we got the fuck outta there.

*   *   *

Shaniqua was just finishing up in her salon before she closed it and jumped in her Cadillac Escalade about to go pick up the kids from Ebony house. When she got to Ebony house she broke down in tears inside her escalade. Thinking about her man and her life and how close she was to losing it. She was one of the lucky ones that got a break like that.

Shaniqua couldn't believe how so much was happening to her the way it was. Dice was in jail and she didn't know if he was going to ever come home. She felt like her whole world was about to end when she lost Dice.

She couldn't focus the way she would normally do. Things were much easier when Dice was around for her. She knew she had to be strong and hold it down for her family now. In her mind things wasn't getting any better it seemed like it was getting worse by the day. Her man wouldn't speak to her or even write to her to let her know what was going on. She wondered why did God spare her life and take Cookies. Nothing made any sense to her the only bright spot she had was Dyemere and Dicecita.

She had them to worry about now and leave the rest up to God. When Shaniqua finally got out her Escalade and was walking towards Ebony's house to pick up the kids she wiped away her tears and went inside.

"Hey what's up girl, you alright." Ebony said. Opening the door letting Shaniqua inside.

"Yeah . . . I'm alright, I just got a lot on my mind." Shaniqua said. Taking a deep breath.

"Well why don't you relax and sit down for a while, cause I know you been going through a lot of shit lately and you beating yourself up is not gonna help it, what you need to do is go see Dice, and talk to him."

"He not excepting no visits from me like did something wrong, he makes me feel like it's all my fault, I don't know why he doing me like this."

"No . . . . Shaniqua, I don't think so, cause when you was gone all that time all he did was worry about you, that man wouldn't eat for days, he kept blaming himself walking and moping, for what happened to you."

"Then why do I feel this way, why he's not calling me." Shaniqua said.

I don't know, he probably upset with the way everything is going right now!

"I just wanna talk to him, and let him know he don't have to worry about me, ain't nothing going to happen to me if I come and see him, but he won't even call me so I could tell him that."

When was the last time you spoke to him?

When he first got locked up, I went to visit him and that was the last time.

"This is probably a phase that he's going through right now, Shaniqua maybe you should give him some time, and see what happens from there, cause the same way you feeling, I know he feel but probably a lot worse.

"I know what you saying Ebony, I just wish this whole nightmare was over and Dice was here with me, look at me, I'm stressed out over this shit."

"It's gonna be alright Shaniqua, you just gotta be strong and pray for him."

"You right, it's just so hard for me to deal with, I love him more than anything, now that he's not here with me it's bringing me so much pain missing him like this, and I can't do nothing to help him the way he made sure that I was alright, when I was kidnapped. I can't even sleep at night thinking about all this, Oh my god, why me, I keep asking myself, why me?"

"Shaniqua, if you want you could stay here with me for a couple of days, until you feel a little better. No I'm alright, I'm a go home and get some rest, can you help get the kids ready."

"Sure, and I'm sorry about what happened to Dicecita's mother, that was fucked up."

"Yeah . . . . I know but I'm a be the mother she needs now, she's a sweet baby."

"After they got the kids dressed Shaniqua and the kids got in the Escalade and went home."

*   *   *

All the way home Shaniqua was thinking about what Ebony was saying to her. She just didn't understand why was Dice treating her the way he was. Shaniqua knew in her heart that Dice really loved her. Not only by the things he did for her or gave her. They shared a special connection between each other. So Shaniqua decided that she wasn't gonna worry about it too much cause she had Dyemere and Dicecita also to think about but no matter what she was going to be around when he decided the time was right.

*   *   *

Ebony was feeling Shaniqua's pain like it was her owns. She felt connected to Dice also from that one night they shared when Shaniqua was gone. Ebony knew that it wouldn't go further than that Dice was into Shaniqua and nobody else. Ebony wanted to apologize to Shaniqua about what had happened between her and Dice. But she didn't know how to and now wasn't the right time to do it so she had to deal with it until she had the guts to tell her. She knew Shaniqua wouldn't be happy about it.

Ebony never told anyone about that night but she wanted to tell Shaniqua so bad and hope that she would leave him so she would have a chance at keeping him for herself. Ebony even recorded that night she shared with Dice and when the time was right she was going to let Shaniqua know about it.

Ebony already had it addressed and sealed ready to be sent to Shaniqua's house.

*   *   *

Anna was at the abortion clinic about to get an Abortion. She was now a couple of months pregnant. Anna been thinking about Dice ever since she last saw him and she was wondering why he haven't called her yet to say anything. Now she knew Dice was serious about her not having the baby but she didn't want to do that without Dice in the baby's life. It wouldn't be fair to the baby or herself so she had came to the decision that she wasn't gonna have the baby alone it would be to stressful for her. Every minute that went by while she was sitting in the abortion clinic she hoped that Dice would come through the door and stop her from what she was about to do. Anna was scared cause this was her first pregnancy and she was about to terminate it. When the doctor's finally called her name she stood up and walked out of the abortion clinic. She decided at that moment she was going to keep her baby no matter what. She also had another plan in mind that might make Dice change his mind cause she wasn't playing with him anymore. But what she didn't know was that Dice and his boys were no longer around at the moment but she was going to find out soon.

* * *

"I don't care, we are the Government, we make the rules in this country, we don't have to let that bastard go, we can keep delaying his case long as we have to, we cant have people like Dyemere Washington running around loose, this is election year, we need this conviction." The US Attorney General said. Talking on the phone in his office.

"I understand sir, but our Agency doesn't have much on this case, we are trying to convince Washington D.C. to bring in the "Rico" and death penalty against this case, but they won't unless we have some substantial evidence against him, which we don't have at this point, or we can make a few calls to see if we can get the president to back us." FBI Chief said.

"I strongly believe that Dyemere Washington had something to do with what happened to our key players on this case, that bastard, I know he had something to do with that explosion on Dean Street, which federal agent Honeytoon was involved, do you have taps on all his phone calls he makes from the jail."

"Yes! We do and theres nothing on them, he hasn't used the phone to call anyone."

"What about mail or his visiting list, it gotta be some kind of connection to all this that's happening involving this case."

"He doesn't expect any mail for anyone or sends out mail, and not only that, he only had two visits since the time he has been arrested."

"Who the fuck does this guy think he is, I'm going to get him, I want you to put a agent inside the county jail where he's at, and let's see if we can get anything that way."

We already have someone inside working undercover.

"Well good! . . . . Let's see if this bastard get outta this one, when is his next court date?"

August 12, 2005.

"When he goes back to court, I want heavy security around him tight like the president, we can't afford anything to happen until we get to the bottom of this."

"Ok. I'll make a note of it, so I'll keep in contact with you, and give you an follow up on the case, have a good day." (click)

* * *

Haitian Black was on his way to New York!

To be continued . . . .